"IT'S BLOOD!"

Now we both saw a whitish heap a few steps ahead. "A body!" the slave boy cried again.

"You'll see lots of them after you've been in the Subura a while," I informed him. "I wish the gangs wouldn't do their dirty work so close to my door."

That was when I saw the red sandals, mark of a patrician. "Not an ordinary corpse after all," I said.

"It's that little patrician who tried to poison you!"

And sure enough, there lay young Appius Claudius Nero, with a neat puncture in his throat and a circular dent in his brow.

Other SPQR Mysteries
by John Maddox Roberts
from Avon Books

SPQR
THE CATILINE CONSPIRACY

THE
SACRILEGE

AN SPQR MYSTERY

JOHN MADDOX ROBERTS

AVON BOOKS ◆ NEW YORK

THE SACRILEGE: AN SPQR MYSTERY is an original publication of Avon Books. This work has never before appeared in book form. This is a work of fiction, and while some portions of this novel deal with historic occurrences, actual events, and real people, it should in no way be construed as being factual.

AVON BOOKS
A division of
The Hearst Corporation
1350 Avenue of the Americas
New York, New York 10019

Copyright © 1992 by John Maddox Roberts
Maps by Loston Wallace
Published by arrangement with the author
Library of Congress Catalog Card Number: 91-92453
ISBN: 0-380-76627-2

First Avon Books Printing: May 1992

AVON TRADEMARK REG. U.S. PAT. OFF. AND IN OTHER COUNTRIES, MARCA REGISTRADA, HECHO EN U.S.A.

Printed in the U.S.A.

RA 10 9 8 7 6 5 4 3 2 1

THE
SACRILEGE

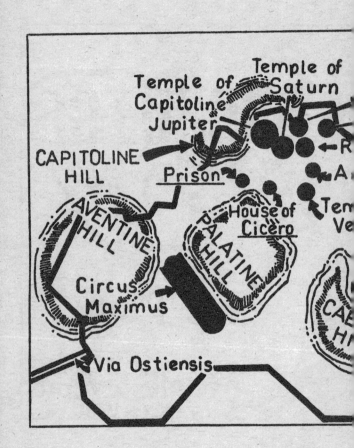

ROME c.70 B.C.
by: Loston Wallace

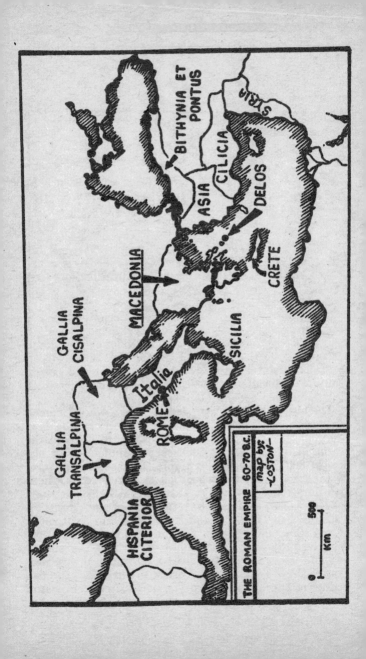

THE ROMAN EMPIRE 60-70 B.C.
map by
~LOSTON~

0   500
Km

I

I wonder sometimes if we can ever know what truly happened. Dead men do not write, so histories perforce are written by those who survived. Of those who survived, some experienced the events firsthand, while others only heard about them. Each who speaks or writes relates events not necessarily as they occurred, but rather as they should have occurred in order to make the teller, or his ancestors, or his political faction, look good.

Once, during one of my numerous periods of exile, I was confined to the beautiful but boring island of Rhodes. There is nothing to do on Rhodes except attend lectures at its many institutes of learning. I chose to attend a course of lectures on history because there was nothing else available that season save philosophy, which I avoided like any sensible man.

The history lectures were delivered by a scholar named Antigonus, who enjoyed a great reputation in those days, although he is all but forgotten now. He devoted the whole of one lecture to this seeming mutability of historical fact. He gave, as example the case of the tyrannicides, Harmodius and Aristogiton, who lived in Athens five hundred years ago. At that time, Athens was ruled by Hippias and Hipparchus, the sons of the tyrant, Pisistratus. Now, it seems that Harmodius and Aristogiton raised a rebellion against the Pisistratids, but they only contrived to kill one of them, I forget which. The surviving and aggrieved brother had both put to death, with embellishments. The anti-Pisistratid party, with the two slain tyrannicides as its martyrs, then raised a successful rebellion and imposed its own enlightened ruler, either

1

Cleisthenes or somebody else. Before you knew it, there were statues of the tyrannicides all over Greece and its colonies. My father had a splendid group, sculpted by Axias, in the garden of his country villa, brought back by an ancestor after we looted Corinth.

But the facts, Antigonus explained, were quite different. Harmodius and Aristogiton were not idealistic young democrats with a hatred of tyrants. They were lovers. The Pisistradid who was killed had conceived a lust for the prettier of the two, who was not about to leave his boyfriend for some ugly old pederast, and so the assassination plot was hatched. It was only after the two were dead that the legend of the tyrannicides was created by the anti-Pisistratid party.

The amazing thing was, everybody knew the true story *at the time*! They all just consented to believe the legend for propaganda purposes. Thus the legend became, in a term created by Antigonus, "political truth." It was a very Greek story, and only a Greek could have come up with such a term.

Antigonus went on to say that only those who directly experienced historical events knew what truly happened, and the rest of us could only perceive them as if through a dense fog, or as blind men tracing the lineaments of a statue with their fingertips. He said that there are sorcerers who, like Proteus in the tale of Ulysses, can summon the shades of the dead and cause them to speak to us, and that it may be only thus that we can ever arrive at a true knowledge of past events.

I thought that made excellent sense at the time, but I have since come to doubt it. About the time I arrived at my present profound knowledge of human nature, the question occurred to me: Would men stop lying just because they are dead? I do not think so. Men of ambition are always concerned about how they shall be remembered after they are dead, and that very end would be defeated were they to start speaking the truth about themselves the moment they found themselves idling by the shores of the Styx, waiting for the ferryboat to come for its latest load of passengers.

One need not go back to a pack of ancient Athenian boy-fanciers to find a warped tale of tyrannicide. Take the assassination of Julius Caesar. There is an official story, sanctioned by our First Citizen, which constitutes Antigonus's "political truth." I know quite another story, and I was there at the time, which our First Citizen was not. Doubtless there are many other versions, though, each shedding the finest light on the teller or his ancestors. If we had one of those necromantic sorcerers, and were he to raise before us the shade of the Divine Julius, and those of Cassius, Brutus, Casca and, say, five of the others (nine is a number very dear to the gods), then I think we should hear nine very different accounts of the events of that fateful ides of March. The fog of men's self-love is as dense as any thrown up by time or distance.

Enough. I shall write of the death of Caesar another time, if age, health and the First Citizen spare me. I write instead of an earlier time, seventeen years earlier, in fact, and of events not quite so celebrated, although they are remembered and certainly seemed momentous at the time.

And you can put your trust in my words, because I was there and saw it all, and I have lived too long and seen too much to care what the living think of me. Much less do I worry about the opinion held of me after I am dead.

I was looking forward to a good year. I always surveyed each new year with optimism, and events almost always proved my outlook mistaken. This year was to be no exception. I was young, not yet quite twenty-nine, and it takes much to overcome the natural high spirits of the young. The wherewithal to crush my optimism was waiting, in great supply.

Everything looked fair as I rode toward the city, though. One reason for my cheerfulness lay outside the walls: a huge encampment of soldiers, prisoners and loot. The loot alone covered acres of land, protected by sheds and awnings. Pompey was back from Asia, and these were the preparations for his triumph. Until the day of his triumph, Pompey could not enter the city, and that was the way I liked it. The anti-Pompeian faction in the Senate had blocked permission for the triumph so far. As far as I was concerned, he could wait out there until the gods called him unto themselves, an unlikely occurrence, whatever he might think.

I knew I would have an active year. My father had been elected Censor, and that is an office with many duties. I expected him to assign me to the census of citizens, since that is tedious and demanding work, leaving him free to concentrate on purging the Senate of unworthy members, which was satisfying, and letting the public contracts, which was profitable.

I did not care. I would be in Rome! I had spent the past year in Gaul, where the climate is disagreeable and people do not bathe. They do not eat well, and a thousand years of Roman civilization will never teach the Gauls to make decent wine. The gladiators were second-rate, and the only saving grace of the place was its wonderful charioteers and racing horses. The Circuses were mean and shabby by Roman standards, but the races were breathtaking. Also, my duties had lain principally with the army. I always had a most un-Roman dislike of military life. There had been no fighting, which was boring and unprofitable, and my duties had been principally as paymaster, which was humiliating. Soldiers always smirk when they see an officer tricked out in parade armor counting out their wages one coin at a time and making them sign the ledger.

All that was over, and my heart sang as I drew nearer the Ostian Gate. I could have taken a barge upriver from the port, but I felt like making an entrance, so I had borrowed a horse from the quaestor at Ostia, had my parade armor polished and bought new plumes for my helmet. It was a fine day, and I made a splendid sight as I rode in, acknowledging the gate guard's salute.

The city walls now stood well beyond the *pomerium*, and I could ride through this part of the town in full military splendor, accepting the admiring hails of my fellow citizens. The popularity of the military stood very high at that moment, as Roman arms had turned in a string of victories with rich loot. I halted and dismounted at the line of the old city wall, established by Romulus. To cross the *pomerium* in arms meant death.

Ostentatiously, I removed and folded my red military cloak and tied it to my saddle. Careful of my new plumes, I removed my helmet and hung it from my saddle by the chin straps. Bystanders helped me out of my cuirass, embossed with muscles that Hercules would envy and much unlike those that adorned my body. I tucked my sword and its belt into a saddlebag and stood dressed in my gold-fringed military tunic and red leather *caligae*. These were permitted within the city proper. Taking my reins in hand, I stepped across the *pomerium*.

The moment I crossed, I felt as if a weight far heavier than my armor had been lifted from me. I was a civilian again! I would have burst into song, had that not been too undignified. My step was so light that the hobnails on the soles of my *caligae* made little sound.

I longed to go to my house and change clothes and go prowl the Forum and catch up on the latest city gossip. My spirit longed for it as a starving man longs for food. But duty demanded that I call upon my father first. I drank in all the sights and sounds and, yes, even smells as I made my way to his house. I find the stenches of Rome preferable to the perfumes of lesser cities.

I rapped at the gate and the *janitor* called Narcissus, Father's majordomo. The fat old man beamed and patted my shoulder.

"Welcome home, Master Decius. It is good to see you back." He snapped his fingers, a sound like the breaking of a great limb. A young slave came running. "Take Master Decius's horse and belongings to his house. It is in the Subura." He pronounced this last word with some disdain.

The slave went pale. "But they'll kill and eat me in the Subura!"

"Just announce that these are the belongings of Decius Caecilius Metellus the Younger," I told him, "and no one will molest you." The dwellers of the Subura couldn't do enough for me since I had brought home the head of the October Horse. Looking doubtful, the boy took the animal's reins and led him off.

"Come," said Narcissus, "the Censor is in his garden. I know how glad he will be to see you."

I sighed. "So do I."

We found the old man seated at a table heaped with scrolls, the winter sun gleaming from his bald head and casting into relief the great, horizontal scar that nearly halved his face. He was Decius Caecilius Metellus the Elder, but everyone called him Cut-Nose. He glanced up as I entered.

"Back, eh?" he said as if I had just stepped out for a morning stroll.

"As events would have it," I said. "I rejoice to find you well."

He scowled. "How do you know I'm well? Just because I'm not dripping blood on the pavement? There are plenty of ways to die without showing it."

This alarmed me. "Are you ill? I—"

"I'm healthy as a Thracian. Sit down." He pointed a knobby finger at a bench opposite him. I sat.

"Let's see," he said. "We have to find work for you. Keep you out of trouble for a change."

"As Censor, you have plenty of work for me, I'm sure," I said.

"No, I've enough assistants. Most of my colleagues have sons who need experience in public work. Even the scut work of the Censorship exceeds the competence of most of them."

"I rejoice to know you think I am worthy of better things," I said.

"As it happens, your services have already been requested. Celer is standing for next year's Consulship, and he wants your aid in canvassing. I could hardly refuse him."

My heart leapt. This would be far more exciting than the Censor's office. Quintus Caecilius Metellus Celer was a kinsman, and he had been my commander in Gaul. He had returned early to campaign for the Consulship, leaving his peaceful province to be governed by his legate.

"I shall be most happy to serve him," I said. "And as for staying out of trouble, that should be no great problem with Clodius out of Rome."

"Publius Clodius is still in Rome," Father said.

"What?" I said, aghast. "Months ago, I had word that he'd won his quaestorship and had been assigned to Sicily! Why is he still here?" The mutual detestation of Pompey and Crassus was as the love of brothers compared to what lay between Clodius and me.

"He has delayed his departure and I don't know why," Father said, still scowling. Scowling was something he did well, and often. "Whatever his reason, you are to keep out of his way. He has amassed a real power base here in Rome. That is how decadent the times have become." He was always going on about the disgraceful condition of the times. I personally do not think the times have ever been anything but decadent. It didn't look as if he was going to offer me dinner, so I rose.

"I'll go home and change, and then I'll call on Celer. With your permission, I shall take my leave."

"Just a minute," Father said. "There was something I was going to give you. What was it? Oh, yes." He signaled and a slave presented himself. "In the cabinet in the atrium," Father said, "in the drawer below the death masks, you will find a package. Fetch it." The slave ran off and was back within seconds. "Take it," Father told me.

Mystified, I took the parcel, wrapped in the finest paper. I stripped off the wrapping and found a rolled-up garment. I shook it out and found that it was a white tunic, severely plain except for the broad purple stripe running from neck to hem. The tunic was the sort worn by every Roman male, but the purple stripe could be worn only by a Senator.

"I gave you your first sword, so I thought I might as well give you this," Father said. "Hortalus and I could think of no pressing reason to keep you out, so we enrolled you among the Senators last month."

To my mortification, my eyes began to film with tears. Father rescued me from disgrace in his usual fashion.

"Don't let it go to your head. Any fool can be a Senator. You'll find that most of your fellow Senators are fools or villains, or both. Now attend me well." He held up an admonitory finger. "You are to sit well to the back of the Senate chamber. You are not to make speeches until you have achieved some distinction. You are always to vote with the family, and you are to raise your voice only to cheer for a point made by our family or one of our adherents. Above all, you are to stay out of trouble, Clodius or no Clodius. Now, you have my leave to go." He returned his attention to his scrolls.

I left. Father could steal the sunlight from a summer day, but that was just his manner. I was happy with my new tunic. I had already ordered several made in anticipation of admission to the Senate, but it meant something to receive this one from my father. His stern instructions were no more that I had expected. Barbarians think that every Roman Senator is a veritable god, but we know better. With or without a purple stripe, I was still a mere son. I made my way through the noon-time bustle of the city and soon stood before the fa-miliar street door of my house. Before I could even rap on its surface, the door flew open and there stood my elderly manservant, Cato, and his equally aged wife, Cassandra.

"Welcome home, Senator!" he cried, causing every head in the street to rotate. Cassandra blubbered as if she'd just received news of my death. Nobody can beat a house slave for sentimentality. It struck me that this was the first time I had been addressed with my new title, and I decided that I liked the sound of it.

I embraced Cassandra and she wept with redoubled fury. "I am so ashamed, master! That boy came by with your horse and belongings less than an hour ago, and I haven't had time to set the house to rights. It's disgraceful."

"I'm sure it is immaculate," I said, knowing they always kept my house so. They were too old to do anything else. "The horse isn't mine. Where is it?"

"I told the boy to leave it at the freedman's stable down the street."

"Good," I said. The stable hired out litters and slaves to carry them, but there were stalls for a few horses and mules. I would go there later and arrange for a rider to take the beast back to Ostia. "The rest of my belongings should arrive sometime soon. I left them with a freighter." I caught sight of someone hanging back in the shadows to the rear of the atrium, shifting nervously from one foot to the other. "Who is this?" I asked.

"Your father sent him a few days ago," Cato answered. "He thought you'd be needing a body servant to dog your heels, now you're a Senator. He's from the house of your uncle Lucius."

I sighed. In my family, we did not just go out and buy slaves in the market. That would have been unthinkably vulgar. We only employed slaves born within the family. This sounds terribly well-bred, but it meant severe dis-advantages. Instead of going out and choosing a slave who had just the combination of skills and qualities you wanted, you got whatever some relative wanted to fob off on you. I knew that before long I would discover why Uncle Lucius wanted to be rid of this one.

"Come here, boy, let's have a look at you." The lad complied. He appeared to be about sixteen, of moderate growth and wiry. His face was narrow and foxy, with a long, thin nose that provided far too little distance between his eyes, which were an alarming shade of green. His dense, curly hair grew to a sharp peak over his brow. His whole look was shifty and villainous, with a touch of surly arrogance. I liked him instantly. "Name?"

"Hermes, master."

I do not know why we name our slaves for the gods, kings and heroes. It must be odd to achieve true greatness and know that someday your name will be borne by thousands of slaves.

"Well, Hermes, I am your new owner, and you'll find that I am a good one, within reason. I never use the whip without reason. On the other hand, when there is reason I wield it very well indeed. Does that sound reasonable?"

"Very reasonable, sir," he assured me with utmost sincerity.

"Good. As your first duty in my service, you may attend me at the baths. Fetch my bath articles, a pair of sandals and one of my better togas. I call on a very distinguished man this afternoon." The boy was about to rush off, but I stopped him. "Stay. Better let me pick out my toga."

With my clucking slaves dogging my steps, I went to my bedchamber to scan my wardrobe. Cassandra had aired the room and placed fresh flowers in the vases. I was touched by this. At this time of year, to get fresh flowers on such short notice they must have bribed the slaves of my next-door neighbor, who had a greenhouse.

I picked out my second-best toga and a pair of sandals. It was a mild winter, so I did not bother with foot wrappings. They always look undignified, and after the chilly climate of Gaul, I felt no need of them.

"I may return late," I told my slaves. "If anyone calls, I shall be at the baths, the Forum, and then the house of Metellus Celer. But nobody knows I am in town yet, so there should be no visitors." I walked as I spoke, and as I walked my aged slaves patted me, dusted me off and all but swept the ground before my feet.

"All will be ready for your return, master," Cato assured me.

"I'll have dinner ready, should none of your friends invite you home," Cassandra said. I knew this would not last. After a few days they would revert to their usual scolding, complaining selves.

I went out into the street with Hermes behind me, carrying the toga, towels, vials of oil and a *strigil* of fine Campanian bronze work, the gift of a friend in younger, more carefree days. Its handle was decorated with lewd images which the imp admired as we walked.

"Are you familiar with the city?" I asked him.

"I've never lived anywhere else," Hermes said.

"Good. I shall probably have more use for you as a messenger than as a body servant." Rome is a chaotic city, and it is difficult to find anything except the Capitol, the Forums and the major temples and Circuses unless you have had long experience of the city.

"Did my uncle Lucius employ you thus?" I asked.

"No, but I ran away a lot and I learned all about the city that way."

I stopped and looked at his forehead. It was free even of pimples, no F branded there.

"Why were you not marked as *fugitivus*?" I demanded.

He had the hypocritical grace to look abashed. "Well, I was very young, and I always came back on my own."

"Turn around," I ordered him. I tugged the neck opening of his tunic wider and looked down his back. Not a mark. I released him and continued walking. "Uncle Lucius is a lenient man. Run away from me once, and your back will have more stripes than an augur's robe. Twice, and I'll collar you. Three times, and you'll have a great big F burned right between your squinty little eyes. Is that understood?"

"Oh, yes, master. But from what I hear, you are a gentleman who likes to get out a lot. If I attend you, I'll be all over town and there'll be no need to run away, will there?"

"I never thought of that," I admitted.

We went to the old bathhouse near the Temple of Saturn, just off the Forum. At a stall on the street I had myself barbered and tonsored, then went inside. The baths of those days were far more modest than those you see now, but this was one of the largest such establishments in Rome, and its interior was cavernous.

I stripped and left Hermes to guard my clothes in the anteroom while I went within. I braced myself, gritted my teeth and plunged into the cold pool. There are many theories about the health-giving properties of cold water, and many Stoic types use only the cold pool, but these theories are nonsense. The reason that we always start with the cold plunge is that Romans distrust anything that affords pleasure, which we think is decadent and weakening. So we suffer first in the cold bath so we can feel all right about luxuriating in hot water afterward.

After my brief gesture to virtue, I hastened, shivering, to the *caldarium* and wallowed in the warmth. I saw a good many old acquaintances and had to make up many lies about my dangerous, savage adventures in Gaul. After I had bored them sufficiently, I summoned Hermes and he rubbed me with scented oil; then I went to the exercise yard, where I rolled around in the wrestlers' pit until I was coated with sand. Then Hermes wielded the *strigil* to scrape off sand, oil and a good deal of skin. This tedious but necessary step is another of the sufferings that make us feel better about bathing.

That done, I went down to the steam rooms. I saw a pack of bearded Stoics in the cold pool trying to converse normally as if their teeth weren't chattering. They weren't the worst, though. Marcus Procius Cato, in his unending quest to become the most virtuous man in Rome, bathed all year round in the Tiber, because that is what he fancied our ancestors did. I don't think it ever occurred to him that the river didn't carry nearly as much sewage in the days of the founding fathers.

When I walked from the bath, I felt quite literally a new man. For the tunic of a soldier I had exchanged the toga of the citizen and the tunic of the Senator. After the heavy *caligae*, wearing street sandals felt like being barefoot. I sent Hermes home with my military tunic and boots and made my way into the Forum. Rome has many Forums, but this was *the* Forum, the Forum Romanum, which always had been, was then, is now and forever shall be the center of Roman life. So much a part of our existence is it that we never bother with the Romanum part of the title unless it becomes necessary to distinguish it from the Forum Boarium or one of the others. It is just the Forum, which is to say, it is the center of the world.

So true is this that, to prove it, we have the Golden Milestone smack in the center (all right, a little off-center, but not by much), from which all distances in the world are measured. You won't find anything like that in some barbarian potentate's main civic center, where they dispense justice, execute felons and sell slaves right alongside the vegetables. It felt good to be at the center of the world again.

I strode across the uneven pavement into the marvelous jumble of monuments, many of them erected to men and events long forgotten. Among the stalls around the periphery I noted with distaste many fortune-tellers. These witches were periodically expelled from the city by aediles and Censors, but they always trickled back. It was bad enough that they influenced political matters with their predictions, but they also ran profitable sidelines in poisons and abortions. Doubtless my father was too busy purging the Senate of his favorite enemies, but he would get to these soon.

The Forum was thronged with citizens, and foreigners gaped at the splendid temples and public buildings to be seen in every direction. The weather was fine, so courts were being held outdoors. Trials are a favorite spectator sport for Romans, and every last street-sweeper fancies himself a connoisseur of the finer points of law. They cheer a clever defense and hurl decaying vegetables at a clumsy one.

As at the bath, I saw many people I knew and smugly accepted their congratulations on my new, exalted status. I received numerous dinner invitations, some of which I accepted, consoled a young kinsman who had been elected quaestor only to be assigned to the treasury, and generally comported myself as if I had achieved some importance. My only sorrow was that no meeting of the Senate had been called for that day, so I could not attend my first session as a full member and strut among my new peers.

When even this new amusement palled, I betook myself to the house of Metellus Celer. He was one of the most distinguished men of the day, and I was unsure what duties he could require of me in his pursuit of the Consulship, which the senior members of my family regarded as all but their birthright. The province he had just governed was one ordinarily assigned to ex-Consuls, but so prestigious was Metellus Celer that it had been assigned to him upon his leaving the office of praetor, at which time he had taken me along to get out of Rome, where I was, as usual, in trouble.

I presented myself at the gate of his town house and was shown to the atrium, where a good many callers idled about, some of them Senators of great seniority. Among them was the last man I expected to see: Caius Julius Caesar. He had held a praetorship the previous year and had been assigned the province of Further Spain to govern. So why was he still in Rome? The extravagance of Caesar's debts was the wonder of the Roman world, and the only hope he had of extricating himself from them was to get to Spain and start looting. He caught my eye and came toward me with hand outstretched, just as if he were standing for office.

"Decius Caecilius, how good to see you back in Rome! And please accept my congratulations for your enrollment among the Senators." He was followed by a band of his toadies, who smiled at me as if my elevation were their own.

"I thank you, Caius Julius," I said. "But I am surprised to see you here. I thought surely you would be in Spain by now."

He waved a hand as if it were a trifling matter. "Oh, certain duties detain me here, most of them of a religious nature." By the most astonishing acts of bribery and corruption, Caesar had got himself elected *Pontifex Maximus* a few years previously and was in charge of all aspects of state religious practice. That reminded me of a question that had bothered me for some time.

"There may be fighting in Spain, may there not?" I asked.

"There is always a chance of that," Caesar said. "I've had disgracefully little experience in military command, but I think I'll be equal to the task."

"I've no doubt at all," I assured him. "But tell me, how will the realities of battle square with the strictures of your pontificate?" The *Pontifix Maximus* may not look upon human blood.

Caesar spoke gravely. "I have consulted the holy books deeply, and I have found that the various strictures of my religious office are binding only within Rome itself, and need not hinder my actions once I am outside the walls."

How convenient for you, I thought. Our religious books were written in such archaic language that they were mostly gibberish anyway.

"Well," I said, "if the supreme pontiff doesn't know about these things, who does? I am sure you will come home from Spain covered with glory." Covered with gold at any rate, I thought.

"I thank you for your good wishes," he said. He might have meant this sincerely. With Caius Julius you could never tell. At that moment Celer appeared in the atrium and began greeting his callers. He started with the most distinguished but quickly came over to me.

"Good to see you back, Decius. Was it an easy voyage?"

"Safe, but not easy," I told him. "I sacrificed to Neptune many times each day." This was the landlubber's wry expression for seasickness.

"The sea is for Greeks," he said. Celer was a squat man with a froglike face, but there was nothing buffoonish about him. He had vast experience in every aspect of public life and was one of the richest men in Rome, although he had acquired it all decently, through inheritance or loot. "Your new tunic suits you well. Wait here while I attend to my guests. I need to speak with you privately."

I waited, trading gossip with the others, until the atrium was empty of visitors. Then I followed Celer into the garden. It was rather bare for that time of year, but beautifully laid out and maintained.

"Have you sacrificed to Jupiter for your safe return?" Celer asked as we walked.

"No, but I did make a *real* sacrifice to Neptune at the temple in Ostia," I told him.

"Sacrifice to Jupiter," he advised. "You are coming up in the state service, and you should be seen to be pious. Romans like to know that their statesmen are punctilious in religious matters."

"Consider it done. My father tells me you wish me to serve you in your campaign for the Consulship. You know I will be happy to be of any help I may."

"Excellent. I expect to win, but I don't want any nasty surprises. You know that winning the office is only half of it. It's no good if you have a colleague you can't work with."

"I see. Who is your choice for colleague?"

"I haven't decided yet. There's a great field of them this year, all busy canvassing the Centuriate Assembly, some of them trying to bribe me. It's generally agreed that I'll be one of next year's Consuls, and most think that the man I choose to support will be my colleague. I am not so sure of that. When I pick my man, I want you to work on his behalf."

"Done," I said. "Have you decided how to divide the office?" In our ancient, unwieldy consular system there were a number of ways the authority of the Consulship could be divided, as agreed before the Consuls took office. Pompey and Crassus, who detested each other and neither of whom would yield an inch, had chosen the most archaic and awkward way: by presiding on alternate days. Others might give the elder colleague senior authority, or one might handle affairs within Rome and the other external matters.

"I'll decide that when I know who my colleague is to be. Honestly, I can't see that it makes much difference. The Consulship no longer has the power it used to have."

This was true. Over the centuries, the praetors had usurped all the judicial powers of the Consuls. As for the military commands, our empire had grown too large for that, and the great generalships went to the men who had already held the highest offices. More and more, the armies were led by men who, like Pompey, had made a virtual lifetime career of soldiering. The last time serving Consuls had led an army had been against Spartacus, and that had ended in disaster.

"Has your father spoken to you of your duties in the Senate?" Celer asked.

"He put me firmly in my place on that score," I assured him.

"You work for years to get into the Senate, and once

you're in, you start at the bottom all over again. That's how it always is. Power comes with seniority."

"What business occupies the Senate these days?" I asked.

"First and foremost, Pompey. The aristocratic party hates and fears him, and it has blocked permission for his triumph. Worse yet, it continues to fight the land grants for his legions."

"If you will forgive me," I said, "I thought *we* were part of the aristocratic party."

"You know that our family has always eschewed the extremes. The aristocratic faction has been in power since Sulla, and it grows increasingly divorced from political reality." I listened attentively. This was inside power politics from a man who knew the subject intimately. "Whatever you think of Pompey, he has earned that triumph. It is foolish and ungrateful of the state to withhold it. And if we deny those legions the land they have been promised and fought hard for, then Italy will be full of thousands of professional killers organized, armed and hating us. I don't want to see a repeat of the last civil war, when contending armies fought within the very streets of Rome."

"Sir, do I detect the slightest of tilts toward the pro-Pompeian faction?"

"We will support him on these two points only. None can deny the justice of giving Roman soldiers the rewards they have justly earned. The family has patched up relations with Crassus, and we don't want Pompey for an enemy because of it. Caesar champions Pompey in the Senate, and he is the coming man in Roman power."

"Caesar?" I said. "He's never even commanded an army."

"Neither did Cicero, and look how far he's come," Celer pointed out.

"As you will," I said. "But I've fallen afoul of Pompey before."

"You were never important enough to bother him much." How true that was. "Besides, to men like Pompey and Crassus, all is forgiven as soon as it is politically expedient. That's how all sensible men should behave."

"Are there any other important matters before the Senate?" I asked.

"One that is not so important, but that concerns us. My brother-in-law is still trying to get himself made a plebeian, and we are still trying to prevent him."

"Ah, Publius Clodius," I said. "Now there is someone who will never forgive and forget, no matter how politically expedient it may become." Clodius was one of the partician Claudians, and he wanted to be a Tribune of the People, an office open only to plebeians. It could be done if he were adopted into a plebeian family, but this was not easy if the Senate were opposed.

"Last year, when Cato was tribune, he put a stop to it by simply interposing his veto. This year, Cicero has been fighting the adoption tooth and nail. Dangerous as he is, Clodius will be ten times as destructive if he is a tribune." In many ways, the tribuneship was the most powerful office in Rome in those days. The tribunes had regained most of the powers taken from them by Sulla. They could introduce bills and veto any action of the Senate. I shuddered at the thought of Clodius having that power.

"Working to frustrate Clodius is something I never need encouragement to do," I told Celer.

"Stay out of his way for now," he cautioned. "I don't know why he's hanging around Rome when his duties lie in Sicily, but I've no doubt he's up to some devilment."

"Always a safe bet, with Clodius."

"Very true. Now, since we are on that subject. We senior members of the family have been discussing what we may have to do when Clodius makes his run for the tribuneship, as surely he will if he lives long enough."

"And what was the decision?" I asked.

"We will want you to stand for a tribuneship the same year."

I felt like a sacrificial ox when he's knocked on the head by the *flamen*'s assistant. "Me? But the family is full of men better qualified."

"Nonsense, you're a perfect choice. Your lineage is impeccable. You'll have a recent Censor for a father, and you have the qualifications for any office. Not that that matters, because any citizen can be elected tribune, so long as he's not a partician. You're an aristocrat, but you're something of a favorite with the commons because of your feat with the October Horse." He grinned at that memory. I winced.

"Now," Celer went on, "I think that Cicero is grooming your friend Titus Milo for the same role. I hate to think of a criminal gang leader like Milo as tribune, but I admit he's a better man than Clodius."

"Milo is an excellent choice," I said, "but I've never even considered the tribuneship. I am flattered that you think me worthy, of course."

"Don't be too flattered," he said. "The main reason we want you is because Clodius hates you so much. He'll be so distracted by your rivalry that he may not do too much mischief."

"I see." My mind was working like a fermenting wine vat. "If both Milo and I are tribunes the same year, we could combine forces to keep Clodius in line."

"You catch on quickly," Celer said. "You may have a future in Roman politics. Well, all this may be years away, but I want you to think about it."

"Rest assured, I shall think of little else," I said. Somehow, I had to get out of this. Clodius hated me enough as a mere enemy. If I were a political rival, his malignancy would know no bounds. In theory, the lives of tribunes were sacrosanct, and to murder one was an impious act. The trouble was, Clodius was a man who specialized in acts of impiety.

"What are you two plotting?" The voice came from the colonnade and we turned to face its source. I knew it instantly, of course.

Clodia was still one of Rome's great beauties, and at this time one of the most notorious. She was also famed for her charm and wit, for her learning and patronage of artists and poets. Most of all, she was feared. She was suspected of complicity in a number of murders, and I happened to know that she was guilty of some of them. However, she was Celer's wife, and certain basic courtesies were demanded.

"You are more beautiful than ever, Clodia," I told her, "and you know that your husband and I haven't an ounce of conspiratorial talent between us."

"How disappointing," she said, extending her hand. I

took it and bowed over the cool, tapering fingers, artfully kissing my thumb instead of her hand. The caution might have been unwarranted, but she was rumored to keep poison under her gilded nails.

"How long has it been, Decius? Not since dear Quintus took the field against Catilina? You left Rome then, did you not?" Needless to say, she had not accompanied her husband to Gaul, to my relief and no doubt to his as well. They were not a good match, but then, the great families always arranged marriages for reasons of policy. They had been betrothed when she was a mere girl and her brother, Clodius, no more that an obnoxious brat.

"I've been away from Rome and you far too long, Clodia." Well, the part about Rome was true. Clodia and I had a tangled and, for me, embarrassing past. Nothing embarrassed her.

"Things have been terribly dull of late," she said. "Now that you are back, perhaps matters will liven up." That sounded ominous.

"Young Decius will be working with me in my upcoming campaign for the Consulship, my dear," Celer said, with the pained look shared by all men afflicted with such wives.

"Oh, what a waste of talent. You couldn't lose the Consulship if the other factions put up gods and heroes as competitors! Still, that means we'll be seeing a lot of dear Decius, so it's all for the good." At that moment a slave came and announced a visitor, so Clodia took her leave and rushed off.

"Well," Celer grumbled, "it's good you and Clodia get along, even if her brother wants to cut your throat."

"I have the highest esteem for Clodia," I assured him.

"Starting tomorrow, I want you to pay your morning call here instead of at your father's house." We began to walk toward the door.

"Shall I bring my clients?" I asked.

"Only if I'm to make an important speech. Otherwise, dismiss them when you leave your house."

"I shall be most happy to comply." I never liked the custom of being followed around by a gang of clients. Even loyalty and devotion become annoying after a while.

In the atrium we found Clodia and the new arrival, a

kinswoman of mine, nicknamed Felicia. She was Caecilia Metella, wife of the younger Marcus Crassus, who was the son of the great Crassus. She made the usual cousinly sounds of greeting.

"What are you and Clodia up to?" I said. I should have known better than to ask.

"We're going to do something scandalous and embarrass our husbands," Felicia said.

"Aren't you a respectable matron now?" I asked. "Surely you're raising a pack of little Crassi."

"Don't be boring," Felicia scolded. "Breeding is for slaves and livestock. Besides, you've reached an advanced age without marrying."

"No woman can pin Decius down that long," said Clodia with a deft twirl of the thumb-screw. "He always makes trouble for someone powerful and has to leave Rome to save his skin."

"Ladies, if you will excuse us, I must see Decius out. He has pressing duties." Celer guided me out the door. "No man should be called upon to deal with both of them," he muttered.

To my surprise I found Hermes waiting for me outside the gate, but in well-bred fashion I ignored his presence while I made my farewells to my eminent relative, promising to arrive early the next day.

Hermes fell in behind me as I walked toward the Forum. "So that's the great Metellus?" he said. "Doesn't look like much."

"He is one of the greatest," I told him. "I, on the other hand, am only a little Metellus. I am, however, far greater than you, which means that you are to curb your insolence."

"As you say, master."

It had been an eventful day, this homecoming of mine. It was to be among the more tranquil.

II

—

The next morning I rose far too early and greeted my clients. I still had only a small number of them, but they are a necessary adjunct of social and political life. I had about twelve at this time, mostly from families long associated with mine or else retired soldiers who had served with me at one time or other. They had little to do except cheer me in the courts or protect me in times of danger, and I was bound to help them legally and financially. They would be asking more favors now that I was a Senator.

I dismissed them with thanks and gifts and then made my way to Celer's house. I found a great mob in his atrium. His clientage in Rome alone numbered in the hundreds, with thousands more in Italy and the provinces. Naturally, even the Roman crowd could not all call on him at the same time. I think they had some sort of system of on and off days.

I wandered among them, catching up with old friends and meeting a few new ones. People spoke mainly of Pompey's upcoming triumph, and what a splendid spectacle it was sure to be. It seemed all but certain that the Senate's muleheaded opposition could not last much longer. Among the crowd I found Caesar again.

"Two days in a row, Caius Julius?" I said. "Surely no Julian has ever been a Metellan client."

Caesar smiled his dazzling smile. "No, I do not come as a client, but as a homeless suppliant. I've come to beg your kinsman for a roof to shelter my head tomorrow night."

"Didn't they ever fix the tiles on the pontiff's palace?" I asked. "They were working on that when I left Rome."

"No, the place is sound, but tomorrow night the rites

21

of Bona Dea are to be held there, and I cannot be present."

"The date had escaped me," I admitted. "But then, I'm not married." This rite was performed in the house of the *Pontifex Maximus* under the supervision of his wife, and all the noblest ladies of Rome attended. It was absolutely forbidden to men, and women were forbidden to speak of it on pain of death.

"You mean even the supreme pontiff can't be there?" I said.

"It is true. I have regulatory power over all aspects of our religious practice, but this one rite I cannot touch, and my wife may not speak to me of it."

"Well, that's—" My words were cut off short when a man standing next to Caesar but with his back to me turned around. His face was malignant, dark and flushing darker. I should have recognized that squat, neckless form even from behind. Somehow I managed to control my natural impulse to reach for a weapon. Just as well, since I was unarmed.

"Why, Publius," I said, "I rejoice to see your face again." And indeed I did. It always did my heart good to look upon the scars I had put on that misshapen countenance.

"My sister said you were back." He almost strangled on the words, but perhaps he just suffered from croup. I swear I saw red veins shoot across his eyeballs like strokes of lightning. Then Caesar put a hand on his shoulder.

"Now, let us have no unseemliness," Caesar said, smiling. "This is the house of Metellus." At his touch and his words and his smile, Clodius ceased to tremble and his color faded. Wordlessly, he nodded. It was the most extraordinary performance. Had the idea not been so absurd, I would have sworn that Clodius was *afraid* of Caesar! I could not guess what the little scene meant, but I learned something from it that was to haunt me for years to come. I wanted never to see Caius Julius smile at me like that.

My kinsman Metellus Creticus was standing near and caught the unpleasant scene, and he moved in to provide a diversion.

"It's no wonder Decius is confused about the date," he

said. "Everybody else is, too. The calendar's gotten all skewed again. That's your job, Caius Julius. When are you going to correct it?" Our calendar was lunar, and because the diurnal year doesn't quite come out even with the turnings of the moon, the calendar would get out of order and every few years the *Pontifex Maximus* would have to slip in an extra month to make it come out even. Caesar had ignored the problem since his election, probably because he was, basically, a lazy man.

"This creaky old calendar of ours is beyond redemption," Caesar said. "I propose to utterly reform the calendar so that it never needs adjusting again."

A good lazy man's solution, I thought. "How will you do that?" I asked him.

"I will assemble the best astronomers and mathematicians to be found and commission them to work out a sensible calendar in which the number of months always stays the same. I think it can be done if we accept the idea that not all the months will have the same number of days and they will have nothing to do with the phases of the moon."

"Sounds too radical to me," Creticus said. At the time I took it merely for more of Caesar's grandiose talk, but a few years later he actually did it, and we haven't had to adjust the calendar since. Even a man like Caius Julius can do something right once in a while.

By this time Clodius's friends had led him away, and it occurred to me that somebody, perhaps Clodia, had passed the word that we were to be kept apart. That was a juxtaposition I could live with. As I waited for Celer to appear, I noticed something that I had begun to suspect the day before, in the Forum: I had become very popular with the *publicani.* Most of these were prosperous *equities,* men in the building or tax-farming trade. They all were eager to make my acquaintance and they all asked pointedly after my father's health. As the Censors were in charge of letting the public contracts, I was clearly a man to cultivate. They hinted that, should I commend them to the old man, I could look forward to some generous gifts at Saturnalia. It looked as if I might finally escape my customary penury.

Mind you, this was not considered a matter of corruption, although our First Citizen would have it so. He claims that we were utterly corrupt in those days and that his "reforms" have fixed everything and corruption is no more. As usual, he flatters himself. He has merely ensured that a fat chunk of every bribe that is passed comes to him.

At one point, while having my ear abraded by a quarry owner, I found myself edging toward a little knot of men surrounding Clodius. I had keen ears, and I always loved to eavesdrop, especially upon conversations where my murder could be the main topic. They were not talking about me, though.

"But just what is it the women *do* at that ceremony, eh?" The voice of Clodius dripped with prurient insinuation. I had to admit, guiltily, that I had wondered exactly that myself.

"Every highborn husband in Rome wonders that," said a man who was obviously uneasy about what his wife would be up to the next night.

"But," said a very young man I did not recognize, "it can't be much, can it? I mean, they're all women, after all." The others drew back and made disdainful noises at such callowness.

"I'll wager it's worth seeing, eh?" said Clodius. I thought of stepping over and hitting him on the head with a vase or something. I just could not abide that voice. It wasn't just the subject. He could comment on the weather and it would come out sounding like that.

"Worth a man's life, you mean," said an older and presumably wiser man. Then conversation ceased as Celer arrived and began greeting the callers. When he got to me he put a hand on my shoulder in that gesture that always says that this is a private conversation. The others turned discreetly away.

"Decius, today I want you to call on Mamercus Capito and sound him out. Politically he's a nobody, but nine in ten Consuls are. More to the point, he's agreeable, which is to say he's pliable, and as an Aemilian, he's as noble as you can get in Rome without being enrolled among the gods. He'd be a suitable colleague for me and he's talked about standing for the office. See if he's amenable to a *coitio*, so long as he agrees that I'll be the senior colleague."

"I'll call on him at once." This was the sort of politicking I liked. It was how a great deal of our public life was carried out. Personal relationships usually had as much to do with it as party affiliations. Debates in the Senate were often just so much noise and bluster, with the real decisions reached and agreed to at dinner parties, in the baths, even in the stands at the Circus.

I hurried out, hoping to catch Capito at home. The Aemilii had been among our most illustrious families, but the line had dwindled and there were few of them left. Those of the present generation were undistinguished except for the name. Capito had plodded his way up the ladder of office, attaining seniority without military or political distinction. He was like two hundred or more of his fellow Senators: colorless functionaries who won office on the basis of family history, served as soon as age and seniority permitted, and lazed through their terms of authority with as little effort as possible, generally using position only as a way to get rich.

In short, Capito was an ideal colleague for an energetic man like Celer, who wanted to pursue the activities of his office with minimal interference. And as senior colleague, he would get the better of the proconsular provinces when he stepped down from office. By that time, the main reason men wanted to be Consul was to get their hands on the rich proconsular provinces. These were supposedly chosen by lot, but everyone knew the choice was rigged. A man who gained sufficient senatorial support would get one of the plums, while one with many enemies in the Senate got a worthless place, rich in nothing but disagreeable natives.

The Senate could come up with some real oddities for unusual Consuls. There had been the time when Pompey was given command over the entire Mediterranean and its littoral to rid us of the pirates, for instance. In later years, Caesar as Consul presided over a Senate that was not only hostile but possessed a sense of humor. Instead of a province, he was given the upkeep of Italy's roads and cattle paths. He made them regret it later, of course.

Yes, the Consulship was an office worth pursuing, although it was not without its hazards. I fully expected to be Consul someday, not because I was particularly ambitious, but because that was what you did when your name was Caecilius Metellus. Not that anyone ever accused me of being a man who lazed through office on his family name. No amiable political hack ever weathered as many murder attempts as I did. A man's seriousness as a public official can usually be gauged by the number and homicidal habits of his enemies.

I reached the house of Capito just as his morning callers were leaving and he himself was on his way to an annual sacrifice given by the Aemilii in memory of some victory or other. I knew him only slightly, but he greeted me hospitably and professed himself glad to see me again. I hinted at political business and he invited me to dinner at his house that evening.

Things were shaping up well, and now I had the rest of the day to myself. It was a short walk to the Forum, where I wandered about, soaking up sun and the attentions of a good number of *publicani*. Most of these were builders, but one intriguing fellow had a novel item to sell: a new design of shields for the legions.

"It's much better than the old *scutum*," he explained earnestly. "Just as thick and protective, but cut off straight at the top and bottom."

"It's hard to get soldiers to accept something new," I said. "What's the advantage?"

"We've given quite a few to the *ludi* in Campania, and the gladiators there say it's a much better fighting design than the old oval style. It's lighter and gives better vision."

"Gladiators don't worry much about arrows and javelins," I said doubtfully. "There's more to warfare than single combat, you know."

"Nonsense, sir," he protested. "A man fighting will always hold his shield just below eye level. With the new design, even less of the soldier's body is exposed."

"But if you give a shield a flat bottom," I pointed out, "the soldiers on guard will rest them on the ground and lean on them and go to sleep. Every officer knows that."

He sighed with exasperation. "But that's why centurions have vinestocks to beat their soldiers with. And what legion ever needs more than one exemplary beheading a year for sleeping when the enemy is near? That's all it takes to keep the lads alert. Now, sir, if you'll put in a good word with your father the Censor, I am prepared to offer the state a very reasonable rate. My shops can outfit a full legion every year, complete with a cheaper version for the auxiliaries."

"I'll speak to him," I said, "but I don't think you'll have much luck. He still thinks the Marian reforms are an outrage. How much per shield?"

"Fifty-five denarii for the legionary model, thirty for the auxiliary."

"That seems steep," I said.

"We're not talking about shoddy materials here, sir. We are talking about first-rate plywood made of seasoned limewood strips and Egyptian glue, backed with the finest felt and faced with rawhide; and on top of that, seasoned bullhide bleached almost white so as to take whatever dye or paint the legion wants to add. Ironmongery of the finest workmanship, sir: boss, rivets and grips and a complete bronze rim. Now tell me that's not worth fifty-five denarii."

"I won't argue the details of your trade," I said. "How does the auxiliary version differ?"

"Identical except the cover is plain brown cowhide and the rim is stitched rawhide instead of bronze. Just between you and me, it's as good a shield, but we both know that the legions will revolt if they see the auxiliaries getting gear as pretty as the legions have."

"That is true," I agreed.

"I'll tell you what: I'll drop the price twenty denarii if they offer the old shields in trade. I can sell those to the Egyptians. But I want the right to refuse any that are too cut up for resale."

I promised to do what I could, and he let me know that he would be not only grateful but generous. As it turned out, the legions tried out the new design and liked it, but they didn't buy new shields. They just cut the tops and bottoms off the old ones. There were few fools among the military purchasing officers.

After this encounter I went to a stall and bought a light lunch of sausage, fried onions and chopped olives seasoned with pungent *garum* and wrapped in flat, unleavened bread. I was washing this down with a cup of watered wine when I saw something over the rim of my cup that made me pause.

A few stalls down, someone was coming from one of the witches' booths. It was a very young man, old enough to shave and wear the toga, but only by a matter of months. He seemed oddly familiar, yet I could not quite place him. He glanced from side to side guiltily as he emerged from the booth. He wore the red sandals with the ivory crescent at the ankle that only patricians could wear. This and some half-familiar cast to his countenance finally placed him for me: He was one of the little group surrounding Clodius that morning. He was, in fact, the one who had spoken and revealed himself to be young enough to think that a group of highborn women couldn't be up to something really unsavory. This was too good an opportunity to miss. I walked over to him, taking care to approach him from behind.

"Good day!" I said loudly. He all but jumped out of his toga as he spun around, white-faced. He cast a frantic glance toward the witch's booth, clearly terrified that I might have seen him leaving it. I clapped him on the shoulder to show that I harbored no suspicions at all. "I saw you at Celer's house this morning, but we weren't introduced."

He looked faintly relieved. "I am Appius Claudius Nero," he said, "and I know who you are, Senator Metellus."

I took his hand. "I am always glad to meet a new-made citizen. You must have donned the man's toga while I was away in Gaul. Are you the son of the Appius Claudius who was legate to Lucullus in Asia?"

"No, I am his cousin. His father and my grandfather were brothers." That made the whelp second cousin to Clodius and Clodia. Clodius had changed his name from Claudius when he decided to become plebeian, and his sister had imitated him.

"It's good to see that our ancient patrician families still produce sturdy young men," I said, beaming at him. One more Claudian was like one more rat as far as I was concerned, but I would give him the benefit of the doubt. Every century or so the Claudians produced a good man. The elder Appius was a decent sort. The fact that this one was consorting with Clodius was definitely not a mark in his favor.

"Thank you," he said. "I—I do not wish to be rude, sir, but I have an—an appointment and I must hurry," he stammered nervously. "I must go."

"By all means," I said, "don't let me detain you. And you must call on me soon. I would like to become better acquainted." I took his hand in both of mine and noticed that it was trembling. Then I noticed something decidedly odd: On the forefinger of his hand he wore a great, bulbous poison ring.

I stared at his fear-stiffened back as he walked away. Why on earth was he wearing one of those? I suppose I should explain here. Back in those days poison rings were not really uncommon, but barbarians often think that we used them to poison our enemies. They fancy that the rings had spring-loaded lids to facilitate the surreptitious sprinkling of poison into an enemy's cup. Actually, they were a means of quick suicide. The domed chamber was cunningly wrought as a seamless capsule filled with poison. There was no access to the poison save by breaking open the capsule. In times of civil strife, when picking the wrong faction could mean death, you saw them everywhere. They were rare in tranquil times. These were relatively tranquil times.

I wore a poison ring myself from time to time. When you knew that at any moment a rampaging mob might break your door down, or your enemies were chasing you through the alleys, it was comforting to have a fast escape. Just bite through the thin gold, suck out the poison, and you might avoid being tortured, or hurled from the Tarpeian Rock, or dragged on a hook into the Tiber.

The boy was far too young to have serious enemies. Perhaps, I thought, he was just trying to get a little drama into his life. It is the common practice of boys just come to manhood to do things like that: wear poison rings or conceal swords beneath their tunics or write dreadful poems. However, nothing remotely connected with Publius Clodius was too trifling to rouse my suspicions.

The booth was typical of the sort: a flimsy construction of poles, roofed and walled with cheap, heavy cloth. Unlike the vendors' booths, this one did not have a table out front for the display of wares. Instead, the front and sides were decorated with magical symbols: crescent moons, snakes, owls and the like. I pushed aside the curtain and ducked through the low doorway. The interior was full of baskets containing all manner of herbs, vials of scented oils and nameless articles, of interest solely to the practitioners of magic. In one rustling basket I saw a knot of writhing black snakes.

"May I help you, sir?" The speaker was an absurdly ordinary-looking peasant woman. She might as well have been selling turnips in the produce market.

"I am the Senator Decius Caecilius Metellus the Younger," I said portentously. "I want to know what the noble youth who just left was doing here."

She looked me over. "Is there any reason I should talk about my clients to you?"

"Your sort is forbidden within the city, you know," I said.

"The stripe's on your tunic, not your toga," she pointed out. By this she meant that I did not wear the purple-bordered *toga praetexta* and therefore plainly had no judicial power.

"No, but my father is the Censor Metellus," I said.

"Is that so? I don't follow political matters much. Well, if that's the case, he's the one I should be talking to, I suppose. Why don't you fetch him here and we'll sit down and have a little chat?"

"Woman, you try my patience. Don't you know how to show the proper respect to a Senator?"

She looked at me pityingly. "Now, sir, you know perfectly well a Senator's just a citizen with a purple stripe on his tunic. If you only knew how many Senators come to me wanting a poison to get rid of their wives, or an abortion for a slave girl, and me just a poor, honest fortune-teller and herbalist. The wives come, too, because the noble husband's been away all year and they're going to have a baby that'll come out looking just like the Gallic stableboy. You'd be shocked at what your peers get up to, sir." Unfortunately, I would not be a bit shocked.

"And you, of course, would have nothing to do with such things?"

"I should hope not!" She made a number of gestures against the evil eye and other supernatural misfortunes. "I read the signs and give advice. Come to me with a cold or a hangover and I'll mix you up a potion to relieve your suffering, but don't ask me to do anything illegal."

Well, I could scarcely expect her to admit selling poisons for purposes other than suicide, since the punishment was a horrible death.

"Fortune-telling is illegal," I pointed out.

"Well, there's lawbreaking that gets you run out of town and there's lawbreaking that gets you nailed to a cross. It's that last kind that I call illegal."

"I am going to stay here until you tell me what that boy was doing here. Then what will you do for customers?"

She threw up her hands in exasperation. "Oh, sir! Wasn't you ever that young? Didn't you always go running to a fortune-teller every time your heart went *thump* over some neighbor's pimply daughter? Lovesick boys outnumber embarrassed Senators any day."

"Very well," I said, "I will accept that for now, but I may be back. What is your name?"

"Purpurea, sir. You'll find me here most days."

I left fuming. Sometimes I envy Asiatic nobles, whose inferiors have to grovel in the dirt before them and lick their toes. Purpurea! When women get to make up their own names, they come up with some strange ones. And her pose of innocence did not impress me. In my lifetime I have known thousands of criminals, and the best of them could make a newborn infant seem a veritable monster by comparison. One thing was certain: That boy had been afraid to be seen emerging from her booth.

If you seek any prominent Roman at midday, it is usually futile to look for him at home. Your best bet is to go to the Forum and wander around until you bump into him. That was how I found Milo. He stood near the Temple of Castor and Pollux, surrounded by a group of tough-looking men, most of them dressed in dark tunics. He was the only one who bothered with a toga. He grinned his great, white-toothed grin when he saw me.

We had been friends for years, a thing most of my peers thought disgraceful. He was the most powerful gang leader in Rome, with Clodius as his only rival. He was a huge man, still young and extraordinarily handsome. He had been a rower in his younger years and was as strong as any professional gladiator or wrestler. We exchanged the usual embraces and greetings and he invited me to his house, where we could talk privily.

The minor fortress Milo called home occupied a whole

block in one of the better slums. It was fully staffed with street fighters, many of them veterans of the legions or the arena. We sat at a table in Milo's enormous assembly room, and one of his men brought us watered wine. Milo was never one for the amenities, so I launched straight into the matter at hand.

"Milo, why is Clodius still in Rome?"

"His presence has not escaped me," Milo said. "Nor has the fact that Caesar shows an uncharacteristic fondness for our city when his fortunes are to be mended elsewhere."

"Caius Julius doesn't amount to much," I said.

"Not yet, but keep your eye on him. And Clodius is Caesar's man."

I remembered the odd tableau that morning. "You think it's connected?"

"I know that Clodius does very little these days without Caesar's permission."

My cup paused halfway to my lips. "That's new. Were some new lines drawn while I was away?"

"The lines are much the same as always, but the number of players in this game has narrowed. There used to be many gangs controlling the streets of Rome. Now there are just two: mine and Clodius's. Once there was a large number of soldier-politicians and lawyer-politicians contending for mastery of Rome and its empire. Most have dropped out or been eliminated. Lucullus, Hortalus and the rest have left the big struggle for power."

"Hortalus is Censor with my father," I pointed out.

"An office with great prestige but no imperium. No, Decius Caecilius, the contenders are now Pompey, Crassus and Cicero, with Caesar soon to join them. See what he is like when he gets back from Spain."

"I trust your instincts," I said. "So you say Clodius has become Caesar's man. Celer tells me that you are now closely linked with Cicero."

"Cicero and I are not friends, but he needs me. The men who want to control the empire must be away from the city much of the time. They must have an ally to control the city in their absence, and there is no constitutional office for that purpose."

I always admired this quality in Milo. He knew the branchings of power as a farmer knows the branching of his grapevines. He knew which branches showed promise and which needed pruning. He was utterly untrammeled by the constitutional precedents and traditions that shaped the political thinking of more orthodox Romans.

"What is Cicero's standing these days with the Senate and the public in general?"

"Precarious for the moment. He has his adherents, but his enemies charge that he was high-handed in executing the Catilinarian conspirators without trial. And many are resentful of his indifferent origins. They can't accept the idea of a new man rising as Cicero has. Some are jealous of his new house on the Palatine. They're charging that he embezzled public funds to build it."

"How do you read the situation?" I asked.

"The Catilinarian scandal will fade in no great time. Nothing gets old as fast as yesterday's scandal. Catilina never had any firm base among the powerful men of Rome. With Pompey coming back, all attention will be on him, and lately Cicero's thrown his support behind Pompey."

"Cicero?" I said. "He was always with the anti-Pompeians before."

"But he understands the inevitable. Something has to be done to placate Pompey's veterans. You know, when Pompey comes into the city for his triumph, it will be the first time in years that Pompey, Crassus and Caesar will all be in Rome at the same time."

"You see a connection?" I knew Milo wasn't just musing aloud.

"There's a rumor floating around. Just a rumor, mind you, but there are those who say that Caesar can't leave because of his debts. Some of those he owes money to are very highly placed."

"But if he can just get to Spain, he'll enrich himself like any other bandit," I said. "Then he can pay his debts."

"Or he may get killed. He has a reputation for recklessness. Remember those pirates?"

It was a famous story. When he was quaestor, Caesar had been captured by pirates and held for ransom. He had behaved arrogantly and demanded that his ransom be appropriate to his rank. He had unbraided his captors, promised that he would return with a flotilla and crucify them all, and made them listen to his speeches. The pirates had been highly amused and treated him as a sort of mascot while he resided among them. In time his ransom arrived and he was sent on to the nearest Roman port. He immediately raised a flotilla, returned and crucified all the pirates exactly as he had said he would. It was the sort of tale that tickled the Roman fancy and made him a minor celebrity for a while.

"So his creditors want some sort of security? What can he do? Caesar spends so freely he barely owns the clothes on his back. *Pontifex Maximus* is a fine old position, but it never made anyone a copper *as* that I ever heard of."

"There is a further rumor," Milo said. "A loan. An enormous loan to stand surety for the bulk of his debts while he is away. All out of one man's purse."

Now things began to make sense. "Crassus," I said.

"What other man in the world has that kind of money?"

"Crassus is not a charitable man. He will want something in return for a loan like that. What can Caesar do for the likes of Marcus Licinius Crassus?"

"That is something I would give a great deal to know," Milo said.

III

The house of Mamercus Aemilius Capito was located in a beautiful district on the Aventine, with a fine view overlooking the Circus Maximus. As I walked up the hill I could smell the incense wafting from the nearby Temple of Ceres. Gazing across the valley, I could see the magnificent new house of Lucullus. It had been under construction when I had last climbed the Aventine, and was said to be far and away the most magnificent dwelling in Rome, built with the spoil of Pontus and Asia. Lucullus was not as rich as Crassus, but whereas Crassus used his wealth to gain more money and power, Lucullus used his to indulge himself.

The guests were already ranging themselves in the triclinium when I entered, and I took my place on one of the couches. Hermes took my sandals and stood behind my place, ready to serve me. I had ordered him to keep absolutely silent and observe closely. For a wonder, he obeyed.

As was customary, Capito had invited a mixed company. He did, however, have more than the usual proportion of exceptionally distinguished guests, a sure sign of his political ambitions for the year to come. Occupying the place of greatest honor was Marcus Pupius Piso Frugi Calpurnianus, one of the Consuls of the year. Like his colleague Messala Niger, he was a time-server of little importance. Like many such men, he insisted on using his whole great epic of a name instead of some shortened form. Men assured of their own greatness prefer to use a single name, as if they alone possessed it. Thus we have Alexander, Marius, Sulla, Pompey, Crassus and, let us not forget, Caesar. Watch out for men who use a single name.

35

At the other end of the head couch resided the pontifex Quintus Lutatius Catulus. Catulus was esteemed one of the greatest Romans of the day, but his star was setting like those of Hortalus and Lucullus as the ambitious military men gained ascendancy. Between Catulus and Piso was our host, Capito.

At the table facing mine reclined Lucius Afranius, a man of some dignity and little importance, like Capito himself. He had served as praetor some years before. The other two at that table I no longer recall, so they could not have amounted to much. My companions on the third couch were an unusual pair. To my right, on the side of the head couch, was the poet Catullus, not to be confused with the great Catulus, who spelled his name with a single *l*. The poet had been mooning around Rome for a couple of years, cadging free meals and writing his verses. Friends of a literary bent assure me that these poems are rather good. Many of those he indited at this time were addressed to a hard-hearted woman of mystery called Lesbia. It was the opinion of most that Lesbia was actually Clodia, who had the requisite cruelty and love of poetry. He had lived in the house of Celer, but I rather doubt that he had been her lover, because he survived.

My neighbor on the other side, at the foot of the couch, was the greatest surprise. It was young Appius Claudius Nero.

"Twice in one day, young Nero," I said. "If I believed that Oriental nonsense about astrology, I would believe that our stars are intertwined."

"The stars had nothing to do with it, Decius," Capito said. "I invited Clodius, but when he learned you were to be here, he sent young Appius Claudius in his stead." Everyone found this uproariously funny, and Nero's face flushed as scarlet as Sulla's. It was always considered witty to pick on the very young, half-witted or deformed, and I felt a bit sorry for him.

"No offense, Nero," I said. "I know you have no control over who your relatives are. I have a good many I'd just as soon not associate with."

"Nepos, for instance?" Afranius needled. My cousin Metellus Nepos was Pompey's firm supporter, unlike most of our family. The year before, Nepos had served as tribune and had been a most inflammatory one. With Caesar's backing, he had tried to have Pompey recalled from Asia to fight Catilina, had even demanded that Pompey be elected Consul in absentia. There had been some rioting and the Senate suspended both of them from office. Nepos fled to Pompey with an aristocratic mob at his heels, and Caesar, ever the adroit politician, patched up things with the Senate and continued his praetorship.

Now that I thought of it, there were no friends of Caesar's here, even though he sought friends everywhere. Catulus hated him because Caesar had tried to rob him of the credit for restoring the Temple of Jupiter Capitolinus and give it to Pompey. Catullus the poet suspected Caesar of having an affair with Clodia. Few prominent women escaped that particular honor. Afranius was of the aristocratic party and opposed Caesar as a matter of policy. The same was true of Piso. It was odd, but seemed no more than coincidence.

As the first course arrived, the conversation turned to the main subject of the day: Pompey's triumph. There was to be a meeting of the Senate the next day and the matter was once more to be discussed.

"This will be your first meeting as Senator, will it not, Decius?" Capito asked.

"It will," I concurred.

"And what will be the subject of your maiden speech?" the great Catulus asked. It was common for new-minted Senators to make a speech on first taking a seat in the Curia. Some made a great splash that way, but more earned ridicule.

"I have been firmly instructed to say nothing until I've attained some sort of prestige in office, with the unspoken implication that several years might elapse before any such event."

"Not a bad idea," Capito said. "I made my first speech back when Decula and Dollabella held the Consulship. I spoke in praise of Sulla's reform of the courts, taking them from the *equites* and giving them back to the Senators. Seemed a safe enough speech at the time. Sulla was dictator, after all. When I left the Curia a mob of *equites* chased me through the streets until I got to my house and barred the gate; then they burned my house down. I escaped over the back wall and fled to Capua until things died down." This, I thought, was before he had reached his present girth.

"Those were exciting times," said Catulus nostalgically. There followed some vintage gossip about the proscriptions and who had whom killed for what advantage. The wine flowed and tongues grew loose.

"What's to be done about Antonius Hibrida, Consul?" Afranius asked. Hibrida was Proconsul in Macedonia, where he had suffered some shattering defeats.

"I intend to press for his prosecution upon his return to Rome," Calpurnianus said.

"Odd, Pompey doesn't have his tame tribunes agitating for him to be given Hibrida's command," Catulus said.

"That isn't Pompey's style," I interjected. "Pompey waits until the war is almost over and then demands the command after someone else has done all the fighting. He did it in Spain, and in Asia and Africa. He's not about to go salvage a situation where Romans have been repeatedly defeated."

"Well, *I* think that Pompey is a great man!" said Catullus the poet.

"You poets are always enthralled by adventurers who pose as gods," said Afranius. "They're all just men, and Pompey's not as much a man as some I know."

"Mucia didn't think so, anyway," said Capito. Now Catullus's face grew as red as Nero's had been. This was an indirect gibe at his infatuation with Clodia. It was widely known that Pompey had divorced Mucia because she had slept with Caesar. This did not prevent Pompey and Caesar from being allies. Politics is politics, and marriage, well, marriage is politics, too.

"I think you are all jealous of his fame," said the poet with some acuity.

"Deserving or not," said Calpurnianus, "it will be a show such as Rome has never seen before. I've been out to visit his camp and he's got a hundred elephants out there, with mahouts drilling them to perform tricks throughout the procession. He has a legion fully armed just to guard his treasure."

This got my attention. "I thought he disbanded his troops when he reached Italy."

"He petitioned to keep this lot under arms until his triumph," Calpurnianus said. "They've been out there practicing for so long that they'll be ready to celebrate the triumph within a few days of the Senate's granting permission."

"I hear that he's celebrating *three* triumphs at once," said young Nero. "The war with the pirates, the war in Africa and the one in Asia."

A slave came in and whispered something to Capito, and our host rose from the couch. "I must go and speak with someone in the atrium. Please continue to enjoy yourselves. I shall return within a few minutes." He left as his slaves began to set plates of sweet pastries before us.

"Pontifex," said young Nero very respectfully, "everyone is talking about the rites of Bona Dea, to take place tomorrow night. I am a bit confused. Just who is Bona Dea?" By "everyone" I presumed he meant Clodius. We all turned to hear Catulus.

"That is a touchy question," Catulus admitted. "We pontifexes are supposed to know all about our native religious practice, but the Good Goddess is rather mysterious. Some identify her with our old Italian goddess Ceres, whom the Greeks call Demeter; others say she is of Asian origin."

"We've always expelled foreign mystery cults," Afranius said.

"That's what makes it touchy," said Catulus. "The college of pontifexes has always been hostile to such practice, but since men are forbidden to ask about this rite, and women are forbidden to speak of it, we don't even know if it's foreign or native."

In the midst of this learned discourse, Hermes leaned forward to fill my cup. As he did, he whispered in my ear: "Don't eat the pastry." I was long experienced at intrigue and conspiracy and gave no sign that I had received a warning.

"Where are the rites being held this year?" asked one of the men at Afranius's couch.

"Caesar's house," I said. "He told me so himself this morning." That caused something else to occur to me. "Isn't it usually conducted by a Consul's wife, or the wife of the senior praetor?"

"It was all rather confused," said Calpurnianus, "because I'm a widower and my colleague Messala Niger just divorced his wife. Caesar was praetor last year, and since he's *Pontifex Maximus,* he said he'd volunteer his official residence. It's a great bother because *every* male must be excluded from the premises, including slaves and animals."

"Even paintings, statues and mosaics of any male creature must be covered," added Catulus the pontifex.

"Who is Caesar married to these days?" I asked. "I remember Cornelia died a few years ago."

"Pompeia," Afranius said, "and rumor has it he's not happy with her."

"More likely the other way around," said Catulus the poet.

"Pompeia?" I said. "Is she Pompey's daughter?" We began to hear voices raised in argument a few rooms away. Not an uncommon sound in a great house.

Calpurnianus shook his head. "No, she's the daughter of Quintus Pompeius Rufus, whose father was Consul with Sulla the year he brought his army into Rome and exiled the Marians. Her mother—let me see—yes, her mother was another Cornelia, the daughter of Sulla."

Between our multiple, political marriages and divorces and the quaint naming practices we inherited from our simple, rustic ancestors, it is remarkable that we can keep track of our own families, much less somebody else's. Pedantic old bores like Calpurnianus always took great pride in keeping these things straight. They were often wrong, but they always talked as if their genealogical memories were infallible.

A loud shout from the front of the house jerked everybody's attention in that direction. We scrambled from the couches and to our feet, aware that this was no domestic argument. As the others rushed out, I hung back and took Hermes by the shoulder.

"Now what was all that about the pastries?" I said.

"They were poisoned," Hermes said.

"Ridiculous. Mamercus Capito has no cause to murder me."

"Wasn't him," said Hermes. "It was that little patrician bugger next to you. He asked the old pontifex about that Bona Dea business, and when you looked that way he

sprinkled something onto those pastries in front of you."
He leaned over and took one from Nero's place and
popped it into his mouth.

"Hermes!"

"Well, he didn't poison *his*! I got hungry, standing there
while you and your friends stuffed yourselves."

I took my napkin from within my tunic and carefully,
without touching them, gathered up some of the pastries. These I wrapped and placed within my tunic.

"Come," I said, "let's see what happened."

The others were gathered in the atrium along with
some agitated slaves. On the tessellated floor lay a stout
body. It was Mamercus Aemilius Capito, dead as Hector.
Appius Claudius Nero stared at the corpse wide-eyed and
pasty-faced. The rest, for whom the sight of a murdered
nobleman was no novelty, were a good deal more composed. Considering that Nero had just tried to murder
me, I found his distress commendable.

"What happened?" I asked unnecessarily.

"As you will discern," Catulus said dryly, "our host will
not be joining us for the after-dinner drinking bout. It
seems that his caller did away with him."

"Did he have enemies?" asked one of the men from
Afranius's table.

"He had at least one," said Catulus. "Come now, man!
What Roman of any importance lacks enemies?"

"How boring," said Catullus the poet. "In the epics
and the dramas, murders are always exciting and terrible. This is rather tawdry."

Calpurnianus turned to Capito's majordomo. "Summon my slaves."

"At once, Consul." The man bustled off. I looked
around for the slave who had summoned Capito from
the table. It was a sizable atrium, but I spotted him and
beckoned him to my side.

"Who called upon your master this evening?" I asked
him.

"It was a man in a dark-colored cloak. He had a fold
of the cloak drawn over his head, so I did not see his
face. He spoke in a low voice."

"Didn't that seem strange?"

"It is not my place to screen my master's visitors. He
said that he was expected."

"Has you master received many such visitors lately?"

"I do not know. I was just working in the atrium when he arrived. The gatekeeper would know."

The Consul's slave retinue came in. Except for a personal valet, each of the greater guests had sent his attendants to the rear of the house. Calpurnianus had at least a dozen, who all tried to pretend that they hadn't been drinking. He summoned a boy who wore the tunic, belt and hat of a messenger. The boy held out a tablet and stylus that were connected to his belt by thin chains. The Consul opened the wooden tablet and began to write on its wax surface.

"Take this to the house of the *Praetor Urbanus* Voconius Naso. He is unlikely to be at home, but wait for him there and see that he gets this. No need to wait for his reply. I'll speak to him tomorrow in the Curia." The boy dashed off and the Consul addressed the rest of us. "I suppose he'll want to appoint a *iudex* to investigate."

I spoke to the slave again. "Were you here during their talk, or was anyone else?"

"My master dismissed me and instructed that he and his visitor were to be left alone."

At that moment, the messenger ran back in. "The gatekeeper's dead," he reported, then ran back out.

"So much for other witnesses," I said.

"The mistress is at Picenum," said the majordomo, "where they maintain a country house. I will see that she is notified and make arrangements for the funeral." From elsewhere in the house began those extravagant mourning noises with which slaves bring a little drama into their lives.

"Any sons?" asked Catulus.

"No. Two daughters, both married. I will notify them as well."

"Nothing more to be done here," said Calpurnianus. "Good evening to you all."

The others sent for their slaves. Our behavior might seem haphazard, but remember that in those days Rome had no police or regular investigative officers. A *iudex* might investigate, or an ambitious young politician might take it upon himself to look into the matter and bring charges against someone. But murderers were often of humble status, and therefore nobody's reputation was to be made by prosecuting them.

I saw Nero gather his slaves together. He had brought no fewer than four. The Claudians were a well-fixed family. I was greatly his senior in years, experience and reputation, and all I could afford was an amoral wretch like Hermes. I summoned that observant youth and whispered to him:

"Follow that little bastard and see where he goes; then report to me tomorrow."

He looked indignant. "Is that all?"

"What do you mean, is that all?" I demanded.

"I just saved your life. That ought to be worth something."

"So you claim. For all I know, you've just accused a perfectly innocent young man. Just follow him. If it turns out you really did save me, I'll be nice to you come Saturnalia." He stalked off. Actually, I had no doubt he had told the truth. If Nero was associating with Clodius, then he had to be guilty. But I knew better than to flatter Hermes. Slaves like that will take advantage of you if you let them.

The pool of blood around the body was growing rather large, but most of it was on one side. I stepped closer on the less bloody side and crouched for a better look. The murderer had cut Capito's throat, but from what I could see of the wound, it was amazingly small, rather like a stab wound. Then I noticed a slightly depressed mark between the brows, as if he had been struck by some sort of cudgel. Most killers find one death-blow sufficient, but I supposed that a little insurance would not come amiss. I stood and backed away from the corpse, my sandals making slight, sticky sounds as I did. I had not been able to entirely avoid the blood.

"Well," I muttered, "that's one who won't be Celer's colleague,"

"What's that you say?" Afranius said. The others had already left, but he had been busy berating his linkboy, who was too drunk to keep his torch alight.

"Oh, a political matter. My kinsman Metellus Celer is standing for the Consulship, and I was to talk with Capito about a possible alliance." It was not the sort of thing that had to be kept confidential.

Afranius's eyes lit up. "A *coitio*? Well, Capito is out of the picture. You know, I think the wine-bowl is still full in the triclinium. Why don't we go back there and talk while my boy sobers up?" We ambled back into the dining room as all around us the house was filled with wails of mourning.

IV

"**L**ucius Afranius, eh?" Celer said. We stood on the steps of the Curia in the dismal light of early dawn. "He wouldn't be a bad choice. I could count on him not to give me any trouble or try to override my acts. In fact, he was one of the ones I planned to have you sound out, eventually. Good work, Decius."

"Always happy to serve," I assured him.

"Pity about Capito, though. The *janitor,* too, you say?"

"Killed with the same two blows, still chained to his gate."

"The killer was probably an ex-gladiator, then. The gangs are full of them, and the stab in the throat is the arena death-blow."

That had occurred to me as well. I had known many gladiators, and among that stalwart confraternity it is a matter of honor to kill the defeated with swiftness and dignity. With a sword, this is best accomplished with a quick jab to the jugular. It is believed to be nearly painless as well, but since none who receive the blow ever talk about it afterward, this is difficult to confirm. Also, there is lots of blood, and the crowds like that.

"Probably a jealous husband and a hired killer," Celer pronounced. "That's what it usually is. Political matters haven't reached the killing stage lately."

"I'm not so sure, " I said. "Business disagreements can get just as vicious."

"He was a patrician," Celer said. "They're not supposed to engage in business. Not that they don't anyway."

While we spoke the Senate was assembling. The curule magistrates, accompanied by their lictors, climbed the

45

steps, stifling yawns like everybody else. Cato was there,
virtuously barefoot. The adherents of Pompey formed a
grim, determined knot, ready once again to press their
suit for his triumph. The usual gaggle of Metellans
formed around us. Creticus was there, and Pius the pontifex, although he was an adopted Metellus, actually a
Scipio. Of the prominent Metellans only Nepos was not
with us. He was always to be found among Pompey's
faction. For a wonder, there was not a single prominent
Metellan governing in the provinces that year.

"I've spoken to you all," said Celer. "You know how
the vote is to go." There were murmurs of assent. Besides
the great Metellans, there were at least thirty like me:
Senators who had served in the lower offices but were
otherwise undistinguished.

"Then to your seats," Celer ordered. Obedient as a
veteran legion, we trooped into the Curia.

The interior of the Senate house was dim, and it was musty
with damp wool, for it had been raining that morning, and
the finest toga is not a fragrant object when it is wet. The
fullers use human urine in their whitening process.

Thus my first Senate meeting was not fully as edifying
as I might have wished. At least, I thought, it would be
the day of a memorable vote. Only the Senate could grant
a triumph, one of the few privileges it had managed to
keep from the popular assemblies.

The first part of the morning was devoted to argu-
ments. Pompey's adherents reeled off the stunning list
of his accomplishments: enemies slain, enslaved or
brought under Roman control; territory added to the
empire; riches brought to the Roman treasury.

Then the aristocratic party had its hour, belittling the
upstart's accomplishments, complaining that the seas
were as dangerous as ever despite his campaign against
the pirates (this was outrageously untrue, but the aristocrats were grasping at straws by that time) and accus-
ing Pompey of offenses against the gods.

Then the presiding Consul, Niger, called for the vote.
The *Princeps* stood. Quintus Hortensius Hortalus was
Princeps of the Senate at that time, and he cast his vote
for Pompey with a brief (for Hortalus) and undeniably
eloquent speech. Even at his advanced age, Hortalus had
the most beautiful voice in the world. Cicero rose and

cast his vote likewise. There were no boos even from the aristocratic party. Everyone knew that Cicero didn't like Pompey. They hated him for the Catilinarian executions and awaited a chance to bring him down on that charge.

Then Metellus Celer was called. He stood and said simply: "I withdraw my former opposition. Let Pompey have his triumph. Let the soldiers of Rome be honored." He sat amid a huge, collective gasp. Everybody knew it was all over. Even such a qualified vote meant that the whole clan of Caecilius Metellus was now behind the triumph.

After that, it was mere confirmation. Permission for Pompey's triumph passed with an overwhelming majority. Even Pompey's bitterest enemies voted in favor, rather than give the appearance of a futile resistance. After all, Celer had given them an out: the assertion that they were honoring the soldiers as a whole, rather than the general in particular. This little qualification was to have serious consequences they did not foresee at the time.

We all went out of the Curia in a mixed mood. Some were jubilant, others subdued. Everyone had a sense that some serious, irrevocable step had been taken and that the Roman state, tranquil for a number of years, was poised on the brink of another period of turmoil. When a leader of the aristocrats was willing to yield even an inch to Pompey, things were unsettled.

On the steps of the Curia, I all but collided with Lucius Licinius Lucullus, celebrated conqueror and enemy of Pompey. He seemed not at all put out by the vote and clapped me on the shoulder.

"Well, that's that, eh, Decius? I hate to see that swine riding in triumph down the Via Sacra, but it was a wise political move."

"A man with an armed legion outside the gates cannot be snubbed forever," I said.

"Exactly. There'll be no more business of note today, and all this has made me hungry. Come to my house for some lunch. Let's see who else could stand a bite." We descended the steps and found Cicero and Milo in conversation. Milo was wearing a splendid white toga, a sure sign that he was embarking on a serious political career.

"Cicero," Lucullus said, "come join me for lunch. You,

too, Titus Annius. And I see Cato's sour face. Cato, you need feeding. Come with us."

Milo grinned hugely. "I shall be most honored, Lucius Licinius." Clearly, this was the first time he had received such an invitation. It was as good as a confirmation by the Censors. Cicero and Cato looked a little peeved.

"Lucius," said Cicero, "you're not going to throw a banquet again and call it lunch, are you?"

Lucullus was all offended innocence. "Now how could I do that? I've given my staff no such instruction. It shall be just the usual simple fare they set out for me every day."

These invitations were much sought after. The whole idea of lunch was rather new to Romans. We made a practice of starving ourselves all day. Dinner was not only the most important social occasion, but virtually the only genuine meal of the day.

By this time an album had been set up on the Rostra announcing the decree of the Senate, and there was much cheering from the populace. Everyone loved a triumph, and this one had been long anticipated. Heralds had been dispatched to Pompey's camp to tell him of the Senate's decision, but his toadies were already heading that way on fast horses.

By the time we reached the border of the Forum, Lucullus had picked up Celer, my father, both Consuls and a gaggle of others for his little impromptu luncheon.

"Prepare to be shocked," Cato said to me as we walked toward the Palatine. "Our host's taste for vulgar luxury has grown legendary. He outdoes the richest freedman in base, wretched excess."

"I'm looking forward to this!" I told him.

"On the other hand," Cato allowed, "he has not been utterly idle in his use of his wealth. He is building a library in imitation of the one at Alexandria, and he has brought cherry trees to Italy for the first time. He's established a cherry orchard near Naples and will make seedlings and cuttings available to all."

"That's indeed good news," I said, "about the cherries, I mean." For all our conqueror's strut, we still took a real delight in agricultural matters. Bringing a new melon to Italy would make your reputation as surely as conquering a new province.

"And his fishponds are extraordinary." Cato had to say these things so that he could endure the guilt of enjoying lunch. There should be a religion for people like Cato. Stoicism is simply not up to the task.

Milo came to join us and Cato walked away to talk with Cicero. His aristocratic soul rebelled at the thought of political adventurers like Milo. I never noticed that this bothered Milo in the least.

"Tell me about last night," Milo said. The story had been all over the Forum by first light. I sketched the details of Capito's murder, then told him about the alleged poisoning attempt.

"That may be my slave's wild imagination," I cautioned, "or an attempt to ingratiate himself with me."

"Best not to take chances where Clodius might be concerned. I'll leave that to you, but I'll see what I can find out about Capito's killer. I don't know of anyone who uses that two-blow technique. It reminds me of the way sacrificial animals are killed: a knock on the head and a cut throat."

"I'd thought of that, too. That's a two-man job, though."

"You like to snoop. Get one of the praetors to appoint you *iudex pedaneus.*" This last was an official appointed to investigate crimes and disputes.

"I'm not on the list of names to be drawn from," I told him. "I won't be old enough for more than a year."

"That's unfortunate, but if Clodius is trying to poison you, you may not have much attention to spare for other matters."

The town house of Lucullus was the size of many country villas, an amazing thing in the tight-packed city. His staff of slaves and freedmen was rumored to number in the hundreds. That was not unusual for a country estate, but town houses were usually more modest. I gaped like any visiting foreigner at the fabulous statuary, the ponds and fountains, the spectacular gardens, where he had had full-grown trees brought in and planted.

A triclinium is supposed to accommodate nine dinner guests comfortably, with room to wedge in a few extras. The triclinium of Lucullus would have housed a full meeting of the Senate. I was told that this was one of several dining halls, and not among the largest. We flopped onto couches upholstered with pure silk and

stuffed with down and precious herbs. The platter set
before me was two feet wide, as thick as my thumb and
made of solid silver.

The opening course was, as usual, eggs. But these had
been wrapped in an incredibly fine foil of hammered
gold. It seemed that we were to eat them foil and all.
Cato fastidiously unwrapped his. The next course was
suckling pigs. They had rubies for eyes.

"This is your modest afternoon repast, Lucius?" Cicero said.

"Yes, when I've nothing in particular to celebrate." He
made a signal and musicians began to play. A troupe of
beautiful Greek boys came in and began a Pyrrhic dance.

"Don't get him started," warned Hortalus, my father's
colleague in the Censorship. "When he wants to show
off, he brings out the gold table service. It's as massive
as this."

"I was wondering what happened to that big golden
statue of Mithridates you captured, Lucius," said Celer.

"Absurd!" Cato protested. "There was a time when
only a single service was owned by the entire Senate, and
it was passed from one member to another when foreign
ambassadors were to be entertained." Cato always talked
as if there were something special about being a small,
poor city-state. The world was full of such places, and he
never seemed to admire any of them.

"I think it entirely fitting and perfectly Roman," said
Lucullus. "Thracian chieftains drink wine from the skulls
of their enemies. Why should we not dine off the statue
of an enemy of Rome?"

"Utter sophistry!" Cato protested. The conversation
turned to other things; Cato was too easy a target. About
this time a group of women of the household entered
and took chairs at the tables. At least they didn't join the
men on the couches. That would have sent Cato into an
apoplectic fit. One of these, a woman about my age who
wore a peach-colored gown, was extraordinarily beautiful. She was as white-blond as a German, but her features
were unmistakably Roman, and of the upper classes.
Milo, who lay on my right, leaned toward me.

"Who is the blond goddess?" He did not say this sar-
castically. He had the stunned look of a man smitten. I

turned to the man on my left, an old Senator who was a regular in Lucullus's circle, and asked him.

"The lady Fausta," he answered. I turned back to Milo.

"Tough luck, Titus. It's Fausta, Sulla's daughter."

"What is wrong with that?" Milo asked. "I want you to introduce me to her." His eyes had a gleam I could only interpret as unhealthy.

"In the first place, I don't know her. In the second, she's a Cornelian, and the gods need permission to call on that family."

He gripped my shoulder and I stifled a scream. Milo had hands that could crush bone. He relented a little and leaned close.

"Introduce me. You are a Metellan, and even a Cornelian will listen to somebody named Caecilius Metellus."

"I'll do it!" I said. To my utterable relief, his hand left my shoulder. I studied the woman. She was something of an enigma in Rome, famous but rarely seen. She and her brother, Faustus, were twins, a portentous enough circumstance without being the children of the godlike Sulla. At his death, Sulla had entrusted their care to his friend Lucullus. Faustus had joined Pompey in Asia and distinguished himself in the wars there. Fausta had remained with Lucullus and for some reason had never married. The twins received their unusual names from their father, in honor of his legendary good fortune. He paid for it at the end, though. He died in terrible, lingering agony of a nameless cancer. The last year of his life must have made him wish he'd not lived the first fifty-nine.

When the luncheon was over, the guests wandered around admiring the grounds, where you almost expected to see naked nymphs burst from the shrubbery, closely pursued by ithyphallic satyrs. Had satyrs not been in such short supply, doubtless Lucullus would have had them.

We found Fausta clipping winter roses in a canopied arbor. She wielded the clippers while a little slave girl held up her skirts to collect them. I walked up to her and made the expected obeisance.

"Lady Fausta, I've not had the honor of your acquain-

tance. I am Decius Caecilius Metellus the Younger, recently returned to Rome from a sojourn in Gaul."

She spared me the slightest of glances, and her eyes
flickered to Milo. "Charmed. And who is your friend?"

I was a bit put out. Granted, Milo was enormous and
handsome as a god, but I was certainly better born.

"Allow me to present Titus Annius Milo Papianus, a—
just what are you, Milo?" I couldn't very well introduce
him as my friend, Milo the gangster, although that was
exactly what he was.

Milo took her hand. "I am the man who is going to
rule Rome, as your father did, my lady."

She smiled up at him. "Wonderful. Men of ordinary
ambition are so common."

"I believe we are related," I said. "Wasn't your mother
a Caecilia Metella?"

"How long have you been in Rome, Titus Annius?"
she asked, utterly ignoring me. Well, it wasn't that much
of a relationship. My family produces even more daughters than sons.

"A little over eight years, my lady." After his initial
burst of arrogance, he seemed almost tongue-tied, a
marvel I never expected to behold.

"Titus Milo, you say? I believe I've heard the name.
Don't your followers get into street battles with the men
of Clodius Pulcher?"

"Not lately," Milo said, bashful at receiving such praise.

"How enthralling. You must tell me all about it."

"Well, I'll leave you two to get acquainted," I said. They
ignored me. I gave it up as a futile task and walked away
from them. I had discharged my duty as Eros.

Full-bellied and with the balance of a fine day ahead
of me, I decided to make another call on a friend, this
time with more than social aims in mind. I headed down
the Palatine toward the river. I had a call to pay at the
Temple of Aesculapius.

For the first time I crossed the splendid new stone
bridge that linked the bank with the island. This had
been built the year before by the tribune Fabricius. At
the temple I inquired after the physician Asklepiodes
and found that he was once again in residence at the
Statilian School, which had been displaced by the building of Pompey's new theater. The new school was situ-

ated in the Trans-Tiber district. Armed with directions, I crossed to the far bank into the city's newest district, which, unconstrained by walls, sprawled over a sizable patch of ground without the suffocating closeness of the old city.

The new school was a splendid affair, with none of the prisonlike air that so many such institutions have. The walk leading to the school was paved with stone and lined with statues of champions of years past. An archway tunneled through the building, leading to a wide exercise yard whence came the clatter of weapons as the men went through their arms drill. I paused to admire the spectacle, and possibly calculate odds for the next games. The trainees fought with practice weapons, but the senior veterans actually used sharp weapons. The blade artistry of some of these men was wonderful to see. No soldier ever gains this sort of expertise, because soldiers spend much time practicing formation fighting and even more on labor details, digging and building. Gladiators do nothing but train for single combat.

Most of the men trained with the large shield and the straight *gladius* or with the small shield and the curved *sica*, and some practiced with the spear, but there was a new category, one that had appeared during Caesar's aedileship.

Caesar had borrowed heavily to put on games of unprecedented magnificence, going so far as to give *munera* in honor of a deceased female relative when he ran out of dead male ancestors. He bought up so many gladiators that his enemies in the Senate panicked, thinking that he was buying a private army. They quickly passed legislation limiting the number of gladiators one citizen could exhibit at any given set of games. Since he could not show as many as he wanted, he began to use bizarre new types: men who fought from elephants, chariot fighters, horsemen and others. Strangest of all were the netmen.

Nobody knew what to make of them whey they first marched into the arena. They looked like fishermen from the Styx with their nets and their three-pronged harpoons. Nobody thought they could be fighters because they wore no armor. We thought perhaps we were to see some new dance. Then a group of big-shield fighters came in and paired off with the netmen. At first, we expected to see the netmen slaughtered. But this was not toe-to-toe fighting of the sort we were used to. The netmen darted all over the arena, casting their nets, running away if they missed, only to return to the fight after retrieving the net by its cord. After a lot of laughter and hooting, the audience began to get into the spirit of the thing and cheered on the combatants. To everyone's surprise, more netmen than swordsmen won their fights. It was all so unexpected that there was no way to decide whether anyone had fought really well or badly, so the crowd withheld the death signal, although a few fighters died later of their wounds.

Caesar had intended this to be a novelty act for that one set of games, but the crowd's fancy was taken and they began to demand the net fighters. Now I saw that Statilius Taurus had added them to his regular categories of fighters. Traditionalists like my father found them entirely too exotic, and Cato, predictably, said it was a disgrace to the tradition of mortal combat.

A slave guided me to the quarters of the resident physician, and there I found my friend Asklepiodes, the world's greatest expert on mortal wounds. We spent several minutes exchanging greetings, for which he had a Greek's fondness. We swiftly brought each other up to date on our doings of the past year or so; then I broached my current business, telling him of the events of the previous night.

"Ah, Decius, how like you!" Asklepiodes said. "Back in Rome only three days and already involved in a murder!"

"One successful," I said. "The other, fortunately, merely attempted." I handed him the wrapped parcel of pastries. "Is there some way to test these, short of feeding them to a slave?"

"I will try an animal. It is difficult to induce a dog to eat sweet pastries, but perhaps a pig will oblige. These tests are not infallible, I must warn you. There are substances deadly to humans but harmless to animals."

"If it is a poison," I asked, "is there any way to determine what sort?"

"That is extremely difficult unless you use a human

subject, who can describe his symptoms. I am, of course, forbidden to do any such thing."

"I wouldn't ask you to," I said. "Do you think you could get a look at Capito's body? Unfortunately, I have no official position just now."

"I am acquainted with the most prominent undertakers. There should be no difficulty. From your description, no detailed examination should be necessary. A quick look should suffice. I shall attend to it this evening."

"I shall be grateful," I told him.

"My friend Decius, life is always so much more interesting when you are in Rome. Please feel free to call upon my services."

"I'll be back tomorrow," I told him.

"Try to live that long," he urged. Asklepiodes had a strange sense of humor, but one must make allowances for Greeks.

As I walked back across the river toward my home in the Subura, I began to regret that I had not thought to arm myself before going out that day. I had been so elated at the prospect of attending my first Senate meeting that it had caused me to be less than cautious. It is forbidden to bear arms within the *pomerium* and doubly forbidden to carry them into the Curia, but I was prepared to risk censure. A recent attempt on my life always lowered my respect for custom.

Now here I was wandering alone through streets that might harbor Clodius's minions. Even as I thought this, I was struck by something else: Poison was not his style. Whatever else you could say about Clodius, he was always perfectly willing to kill his enemies with his own hand, right out in public.

But who else was my mortal enemy? I hadn't offended anyone lately. Only madmen like Clodius nurse grudges year after year, awaiting a chance to strike. I had made my peace with most of my enemies, and the rest of them seemed to have forgotten me. It was all a great puzzle.

I managed to reach my house without homicide and sent for Hermes. My aged slave Cato clucked dolefully.

"Nothing good will come of having that young lout in the house, master. He's destined for the cross."

"Most likely. But until that sad day, let's see what use we can get out of him. Send him in."

Hermes came in, smirking and swaggering as if he had done something heroic, something praiseworthy. I would have been astounded to learn he had done something moderately honest, but slaves perceive things differently from the freeborn. Sometimes one must humor them.

"What have you to report?" I asked him.

"I followed your friend from the dinner party just like you told me to. He stopped twice on the way to vomit."

"That's odd," I said. "Dinner wasn't all that rich, and the drinking had hardly started when Capito's murder broke things up. It must have been the first time he had tried to murder somebody. It may have made him nervous."

"Ha! So you admit I saved your life!" Hermes crowed.

"Not yet. I'm having the pastries tested. Go on with your report."

"I followed him over past the Circus and up onto the Palatine to a big town house—"

"I knew it!" I said. "He went to Clodius's house to report that he'd failed to kill me. I wish I could have seen Clodius's ugly face when he heard the news!" Then I noticed that Hermes had that smug expression slaves get when they know something you don't.

"He didn't go to the house of Clodius, master."

"Whose, then?" I demanded.

"He went to the house of your kinsman Metellus Celer."

V

I did not really believe that Celer would try to kill me. We were on good terms, and he and my father were close. I had not forgotten who his wife was, though. But it had been years since Clodia had last tried to have me killed, and I could not think why she would try to do away with me now. Her only possible reason would be that she thought I threatened her brother, for whom she had a more than sisterly fondness.

These things were much on my mind as I prepared for the day. This time, I did not neglect to tuck my dagger and my *caestus* into my tunic. Best to be safe. Accompanied by Hemes, I set out for Celer's house. I had no intention of confronting him with Nero's doings. In the first place, I did not yet have confirmation that any murder attempt had taken place. I would wait and watch.

I stopped at a corner barber's stall for a shave, then proceeded on toward the Palatine. I was at the base of the hill when I met a well-dressed procession headed toward the Forum, a grim-faced Celer at its head. He did not spare me a glance, and I was not about to attract his attention. I had seen that look before, in Gaul, and it usually meant that traitors were about to be executed. I fell in with the crowd of clients. I noticed that Caesar was there as well, equally grim-faced. I spotted my cousin-by-adoption Scipio Nasica the pontifex and stepped to his side.

"What's happened?" I asked him in a low voice.

"We don't know," he said, equally quiet about it. Everyone looked as if something terrible had happened. "A messenger came during the morning call. He took Celer and Caesar aside and spoke to them in private. Then they came out looking like they do now. Celer announced that an extraordinary meeting of the Senate has been called and has said nothing more."

My spine tingled. Ordinarily, this meant a major military disaster. I wondered where it had happened. Antonius Hibrida had turned in a string of defeats in Macedonia, so that should not come as a surprise. Perhaps the Germans were on the march again. I shuddered at the thought. The last time they had terrorized all Italy, and it had taken Gaius Marius to defeat them. Despite all his posturing, Pompey was no Gaius Marius.

The Forum had that look it always gets when everyone knows there is bad news in the air. Instead of the usual drifting, shifting mass, people gathered in tight little knots, each one feeding the other's ignorance with rumors and omens. I overheard talk of military disaster, civil war, invasion by foreign enemies, plague, famine, earthquake and wondrous visitations by the Olympian deities, all before we reached the steps of the Curia.

Senators were bustling up the steps, eager to find out what had transpired. The lictors of the magistrates stood leaning on their fasces, trading omens like everybody else. As we reached the steps, Caius Julius left our little procession to speak with a matron so hatchet-faced she made him and Celer look cheerful by comparison. I asked my companions who this might be, and someone identified her as Caesar's mother. This was strange indeed. Roman women, however prestigious, were not supposed to take part in political matters.

Inside, the Curia vibrated with a low buzz, everyone apprehensive but also eagerly curious to know what had happened. Down in front, where all the greatest men were, stood the Consuls and the senior magistrates, the pontifexes and the *Princeps*. Something seemed decidedly odd about this group. Some of them, the Consuls in particular, looked *amused*.. There was an aura of barely suppressed hilarity among them, until Caesar joined them and they resumed their stony faces. The Consuls took their curule chairs and the rest of us sat on our benches. When all was properly ordered, Hortalus stood to address the Senate.

"Conscript fathers," he intoned, "I must address you on a grave matter." His voice to the ear was like honey to the tongue. "Last night, here in this sacred city of

Quirinus, a most heinous act of sacrilege was perpe-
trated!" He paused for effect, and he got it. This was the
last news anyone was expecting to hear. Serious offenses
against the gods were rare, and usually involved unchas-
tity in a Vestal Virgin. I noticed, however, that Hortalus
had used the rare word *sacrilegium*. Sexual relations with
a Vestal was always referred to as *incestum*.

"Last night," Hortalus went on, "during the ancient,
holy and most solemn rites of Bona Dea, an impostor
was discovered spying upon this ritual, which is forbidden to all men! It was the quaestor Publius Clodius
Pulcher, who entered the house of the *Pontifex Maximus*
by stealth, dressed as a woman!"

The Curia erupted into total uproar. There were calls
for trial, calls for death. Mostly, there was just jabbering
and whooping, and I did my share of it. I jumped around
like a boy, clapping my hands with sheer joy.

"Now we'll be rid of him!" I said to someone near me.
"Now he'll be condemned and given some awful ritual
punishment, buried alive or pulled apart with red-hot
pincers or something." It was a cheering thought, but my
neighbor dampened it.

"He'll have to be tried first. Sit down and let's see what
the pontiffs and lawyers say."

I hadn't thought of that. Cicero had gotten himself in
plenty of trouble by urging the Senate to condemn the
Catilinarians without jury trial, and no one had forgotten that. I sat. The Senators would be cautious about
prosecuting him, worse luck.

The Consul Calpurnianus stood and held up a hand
for silence, which he finally accomplished.

"Conscript fathers, before we can even discuss action,
we must have some definitions so that we know what we
are talking about. The distinguished *Princeps* Quintus
Hortensius Hortalus has used the word 'sacrilege.' I will
ask another distinguished jurist, Marcus Tullius Cicero,
to explain this term for us."

Cicero stood. "In earlier times, 'sacrilege' was defined
as the stealing of objects consecrated to a god, or deposited in a consecrated place. In more recent times, this
word has been extended to cover all damage or insults
done to the gods and to sacred places. If the conscript
fathers so direct, I shall be most pleased to prepare a

brief listing the sources and precedents for the legal charge of sacrilege."

"Caius Julius Caesar," said Calpurnianus, "as *Pontifex Maximus,* is it your judgment that this offense merits the name of sacrilege?"

Caesar stood and walked before the Senate as if he were officiating at his father's funeral. He pulled a fold of his toga over his head, solemn as a tragic actor.

"I do so judge it," Caesar intoned, "and it is to my unutterable shame that this unspeakable act should happen within the house of Caesar." This was the first time I heard him refer to himself in the third person, an annoying habit with which we were to become all too familiar.

"Then," said Calpurnianus, "with the concurrence of the Senate, I shall direct the praetor Aulus Gabinius to go with his lictors to the house of Clodius and place him under arrest."

"Just a minute, now!" shouted a Senator named Fufius, a notorious lackey of Clodius. "Publius Clodius is a serving Roman official and cannot be arrested or impeached while he is in office!"

"Oh, sit down and stop talking like an idiot!" barked Cicero. "Clodius is a mere quaestor, with no more imperium than brains. What's more, he has not yet gone to his place of duty to take up his office, and this offense has nothing to do with the discharge of official business."

"And let us not forget," said Metellus Nepos, all bland malice, "that during the Catilinarian emergency, serving Roman officials, including a praetor, were arrested. Might not a charge of sacrilege be as serious as one of treason?" This, of course, had nothing to do with Clodius but was aimed directly at Cicero, who had ordered those arrests.

I must say that, in the midst of all this legal and ritual dispute, the mood of most of the Senate was one of merriment. The whole affair was so absurd that it was like something happening in a play by Aristophanes. We would not have been surprised to see the principals don comic masks with wide-stretched mouths.

"Gentlemen," said Hortalus, "before we speak seriously of arrests and trials, I must remind you all of something. If we bring Publius Clodius into court, there will be testimony. In the course of that testimony, *somebody*, sooner or later, must speak of the rites of the Good Goddess." That gave us all pause.

Cato stood up. "Unthinkable! These sacred matters must not be made the subject of vulgar gossip in the Forum!"

"Step outside, Cato," shouted someone. "I'll wager a hundred sesterces nobody's babbling about anything else right now!"

"How can we have a trial," said the praetor Naso, "when the women who were present at the offense can't speak of what they were doing and no man can hear about it?" That set off another round of calls for action and protests against any such thing. I began to despair of anything constructive being decided. By now, I thought, Clodius must be on a fast horse headed for Messina, there to take ship for Sicily, where he could hide under the cover of his office until the furor died down in Rome.

Toward noon, there occurred a remarkable exchange. Everyone has heard some version of it, usually distorted beyond recognition by those who were not there or those who were but in later years grew too fearful to tell the truth. I am the only man now alive who was there that day, and this is how it truly happened, not how it ended up in Roman legend.

"Caius Julius," said the Consul Messala Niger, "without your speaking of forbidden things, do you know if any of the ladies who were present last night have any idea of what Clodius was up to when he entered your house dressed as a woman?" Everybody wanted to hear about this.

"My mother, the lady Aurelia, has told me there was talk that Clodius thus gained stealthy entrance to carry on a liaison with Pompeia." He drew himself up so straight and tall that I suspected him of wearing actors' buskins on his feet. "I have therefore resolved to divorce Pompeia forthwith!"

Celer stood. "Don't be hasty, Caius Julius. There is nothing going on between your wife and Clodius. He just wanted to spy on the rites. The fool has talked about nothing else for days."

Then Caesar made history, of a sort. Gazing around him like an eagle, he said, "She may well be innocent, but that is immaterial. Caesar's wife must be above suspicion." You could have heard a pin drop in the Curia. The appearance of a god among us could not have been so stunning.

One of the many banes of my existence has been my laugh, which is high-pitched and raucous, and has on more than one occasion been likened to the braying of a wild ass. I could not help myself. I held it in as long as possible, then let it loose when the pain of suppression grew insupportable. It started as a snorting wheeze high up in my aristocratic Metellan nose and, an instant later, emerged like the sound of a legion's pack-train demanding their ration of oats.

In an instant, the Senate was convulsed. Vinegary old politicians who didn't laugh from one year to the next doubled over, laughing until their guts cramped. Solemn pontifexes had tears rolling down their wrinkled cheeks. Just outside the chamber, a whole bench of tribunes rolled about so helpless with laughter that they could not have interposed a veto if we had called for the beheading of every plebeian in Rome. I am sure that I saw even Cato smiling.

Since he is now a god, people think that Caius Julius must have been held in reverent awe since earliest youth. Nothing could be farther from the truth. At this time he was forty years old, completely undistinguished politically and militarily, and highly regarded only in the popular assemblies, where he was good at currying favor with the mob. In the Senate he was a nobody. He had bribed his way to the supreme pontiff's position and he was renowned only for his extravagance and his questionable morals. Of Caius Julius Caesar two things were generally agreed: He had the biggest debts in history and he had almost certainly been buggered by King Nicomedes of Bithynia.

It was hearing that unbelievably sanctimonious pronouncement from such a source that convulsed the Senate. During all this hilarity Caesar stood like a statue of himself, his face devoid of expression. In later years, I lost a great deal of sleep wondering if he remembered that I was the first who laughed that day.

The meeting broke up with nothing decided. In no time at all, the story was all over the city. For months afterward stage comedies and wall scrawlings referred to Caesar's famous dictum. Anytime conversation flagged or a party seemed to be growing dejected, somebody would draw himself up and intone: "But Caesar's wife must be above suspicion," and everybody would laugh like rabid hyenas.

I walked down the steps of the Curia, mopping the tears from my face with a corner of my toga. No one could ask for better entertainment than this. Hermes came running up to me, and of course I had to explain everything to him. The jabber of the multitude in the Forum grew deafening. Between them, Clodius and Caesar had concocted the most memorable event of the year.

I went to the baths and was swamped by men who had not been there, demanding to know what was going on. I held forth for some time, not neglecting to call for the immediate arrest and trial of Publius Clodius. It was all so congenial that I had to remind myself that I was involved in deadly matters as well.

"I hope there's a trial," said a fellow Senator. "I've wondered for years what it is my wife does at that rite." It turned out that he spoke for a great many highly placed husbands. Others were more fearful of divine wrath.

"That woman Clodia must be involved," said a prominent banker. "She's his sister, and everyone knows that woman will do anything." This had occurred to me as well.

From the baths I went to the Statilian *ludus,* where I had to explain everything all over again to Asklepiodes. He knew little of Caesar and therefore missed the humor of the situation. And he had a Greek's love of mystery cults, so he was mildly scandalized by Clodius's sacrilege.

"Your Italian gods seem to lack the proper subordinates for punishing such transgressors," he said in his superior fashion. "Greek deities would have set the Friendly Ones after him."

I thought of those winged, serpent-haired creatures pursuing Clodius through the alleys of Rome, blood dripping from their eyes and their claws extended to rip flesh.

"It's a great pity," I admitted. "We don't personalize our gods in quite the way you Greeks do, and give them minions and servants. Some of our gods don't even have images."

"That is a very poor sort of religious practice, if you ask me," Asklepiodes maintained. "And the way you elect and appoint your priests, as if they were just ordinary officials. And most disgraceful is the way you appoint your augurs and give them a rule book for taking omens. Where is the art of divination without the divine afflatus?"

"That is because we are a rational and dignified people, and we are not about to conduct public affairs according to the ravings of a demented ecstatic. In times of crisis, I admit, we consult a sibyl, but I never heard that it did any real good."

"Because you Romans lack a true understanding of divine nature," he said stoutly.

"Nor have I ever heard of it doing Greeks any good. Even when their prophesies proved to be correct, the supplicant usually misinterprets it and comes to disaster."

Asklepiodes looked down his nose at me, a considerable feat since he was shorter. "It is always the occasional tale of irony that makes its way into legend. When approached in the proper spirit, sibylline oracles are usually quite reliable."

"I'll take your word for it," I told him.

"Now, on to less exalted matters. I fear I must bill you for one pig. A small one, originally intended for the gladiators' dinner."

My heart sank. "Then it was truly poison?"

"Healthy pigs are seldom struck dead by natural causes or the wrath of the gods. I fed it the pastries you gave me, and it was dead within an hour."

"An hour? That long? It must have been a weak poison."

"Not necessarily. Those instantaneous poisons one always hears about are fictitious. I have never encountered one that took less than an hour to kill a grown man, and most of them take much longer, accompanied by agonizing pains and convulsions. Somebody wanted you dead, my friend."

"Any idea what sort of poison?" I asked.

"I spoke before of the difficulty of this. I dissected the animal afterward and found no signs of hemorrhage. It did not go into violent convulsions. The poison might have been an extract of certain mushrooms, but it might as easily have been a decoction of Egyptian cobra venom which had been reduced and concentrated, then mixed with a stabilizing agent to form a powder."

"Cobra venom? That's a bit exotic. The boy had just visited a peasant herb-woman in the Forum. Do they traffic in such things?"

"They most certainly know mushrooms. Do not be fooled by appearances, Decius. She may never have attended lectures by learned physicians, but a peasant herbalist will have an intimate knowledge of the local plants and their properties. For all I know, there may be an herb or a root native to some local valley that produces a poison deadlier than any known to the school of Hippocrates."

"Or he might have obtained it elsewhere," I said.

"I marvel as always at your discernment in these matters. Most men are inclined to accept the quickest or most convenient answer to everything."

"It's what makes me so good at my work," I admitted. "There is a faculty in me that refuses to accept face value. If an explanation is easy or obvious, I get suspicious. If someone wants me to believe something, I suspect an ulterior motive."

"It must be a useful faculty indeed. In kings it becomes overdeveloped and they see assassins everywhere and overindulge themselves in executions."

"It's a good one for a man on the service of the Senate and People of Rome," I maintained. "And sometimes the lethal designs of enemies are real, as witness the unfortunate pig. How much for the animal, by the way?"

"Twelve sesterces."

"Twelve? That seems a bit steep for a small pig. Couldn't you have gone ahead and fed it to the gladiators? Surely the poison affected only the vital organs and could not have permeated the flesh."

"It is always inadvisable to take liberties with the diet of professional killers. Twelve sesterces, Decius."

I took out my purse and counted out the coins. "Now,

as I see it, the boy may have been consulting the woman in her fortune-telling capacity, as she claimed. When I took his hand, I noticed that he was wearing a suicide ring. My slave Hermes followed him home and he vomited twice on the way. These seem to me to be signs of a very young and inexperienced conspirator, unused to murder. Well, he will be sorry he picked me for his maiden effort."

"And the fortune-teller?" Asklepiodes inquired.

"He probably wanted to confer about favorable signs or some such. I rather doubt he confided to her the nature of his mission, but a boy nervous enough to wear a poison ring would want to be sure that the gods favored that day for a momentous enterprise, or perhaps he wanted confirmation that he has a long life ahead of him."

"Yet he was a stranger to you. Who do you suspect set him upon you?"

"I have a short list this time, but more names may be added as I investigate further. Clodius, of course, but I think he would rather do me in with his own hand."

"Even Publius Clodius may have attained a certain discretion and maturity with the advance of years," Asklepiodes said. "I hear him spoken of as a promising figure in city politics."

"Oh, that. It just means he's the most successful criminal now operating."

"I also hear your good friend Titus Milo spoken of in the same fashion," he added.

"That's just because they're rivals. But Milo is my friend!" Sometimes I just could not understand Greeks.

"Now, you asked me to view the corpse of Aemilius Capito," the physician reminded me.

"Oh, right. I almost forgot. Being the would-be victim of a murderer makes you forget other people's problems in that area. What did you make of it?"

"Most odd," Asklepiodes said.

"How so?" My attention sharpened. "I thought it seemed rather ordinary, apart from the two-blow style of dispatching."

"That was the oddity. I persuaded the undertaker's men to allow me to examine the wounds closely. The persuasion will cost you another ten sesterces, by the way."

"Ten sesterces just to handle a corpse?" I said. "The necrophiles who lurk around the amphitheaters only pay five."

"Please!" he said, offended. "I did not 'handle' the corpse. That would be unclean. I examined closely. And one would expect the price to be higher for a Senator than for some poor, condemned wretch."

"It had better be worth it," I said, counting out yet more coins.

"It was most intriguing. The cut, or rather, *stab* in the throat was delivered with the most precise expertise. The blade was double-edged, no more than an inch wide, not a *sica* or a *pugio*, but rather an extremely sharp, flat-ground blade with a short point section." He gestured at the armory hanging on his walls. "I have nothing quite like it among my collection, but I think it must be rather like the sticking knife used to slaughter animals."

"That *is* odd," I admitted. "I know of nobody in Rome who kills like that. Perhaps that's why he knocked poor old Mamercus on the head first—to set him up for the artistic death-blow."

"Now I come to the oddest part," Asklepiodes said, relishing this slow process of revelation.

"Come to it quickly," I said.

"When I examined the depression on the brow, I had no difficulty in identifying the weapon. It was a hammer, one with a round, flat face approximately one and one-half inches in diameter. The circular depression lay just above the nose, and it was twice as deep on the lower or nose side as on the upper side, toward the hairline."

"You speak as if this unevenness of depth were fraught with significance," I commented.

"And so it is. It means that the hammer blow was not delivered first, to stun the victim. Had that been the case, the depression would have been deeper toward the hair-line. No, the murderer struck Capito with the hammer after he lay on the floor. He stood behind the body, about a foot from the top of the head, and struck downward at a rather sharp angle."

"*After* he was already down!" I said. "Whatever could

have been his purpose? Capito was as good as dead when the knife blow was struck."

"Decidedly. A severed left carotid brings unconsciousness within a very few seconds, and death only a few seconds after that. There is no saving the victim. The hammer blow must have been for another purpose." He wandered over to his window and gazed down at the men practicing in the yard below. "It reminded me of something, and I think it was a thing I saw many years ago, but I cannot call it to mind. I do not have your facility for summoning up odd facts and putting them together."

I might have known. He probably knew something vital, but he couldn't remember what it was. I decided to be patient. My near-poisoning concerned me far more than the unfortunate Capito.

"Well, should you remember, please send for me."

"I shall. And should there be more of these murders, please feel free to consult me." He patted my shoulder as I left his quarters. "If I know you, there well be more of them."

VI

The next morning, at the house of Celer, I eyed the callers most closely. Clodius was not there, nor was Nero. Neither was Caesar, but he might have been busy divorcing his wife. I saw my kinsman Creticus and went to pay my respects. He wasn't much of a figure as the senior members of my family went, but he had once stood up to Pompey and came out on his feet, for which I respected him greatly.

"Decius, good to see you," he said. "Odd business the other night, wasn't it?" Nobody in Rome was talking about anything else.

"What does Felicia tell you?" I asked. Felicia was the daughter of Creticus.

"She just takes a smug attitude and claims she can say nothing while hinting she knows things we men can only dream about. What's your wife say?"

"I'm not married, Uncle," I said. He wasn't Father's brother, but I had always called him that. He was actually a second cousin, or perhaps it was a third.

"Lucky you. Well, my money is on Clodia as the instigator, and Felicia and Clodia are as close as two women can be, but I can't get a thing out of the girl. I've told her husband to put a stop to it, but the boy dotes on her and won't say a word to offend her."

The boy was the younger Crassus, and it was true. His love for Felicia was the talk of Rome. They had been united in a typical political marriage, but some people are just meant for each other. When she died he built her the most splendid tomb ever seen in Rome.

"When it comes to Clodia," I said, "it is often best not to inquire too closely."

"Jove has spoken," he vowed. Our conversation was

interrupted when Celer beckoned for me to join him. I went over, and he excused the two of us from a knot of magistrates and foreign ambassadors. We walked not merely to a private corner of the atrium but all the way out into the peristylium, where we could be sure even the slaves wouldn't overhear.

"Decius," he said, "I'm taking you off all political duties. I have a job of investigation to be done, and I know you're the best for that. Your father acts like it's unworthy, but he takes a real pride in your accomplishments. When I broached my problem at the family council last night, he recommended you as the one to appoint."

"I am flattered," I said. I had not been informed that a family council had been called, but I didn't amount too much in those days.

"Here is the task: You know what everybody knows about the profanation of the rites of the Good Goddess by my odious little brother-in-law. Today the college of the pontifexes meets to officially declare the charge of sacrilege. That means nothing. All they can do is turn it over to the courts. A trial will be—messy. I would rather not see it happen. As for Clodius, it would not bother me greatly if the little swine were to die on the cross. But I don't want my wife involved. Do you understand?"

This was discomforting. "I understand, sir. But I cannot guarantee that I will be able to—"

He grabbed me by the upper arm, painfully. "Decius, find out what happened. Find out who was responsible, compile evidence, but *keep Clodia out of it*! Do you understand?"

"Perfectly, sir," I said. It was not the first time I had been told to suppress evidence. It was the first time the demand had come from my family, though. It seemed odd, since they should have known better than anybody else that I couldn't do it. It was not that I was especially honest, or that I did not want to act as demanded. It was just that some mischievous *genius* in me made me ferret out the truth and make it public. It was another part of that faculty Asklepiodes and I had discussed. One thing I could be sure of. My father had no illusions about me. If he had recommended me for the job, he understood what might come of it.

The truth of the matter was that this caused me no

great crisis of conscience. The profanation of the Bona
Dea ceremonies seemed ludicrous rather than shocking.
I did not classify mere scandal as crime, whatever the
pontifexes might think. Besides, she was not really one
of the official state deities. When someone was trying to
poison me, the indignation of some highborn Roman
ladies seemed a small matter, indeed.

"What is to be my official capacity in all this?" I asked
him.

"Oh, say that you're acting on my behalf as Consul-
elect."

"I can't do that! Granted you'll win the election, but if
you assume the authority so far ahead of time, people
will regard it as high-handed. They'll vote against you
out of spite."

"You're not going to be making speeches to the Centuriate Assembly," he said testily. "You're going to be
questioning in the houses of Senators, discreetly and in
privacy. They know how these things work."

"Where should I start?"

"You're the investigator. I leave it up to you."

I took a deep breath. "I will have to question Clodia."

He glared from beneath his bristly eyebrows. "If you
must," he all but muttered. "Just keep my admonitions
in mind."

"Well," I said, "I'll be about it." I dreaded confronting
Clodia, but the chance of doing Clodius a bad turn was
too good to miss.

I didn't question Clodia first, though. I left Celer's
house and made for the Forum, with Hermes dogging
my steps. The day was blustery and the law courts had
moved indoors. I found Cicero in the Basilica Porcia, the
oldest of our permanent law courts. He had been listening to a defense conducted by one of his students and
readily stepped aside with me into one of the aisles. I
briefly sketched my commission from Celer and asked
Cicero's opinion, wanting to be sure of my legal ground.

"Since no official investigator has been named, you
may do what you like as an interested citizen. Celer, of
course, has no authority, and I suspect that he is moti-
vated primarily by personal interests."

"Keeping Clodia out of it, you mean?"

"Not that any involvement of hers matters greatly," he

added rather hastily. "If she had anything to do with it, the pontifexes may reprimand her, but no more. The sacrilege was committed by Clodius, who as a man was forbidden to look upon the rites. If formal charges are brought, they will be against him alone."

"That sets my mind at ease, a little," I said.

"Has Celer indicated his preference for a colleague?" Cicero asked, changing the subject rather abruptly. He was a politician, and power interested him far more than ritual matters.

"He asked me to broach the matter to Mamercus Capito," I told him.

"Now disqualified."

"Decidedly. The main contender now seems to be Lucius Afranius," I said. "Did I just hear you groan, sir?"

"I groan because I am not a philosopher," Cicero said, "and only a philosopher could look upon Lucius Afranius without groaning. The man is a nonentity."

"I think that's what Celer likes about him," I admitted.

"These times call for firm direction from our Consuls. I shudder to think of Afranius in such a position."

"It will essentially be a one-man administration, and Celer will be the man," I said. "You must admit that his withdrawal of opposition to the Pompeian demands was a wise political move, however much he may have disliked it."

Cicero shook his head. "No, no, I mean no disrespect to your kinsman, but he is too firm an adherent of the aristocratic party. It was foolish to oppose the triumph, that is obvious. But the settlements for the demobilized veterans are another matter entirely. This involves land, and lowborn men getting control of it, a thing that horrifies the extreme aristocrats. And it means a landed power base for Pompey, whom the aristocrats hate. Believe me, Decius, by this time next year Quintus Caecilius Metellus Celer will be firmly aligned with the extreme end of the aristocratic party."

It did not escape me that Cicero spoke of the "extreme" aristocrats. He was an adherent of that party himself, despite the fact that many of its leaders openly snubbed him. Cicero had an ideal of a Republic led by the "best" men, who would be drawn from the prosperous and propertied classes of free citizens, who would be educated, patriotic and concerned with the welfare of the state. It was a fine ideal, but Plato had had such a concept and had not had conspicuous success in convincing his fellow Greeks to adopt it as a governing principle.

I would never claim that I had more than a fraction of Cicero's intellectual capacity, for he had the finest mind I have encountered in my long lifetime. But he had a certain blindness, an almost naive belief in the inherent capacity of aristocrats to govern.

I was born an aristocrat, and I had no illusions about my class. Aristocrats are persons who possess privilege by virtue of having inherited land. They prefer rule by the very worst of aristocrats to that by the most virtuous of commoners. They detested Pompey, not because he was a conqueror of the Alexandrine mold who might overthrow the Republic, but because he was not an aristocrat, and he led an army of the Marian type that was not composed of men of property.

At the time of which I write, my whole class was engaged in a form of mass suicide by means of political stupidity. Some rejected our best men for reasons of birth, while others, like Caesar and Clodius, curried favor with the worst elements of Roman society. Most wanted a return to their nostalgic image of what they thought the ancient Republic to have been: a place of unbelievable virtue where an aristocratic rural gentry lorded it over the peasants. What they got was our present system: a monarchy masquerading as a "purified" Republic.

Cicero was right about Celer, though. Within a year he was back among the most extreme aristocrats, opposing the land settlements for Pompey's veterans.

"It is not surprising that they dislike the idea of Pompey having a powerful private army settled near Rome," I said. "I find the idea rather upsetting myself."

"I am not so easily terrified," Cicero said. "With the Asian menace settled, there are no glorious campaigns in the offing. He will have no interest in the sort of desultory combat that Hibrida is bungling so terribly in Macedonia."

"Meaning?"

"Meaning that, for now, Pompey must stay home and

devote himself to politics. The very concept is ludicrous. Pompey is a political dunce. He held most of his military commands without holding any of the offices required by the constitution. He was made Consul by force alone. He has no experience of civil administration or the real politics of the Senate. The man's never even served as quaestor! You'll be a more effective Senator than Pompey, and you've had less than a week's experience as Senator."

It was an odd sort of compliment, if compliment it was. At least I was now fairly certain that I would not be hauled into court for snooping.

I now had some people to call upon. I decided to begin at the very site of the enormity. I went to the house of Caius Julius Caesar, whose wife, we were given to believe, must be above suspicion. The house of the *Pontifex Maximus* was a sizable mansion, one of the few residences in the Forum, adjacent to the palace of the Vestals.

The gatekeeper let me in and conducted me through the atrium, where the household slaves went about in the gingerly fashion that bespoke uncertainty in their lives. Doubtless they were wondering which of them would stay with the master and which would accompany the divorced mistress. I noticed that the male statues still wore palls. The sun had broken through the clouds and I was conducted to the enclosed garden, where the rooftiles still dripped musically. In a corner stood a small statue of Priapus, covered by a scarlet cloth. In front, the cloth hung from the god's outsized phallus like a ludicrous flag.

"May I help you?" I turned to see that a woman had come into the garden. I did not recognize her, but I was greatly taken by her wheat-colored hair and large gray eyes, and by the sound of her voice.

"I am Decius Caecilius Metellus the Younger," I said. "I need to speak with the *Pontifex Maximus*."

"He is not here at the moment," she said. "Is it a matter in which I might be of assistance?" Her grammar and diction were perfect. Her poise was elegant, her manner open and helpful without being obtrusively familiar. In a word, patrician.

"I am engaged in an investigation of the recent, ah, unpleasantness at the rites of Bona Dea in this house."

She did not look pleased. "On such a matter," she said, "who has the authority to question the *Pontifex Maximus?*"

This was an embarrassingly penetrating question. "This is not an interrogation, my lady. I've been instructed by one of the most distinguished members of the Senate to make an informal inquiry, not to bring charges, mind you, but merely to . . ."

"Metellus Celer," she said.

"Eh? Ah, well, you see, you are not totally incorrect in this, but actually . . ." It has never been my habit to babble, but this woman had caught me completely off guard. "Who did you say you were?" I asked.

"I did not say. I am Julia." This narrowed things somewhat. She belonged to the fifty percent of *gens* Julia that were female.

"I knew that Caius Julius had a daughter, but I had thought she was . . . well, I had the impression that she was, shall we say, younger."

She kept her face patricianly impassive, but I sensed that she was laughing inwardly at my ridiculous discomfiture.

"Caius Julius is my uncle. I am Julia Minor, second daughter of Lucius Julius Caesar."

"I see. I knew you had to be one of those Julias. I mean, I should say . . . how did you know it was Celer?"

"You are a Caecilius Metellus and he is the husband of Clodia Pulcher."

"You have a very well-developed faculty of deduction," I said.

"Thank you. I take that as a compliment, considering its source. You are famed for that very faculty."

"I am?" I said, not sure whether to be flattered.

"Yes. My uncle speaks of you often. He says you are one of the most interesting men in Rome."

"He does?" I was truly astonished. I knew Caius Julius only slightly. It had not occurred to me that he spoke of me, with or without approval.

"Oh, yes. He says there's no one like you for snooping and prying and drawing deductions. He says your skill merits classification as a branch of philosophy." I did not believe that she was deliberately flattering or gulling me. She seemed as open and honest as anyone I had ever met. Of course, no one was more aware than I of my susceptibility to attractive women.

"I have always avoided philosophy," I told her, "but who am I to dispute definitions with such a master of the rhetorical arts?"

Finally she smiled. "Exactly. Well, I am sorry that Caius Julius is not here to speak with you, but I am pleased to have met you at last." She made to leave, but I did not want her to go.

"Stay, please," I said.

"Yes?" She was a little puzzled, as was I.

"Well." I groped for words. "Perhaps you could help me. Were you here that night?"

"Only married ladies attend the rites of Bona Dea. I am not married."

"I see." I was inordinately pleased to know that she was not married. "How wonderful. I mean, I am not happy that you were not here." My words were getting tangled again.

"I didn't say I was not here, just that I did not attend the rites."

"Ah. Well, it is a rather large house."

"You're going about this all wrong, you know. I fear that you disappoint me."

"I fail to understand," I said.

"Just going into great men's houses and asking direct questions. That's no way to get to the bottom of this matter."

I was a little crestfallen. After all, who was famed for this sort of thing?

"Well, it is a little different from investigating a throat-cutting in the Subura. Could you suggest a better method?"

"Let me help you."

"You have already very kindly made that offer," I reminded her.

"I mean, let me be your helper in this investigation. I can go places you cannot."

This took me greatly aback. "Why should you want to do that?"

"Because I am intelligent, well-educated, personable

and bored to a state of Medea-like madness. I've followed your career for years by way of gossip among women and table discussion among my father and his brother and their friends. It is just the sort of activity I feel drawn to. I can go places you cannot. Let me help you." In true patrician fashion she demanded this as her right, but I could detect a pleading tone in her voice.

"This is most unexpected," I said. Immediately, though, I could see the advantages of such an arrangement. Among other things, it meant that I would see more of Julia. "But let's discuss it."

She sat on a stone bench and patted the place beside her, which was only slightly damp. "Sit here with me."

I looked around the garden. "We are not chaperoned. Will your family think this is correct?" The men in noble old families could behave like goats or worse, but their women had to be chaste, or at least perceived as such. Caesar's wife, etc.

"Gaze over my left shoulder," Julia said. "Do you see a shadow lurking beneath the colonnade?"

I complied. "I see such a shadow."

"That is my grandmother, the lady Aurelia. Rest assured, if she sees anything untoward, she will interpose herself between me and dishonor. She has the eyes, the instincts and the claws of a bird of prey."

"Oh, good. Now we can plot. Just how would you go about being my assistant?"

"Colleague, if you please."

"Very well." This concession cost me nothing.

"Most of the highly married ladies in Rome were here that night. I shall call upon some of them and pump them for information."

"Aren't they forbidden to speak of the rites to one who is not an initiate?"

"Certainly. But some of the most scandalous ladies of Roman society were there, women known for their indiscretions. Besides Clodia, I know that Fulvia and Sempronia were there, along with that whole lot from Lucullus's household: his wife Claudia and his ward, Fausta the daughter of Sulla, and your cousin Caecilia, the wife of the younger Marcus Crassus. If I can't get information out of some of those women, I'll take vows and become a Vestal."

"That would be valuable," I admitted. "But if your grandmother over there were to hear of you being in the company of any of those ladies, she would open her veins."

"I will be suitably cunning. I can contrive to run into them at some innocuous location—the baths, for instance."

In those days, there were several baths in Rome exclusively for women. The thought of Julia soaking in the *caldarium* with any of those notorious ladies instantly filled my head with distracting images.

"That seems safe enough," I allowed. "But stay away from Clodia. She is a truly dangerous woman, whereas the others are only mildly wicked. I have Celer's permission to question her myself, not that I expect to get much out of her. How will you get in touch with me?"

"Have you a slave you can trust?"

"I have a boy named Hermes, but he is a duplicitous rascal."

"Then I will send someone to you when I have something of worth to report."

"I would like to know one thing. Why are you doing this? Besides being bored, I mean."

"I find that quite sufficient reason. And, like most decent Roman women, I detest Clodia."

"That's intriguing. Most of the men feel the same way about her brother. Just keep clear of her."

"That will not be difficult. I am afraid of her."

"And well you should be. Personally, she terrifies me. She if far subtler than Publius." I debated telling her about the poisoning attempt, but restrained myself. I was being far too trusting as it was. I rose from the bench.

"I will take my leave, then, and hope to hear from you soon." She saw me out with all the usual courtesies, most of them, I presumed, for the eyes of the dragonlike grandmother.

I walked away greatly bemused. It might be wondered that I would even consider trusting someone from the family of Caesar. A major reason was that I *wanted* to trust her. This tendency to confuse desire with reason has landed me in more trouble than I care to remember. Nonetheless, my instincts, which were sometimes reliable, said that she was sincere.

In a way, it was not a good time for me to be so distracted, for my next stop was the house of the man I genuinely feared. Marcus Licinius Crassus and I had crossed paths more than once, and although our relations were cordial for the moment, I did not mistake this for any sort of permanent arrangement.

Marcus Licinius Crassus Dives was believed to be the richest man in the world, and his house did nothing to dispel the belief. It was not far from the house of Celer, on a broad stretch of ground that had once belonged to several enemies of Sulla's. Crassus had eliminated the owners for the Dictator and was given their estates as a reward. He had demolished the old structures and had built his own palace, surrounded by spacious grounds landscaped by the best Greek artists and populated with the most sumptuous statuary imaginable. The whole collection was something of an oddity in Rome, for Crassus had actually bought most of his treasures. He had acquired little of it decently through inheritance and almost none of it as loot from foreign wars. This was still a rather new concept in Rome, where we associated great purchasing power with wealthy *equites* and freedman.

Making money was a passion with Crassus, almost a sickness. Many of his contemporaries strove for power, believing that wealth would come to them as the natural concomitant of power. Crassus was the first Roman to understand that wealth *was* power. Others struggled for years to obtain high military commands so that they could win loot and glory in foreign lands. Crassus knew that he could buy an army at any time.

I was suspicious of Crassus at this time. Of course, it was all but impossible not to be suspicious of him. He was involved in so many intrigues, most of them involving money, that it was unthinkable to sort through them all. We all knew that he had dealings with Ptolemy the Flute-Player, the putative King of Egypt. But Ptolemy always needed money, so it was natural for him to court Crassus. Crassus was angling in the Senate for a war with Parthia. We had no particular quarrel with Parthia, but it was the last really rich nation on our borders and he wanted a chance at it before Pompey got it. Pompey's single-minded pursuit of military glory matched Crassus's passion for money. They hated each other, but they could cooperate on occasion.

My reasons for calling on him were a bit devious. Ordinarily I took pains to avoid Crassus, but I was curious about his political orientation, which might well have shifted while I was away from Rome. Most especially, I was unsure of his attitude toward Clodius. My quasi-official status gave me the opportunity to pry.

I found him in his atrium with a pack of cronies. They watched him when I entered to see what attitude they should take. He smiled and came to me with hand outstretched, so they relaxed. Crassus could be as jovial as Lucullus when it suited him, but his good-fellowship never extended as far as his eyes. We exchanged the usual greetings and he asked after my father's health. I glanced around the room and did not see his son, the younger Marcus Crassus.

Briefly, I explained to him my mission, and he nodded his understanding of its political subtleties.

"Messy business," he said. "I quite understand Celer's concerns about Clodia. That woman never brought any man anything but trouble."

I did not point out his own sinister dealings with the woman. It was a part of such unspoken truces as lay between me and Crassus that such things *remained* unspoken until hostilities broke out afresh.

"Then you can understand my difficulty," I said. "I can't very well confront Felicia directly"—I did not mention my agreement with Julia, naturally—"and Marcus the Younger would be gravely insulted if I approached him, but as paterfamilias, you could handle these matters." I expected no help from him. This was for the sake of form.

"I shall be more than glad to," he lied jovially.

"What do you think Clodius was doing?" I asked.

"Just another of his idiotic pranks, no doubt. What genuine mischief could he accomplish at a women's religious ritual? His ideas of fun are as harebrained as his political ideas."

This was new. "I hadn't heard that he had any political thoughts. Thoughts of any nature whatever, for that matter."

"Say you so? That's right, you've been out of Rome this past year, haven't you?"

"Enlighten me," I said. "I know he wants to be tribune if he can switch his status to plebeian, but I had thought that he had no purpose in mind except to make trouble."

"Trouble is the very word. He has become a man of the people, you see. He plans to make the grain dole a permanent right of every citizen, free of charge."

"That is radical," I said, my mind turning over the possibilities. The grain dole had been around from earliest times as an emergency relief measure. It had been instituted in the days when the farmers of the countryside had taken refuge within the walls of Rome in times of siege. It was revived frequently in times of famine or other want, and sometimes as a celebration to mark an important occasion. Every citizen had his name enrolled on the dole. In fact, the old expression "receiver of the dole" meant "citizen" and was used as such even by the wealthiest of us, who would never actually have to apply for relief.

"That's not the worst of it. He's already canvassing among the plebian tribal assembly, promising to pass this outrageous legislation if they will elect him tribune."

I was stunned. This was beyond the most outrageous excesses of our electoral process. Ordinarily, one devoted years of service to the public, and then demanded election as a reward, never omitting to cite one's distinguished ancestry. No one had ever thought of promising the electorate favors *after* being elected. Even Caesar had not come up with that one. This thought led me into some speculation, which was interrupted by Crassus.

"And he is siding with Pompey on the land grants."

"That is at least consistent," I observed. "If you're going to curry favor with the mob so outrageously, you might as well get the veterans on your side."

"My thought exactly. I find myself wondering if he plans to ask Pompey for a few of those veterans. A man as important as Clodius intends to be needs a proper escort."

"A private army? He already has a great mob of ex-gladiators and street brawlers."

"Pompey's veterans would add a certain tone, not to

mention demonstrating solidarity between the two." This sounded reasonable enough, but I suspected it to be pure malice on the part of Crassus. He wanted to cast suspicion on his old rival. As if I needed encouragement to be suspicious of Pompey.

"And," Crassus went on, "I've noted that Pompey has lent him some Etruscan soothsayers. Tame soothsayers are always an advantage to an ambitious man."

"I didn't know that Pompey was cultivating the entrail-examiners." All our haruspices in those days came from Etruria.

"Oh, very much so," Crassus assured me. "You know the common people hold them in awe. And there are certain, shall we say, military-political advantages to a power base in Tuscia." He used the common Latin word for the old Etruscan nation. There were, indeed, advantages to a power base there, considering that you had only to cross the Tiber to be in Tuscia. The very Trans-Tiber district lay on Etruscan land. Tuscia had been a part of the Roman hegemony for a long time, but like many of our allies, its people were an independent lot and considered us upstarts.

And the Claudians had Etruscan blood, although they always claimed to be Sabine in origin. In recent years there had been a veritable mania for things Etruscan. People claim Etruscan descent whose ancestors came to Italy as slaves two generations ago. Others pay absurd prices for authentic Etruscan art, and there is a thriving trade in forgeries. Now that the people are all but extinct, there is something romantic about them that was not apparent when they were around to plague us. Back then we still remembered that they had once lorded it over us as kings and we had little love for them. Their primary reputation lay in the fields of magic and soothsaying, which always struck me as an easy way to make a living without actually having to do anything.

I had a few more questions to ask, but we were interrupted by the arrival of none other than Caius Julius Caesar with his whole retinue.

"I fear I must take my leave, Decius," Crassus said. "The *Pontifex Maximus* and I have a little business to discuss." He lowered his voice as if letting me in on a deep secret. "I've just about persuaded him to let me

have the first plebeian vacancy in the college of pontifexes."

"Then please accept my congratulations in advance,"
I said. I did not doubt that he was telling the truth, but
I also did not doubt they had far more serious business
than mere sacerdotal honors. Caesar had debts. Crassus
had money. It didn't take Aristotle to figure out the connection there.

As I walked away from the house of Crassus, I pondered the connections between Caesar and Crassus. What
I needed, I decided, was a good, unbiased source for
rumor, gossip and calumny. And I knew just where to go
to find it.

VII

A foreign embassy might seem a strange place to go looking for semi-reliable information on internal Roman politics, but I knew better. Ambassadors live on inside information and rumor. They freely discuss among themselves things avoided by Romans. They hear everything and are always anxious to curry favor with well-connected Romans.

The Egyptian ambassador at this time was a fat old degenerate named Lisas. He had been in Rome forever and he knew everybody. I have already mentioned the connection between Crassus and Ptolemy, which made Lisas a natural source to sound out. Besides, I was hungry and Lisas was a famous host.

The Egyptian embassy was a great sprawl of buildings outside the city walls on the slope of Janiculum. Its architecture and decor displayed the great Hellenistic mishmash of Egypt and Greece that characterized Alexandria. Hermes goggled at the place as we trudged toward the main gate.

"Did you ever come this way when you ran away?" I asked him.

He shook his head. "I've never been outside the city walls before."

"A good thing. When the Egyptians catch a runaway, they feed him to the crocodiles in their pool." Just then one of those torpid beasts bellowed from the other side of the wall surrounding the compound.

"I've heard that," Hermes said, his face pale. "Is it true?"

"Absolutely," I assured him.

A liveried slave stood in the gateway to greet visitors,

and when he saw my Senator's insignia, he bowed so low that his nose could have brushed his ankles.

"Senator Decius Caecilius Metellus the Younger to see the Ambassador Lisas," I said grandly. The slave conducted me into a wide atrium and hurried off in search of the master. In the center of the room was a sphinx of white marble with the face of Alexander the Great.

A few minutes later Lisas waddled in amid a cloud of greetings. Besides his great girth, he was distinguished by a huge black wig and grotesquely heavy facial cosmetics. Like all the ruling caste of Egypt, he was of Macedonian descent, but he affected the trappings of the pharaonic past. He was famed for his many perversions, some of them unknown outside Egypt until he brought them to Rome. In spite of all this, I liked the man, who was genuinely kind and thoughtful.

"It is so good to have you back among us, Decius Caecilius," Lisas said, eyeing Hermes wistfully. I knew he would do no more than look. He was too well-mannered to make an indecent proposal concerning another man's slave. "But I can see that you're faint with hunger. Please come with me and we'll remedy that." I went with him into a triclinium laid out as if for a minor banquet. It was not a regular dining-hour, but Lisas kept a buffet in this room at all hours for unscheduled visitors. I heaped a plate with smoked fish and pickled tongue and other items such as did not have to be served hot. Lisas did likewise and we sat down to talk. Since this was purely informal, we dispensed with couches and servitors. I brought up the subject on my mind and he mused for a while, popping sugared dates into his mouth.

"Crassus and Caesar ..." His pudgy fingers sketched idle designs in the air between us. "One hears so many rumors."

"What sort of rumors?" I asked.

"You recall the year of Caesar's aedileship?"

"Who could forget that year?" I said. "He put on the greatest games in history."

"There was a rumor at the time, just a rumor, mind you, that he had more than public duty and splendid games in mind. He is supposed to have taken part in a conspiracy to overthrow the state, in league with Crassus.

You recall that the Consuls-designate of that year were not allowed to take office?"

"I remember," I said. The year before, the consular election had been won by Publius Autronius Paetus and Publius Sulla, nephew of the Dictator. They had been convicted of bribery before they had a chance to take office, and the two runners-up were chosen to serve in their stead.

"The plan, it is said, was that Caesar and Crassus would attack the Senate house on the new year and kill all their enemies while they were gathered in one place. Then Crassus was to assume the Dictatorship and name Caesar his Master of Horse. Publius Sulla and Autronius would then serve as Consuls."

"That sounds like malcontent talk to me," I said. "Not that I'd put it past any of them, but it's rather farfetched. Neither Caesar nor Crassus had enough followers to pull it off. Now, Sulla I can understand. He's harebrained enough to try something like that. Ever since the old Dictator died, every adult male bearing the name Cornelius Sulla has been involved in every crackpot conspiracy that's come along. He was tried for throwing in with Catilina, and it took a defense by Cicero to get him off. His brother was accused and convicted, although he escaped execution."

"It was Caesar's intervention that spared him, was it not?" Lisas said blandly.

"Now that I think of it, it was. Servius Sulla was so guilty, Jove himself couldn't have got him free, but Caesar got his sentence commuted to exile." This looked suspicious, but by this time I was seeing conspiracies everywhere. I shook my head. "No, Caesar and Crassus are too shrewd for anything so desperate."

Lisas smiled his man-of-the-world smile. "So it may seem to you, my young friend, but that is not at all apparent to me. In Crassus I see a man of thwarted ambition who yearns for supreme power and glory, only to see it all go to Pompey. Caesar is a man who has watched his best years pass by without performing any deeds of note. They may have perfected a pose of serene majesty, but they are desperate men. Historically, such men have always been the overthrowers of states and the establishers of tyrannies."

"Well, perhaps among Greek and Asiatic states," I said. "But we are Romans."

"And what of that? Was Gaius Marius any different, or the great Sulla? Was Romulus, for that matter? The other great men were away from Rome that year. Had they shown enough resolution, they might well have carried out such a coup." He made a gesture intended to acknowledge the mastery of the gods in all things. "They might have, that is, had this matter been anything other than a mere rumor, which, I remind you, is all it is."

"And now," I said, "Caesar is so buried beneath his debts that he needs a province and its legions to dig him out."

"And soon he will have just such excavationary resources," Lisas said.

"Then why," I asked, "is he still in Rome?"

Lisas performed an expressive shrug. "More rumors. His creditors will not allow him to leave until he posts some surety for his debts."

"A surety only Crassus can provide," I said.

"I know of no one else."

I thanked him for his hospitality and his enlightening gossip and took my leave. A slave fetched Hermes and brought him to the atrium. He looked a bit distressed.

"They took me to see the crocodiles," he said. His breath smelled of Egyptian date wine. "There's one in there that must be twenty feet long. Biggest lizard I ever saw."

"Did you see them eat?"

"No, but I saw bones in the bottom of the pool. They looked like human bones."

"It makes you think, doesn't it?" I said. The tour of the crocodile pool was a service the embassy provided for the slaves of their guests. The "bones" were made of marble. It seems that crocodiles crunch bones to tiny fragments.

We almost made it to the door before a house slave scurried up to me with a wrapped parcel.

"The master said that you forgot this. It is for your slaves at home." At a dinner, of course, I would have wrapped some goodies in my napkin to take home to my slaves. It had not occurred to me to do so at this informal

lunch. As I have said, Lisas was uncommonly thoughtful.
I handed the parcel to Hermes.

"I want you to take this home to Cato and Cassandra.
Don't unwrap it and eat along the way. Cato is to divide
it among you after you get there."

He shrugged. "They fed me here. Better than you do."

"Lisas can afford it. Do you know where Milo lives?"

"Everyone in Rome knows that."

"Then you are to rejoin me there when you have delivered this. Wait for me in Milo's atrium and don't frat-
ernize with his household staff. They are very bad
people."

He grinned with gleeful anticipation. "Yes, sir!" That
I was a Senator and a Caecilius Metellus meant little to
him. That I was the friend of Titus Milo impressed him
no end.

I was glad of the opportunity to walk alone and think
things over. I often had my best thoughts in this fashion,
ambling along in a semi-unconscious state, letting my
feet take me where they would. Sometimes, my feet
would lead me to a place crucial to the solution of my
problem. I have often wondered why this should be, and
I think it may be that the small gods of the crossroads,
whose shrines I passed at every intersection, were aiding
me. They are the most Roman of deities, and it was only
natural that they should take an interest in my ponder-
ings, which usually involved protecting our ancient city
in some fashion.

I thought about Caesar, and Crassus, and Pompey and
all the others who plagued us with their power games.
And I thought of Julia. Something she had said had
raised a question in my mind, but I had been so distracted by her presence that I had not been able to concentrate, and now I had forgotten what it was. I dismissed
that as a lost cause and went back to Crassus and Caesar.

Crassus was unthinkably rich, but he was woefully
lacking in the sort of military leadership we considered
crucial to a successful political career. To wit: one that
involved plenty of loot and glory. He had all the requisite experience under senior commanders. He had commanded legions in one campaign, the Servile War against
Spartacus and his slave army.

Spartacus might have been the wiliest, ablest, most

dangerous enemy Rome had ever faced, but he was a slave and his followers were slaves, and Romans refused to acknowledge a slave army as a worthy enemy. Worse, Crassus had conducted a prudent, plodding war of maneuver, making best use of the legions' skills of discipline and engineering. He turned in a victory that was shatteringly complete and low in Roman casualties, but lacking in the sort of dash admired by the public. As usual, Pompey had arrived from Spain after all the real fighting was over, mopped up a few bands of fleeing slaves and claimed credit for the victory. Crassus had never forgotten. He was itching for a good war, but perhaps, given his mentality, a coup was not out of the question.

As for Caesar, then as now he was an enigma. He was a man of immense capability who had done nothing. He was an aristocrat of one of the oldest patrician families who posed as a man of the people. He was an old Marian in a Rome that had belonged to the supporters of Sulla for twenty years. We Metellans had been his supporters, as had the Claudians, the Cornelians naturally enough, and most of the other great families, such as the Crassi. Even some Julians had backed him, but Caius Julius had always stressed his marriage connection to Gaius Marius, even during the years when his fortunes were the lowest. Could there be more to Caesar than I had thought? He even backed the Greens in the Circus.

On this day, the guardian deities of the city did not seem inclined to guide my steps in any fruitful direction. I walked completely around the Circus Maximus, no mean undertaking. I rounded the base of the Palatine and ascended to the Forum, which was rapidly emptying of its day's occupants. I climbed the Capitol all the way to the Temple of Jupiter. I walked inside and stood watching the priests as they went through a scantily attended evening ceremony. The new statue of Jupiter still seemed out of place, although its majesty was impressive. The haruspices had declared that a new statue of the god was necessary to protect the state and expose plots against the constitution. They must have been right, because no sooner had the statue been tamped in place than the conspiracy of Catilina was exposed.

I have always found the services in our temples to be

restful and conducive to meditation, as long as they were not sacrificing something large and protesting. This was one of the oldest of our temples, exceeded in antiquity perhaps only by the Temple of Vesta. It had been rebuilt many times, and at one time had been a sanctuary containing no image, for the practice of giving our gods the form of human beings was relatively recent. When the Greeks became our slaves, they began reordering our city to suit their own ideas of propriety. I have never understood how it comes about that our slaves take over our lives, but it seems to be a universal rule.

With the smell of incense clinging to my hair, I left the temple and made my way to Milo's house. It was not an hour usually considered proper for calling on a citizen, but Milo was not an ordinary citizen. He never seemed to sleep, and it was a point of criminal/political principle with him to be available to citizens at all hours. When it came to giving the citizens individual attention, Caesar was an amateur compared to Milo. But then, Milo was not distracted by armies and provinces and rival generals. Milo did not want to conquer the world. Milo just wanted to control the city of Rome. To that end he had assembled an immense clientele, and by no means were all of them drawn from the criminal classes. His gang of brutes remained the hard core of his strength, naturally enough, but he had expanded his relationships to include many of the highest personages of Roman society, as witness his recent invitation to lunch with Lucullus.

Milo had accomplished his astonishing rise from street thug to political contender through driving energy, immense charm and a ruthlessness that was breathtaking even in that age of men without compunction. His aims, I suppose, were no different from those of Clodius, but they were different men. Clodius began with wealth, high birth and social position. An easy mobility in the highest circles was his birthright. Milo began with nothing. Milo had, I will not call it honor, but rather a consistent and punctilious regard to his loyalties and obligations. Milo had friends whereas Clodius had toadies.

Admittedly, I may have been prejudiced in his favor because I detested Clodius so heartily, but then, Clodius was a detestable man. I have never considered myself to be unfair or arbitrary in these matters.

Milo greeted me warmly when I arrived. I was lucky enough to find him alone, by which I mean that he had no other visitors of consequence, although he had a somewhat understrength century of thugs lounging about the house. He conducted me to a side room where we relaxed on couches.

"You look tired, Decius. Have some wine." He poured two cups and handed me one. It was a good Falernian, mixed with no more water than what was necessary to avoid charges of incivility. I drank gratefully.

"I should be tired. I started the day at the house of Celer, went from there to the Forum, thence to the house of Caesar, from there to the house of Crassus and then to the Egyptian embassy. After lunch with Lisas I went to the Capitol to see if Jupiter could sort things out for me, a favor he declined. Now I've come to talk with you. I should have stayed in Spain. The legions are less strenuous."

"If you are going to get ahead, you must expect to exert yourself." Milo had scant sympathy for those whose energies were less formidable than his own. "Still the matter of the sacrilege?"

"Yes, and now the murder of Capito has taken a new turn." I described to him the peculiar wounds as interpreted by Askledpiodes, and he listened with great attentiveness. The arts of mayhem were always of deep interest to Milo.

"So the hammer blow came *after* the fellow was dead?" Milo mused. "That sounds—I can't say—it sounds more like ritual than ordinary murder. I've been inquiring among the *sicarii*, looking for someone who uses that two-blow technique, but I've been assuming that the hammer blow was to set the man up for the kill. This changes things. If it's ritual, it isn't Roman ritual. You may have to look into the foreign community."

"Wonderful. Rome is full of foreigners and their loathsome religions. I cannot go knocking on the door of every Asiatic or Gaul or African in Rome."

"You can eliminate most of them easily enough," Milo said with his usual perspicacity. "It will have to be someone who had doings with Capito. Surely he wasn't involved with Nubian tribesmen or Arabian camel-herders. Find out what Capito was involved in and you will probably find which foreigner had cause to kill him."

"That makes sense," I admitted. "Will you aid me in this as well?"

"Certainly," he said. "Favor for favor?"

"Whatever you wish," I said, "but what can a political nobody like me do for you?" I was never under the misapprehension that Milo's favors were the result of purest generosity and that someday he would require favors of me, but I had assumed that this would happen after I had achieved eminence and influence.

"It is not your political importance that I need just now, but your social prominence. I want you to help me court the lady Fausta."

I should have seen it coming. "You aim high, my friend." The moment I said it I knew how stupid it was. Why would a man who planned to control Rome aim low?

"I don't think the lady herself will see it that way," Milo said. "She is a Cornelian, but her father came of the poorest branch of the family. Sulla was a patrician beggar who rose high. And she realizes it. Fausta knows that the day of the patrician is past and the future of Rome belongs to men like me." This was characteristically blunt and perfectly true. Milo was clear-sighted in a way that even Cicero, with his preconceptions and ideals, could never match.

"I shall, of course, be happy to help in any way I can. What would you have me do?"

"As yet I lack the prominence to call upon Lucullus casually. You can do that. Fausta seems to have complete freedom of the house. You should have little difficulty in finding ways to speak with her. Press my suit and see how she reacts."

"Ahh, Milo, my friend, it is usually customary to approach a woman's parent or guardian in these matters. In accordance with Sulla's will, Lucullus has that authority."

Milo waved a hand, peremptorily dismissing all custom. "As I have said, certain aristocratic practices are of diminishing importance. They are of no concern to me, and I doubt that the lady in question has any use for them either."

"In that case, I shall be pleased to act for you."

I left his house amid effusive thanks. This was behavior I did not expect from Milo, whose words were always sincere but usually laconic. It was an indication of how his infatuation with Fausta was altering his manner. I had never seen him change countenance in the face of mortal danger, but this woman made him preoccupied.

It grows dark early at that time of year, so Milo provided Hermes with a torch to light our way home. I was pleasantly befuddled by the wine and greatly bemused by my new commission from Milo. I did not like the idea, but he had done me many favors and I could not refuse him this. I felt that by pursuing Sulla's daughter he was storing up much trouble and grief for himself, and I was right, but it was not something I could say to him when his motivation was so obviously emotional rather than political.

There were some families I thought it best to avoid. The whole pack of Claudians bore that distinction, as did the Antonines. The family of Sulla was another such. People who have a tyrant among their immediate ancestors are apt to have a magnified idea of their own importance.

Thinking about this led me back to the thing Julia had said that morning that I still could not call up to the surface of my mind. I could not think what the connection might be, but I knew that it was there. I was being more than ordinarily dense, I knew. I could attribute this partly to the wine and partly to the very complicated turns my life had taken since my return from Gaul. And I was about to receive a distraction that would drive it completely from my mind.

"It's black as Pluto's bunghole out here," Hermes groused as we neared my gate.

"That's because it's night," I reminded him. "Night is when it's dark. It's daytime that is light."

"It's just that it's dark even for Rome on a moonless night. This torch is about as much use as a one-wick lamp on a night like this." A second later, he squawked and fell and the torch went out. Without thought on my part, my hands went into my tunic and reemerged with my *caestus* on one and my danger in the other.

"What happened, you little idiot?" I demanded.

"I slipped! There's something slippery on the cobbles." He cursed mightily as he struggled to his feet.

"Someone's probably dumped a chamberpot here," I said. "See if you can get that torch going."

"Doesn't smell like shit," Hermes insisted. "It's sticky, though." He whirled the torch around his head and the flames sprang to life again. By their light he examined the stains on his hands, legs and tunic.

"If you've ruined that tunic, I'll flog you to—"

"It's blood!" he cried, interrupting rudely. Now we both saw a whitish heap on the cobbles a few steps ahead. "A body!" he cried again.

"You'll see lots of them after you've been in the Subura a while," I informed him. "I wish the gangs wouldn't do their dirty work so close to my door." We went closer and Hermes lowered the torch. That was when I saw the red sandals decorated with the ivory crescent at the ankle. I gripped my weapons more firmly.

"Uh-oh. Not an ordinary corpse after all. Well, let's see who we have here." I crouched by the head and Hermes lowered the torch further. "Well, well," I said. "Here's somebody we know. Pity it isn't Clodius, though."

"Pollux!" the boy exclaimed. "It's that little patrician shit who tried to poison you!"

And sure enough, there lay young Appius Claudius Nero, with a neat puncture in this throat and a circular dent in his brow.

VIII

I left him there until morning. He'd been no friend of mine, and I saw no point in waking up a lot of citizens just to come and gape at the little lout. Still less did I feel like losing a night's sleep on his account. I'd had a long day and I was tired. So I just tossed a handful of earth over him and went inside. I bade Hermes soak his tunic in a bucket of water before he retired. As usual I was low on funds and did not want to have to buy him a new tunic.

I slept like a corpse myself and woke feeling much better. Cato brought in a basin and my breakfast at first light. I splashed my face and downed a mouthful of bread and cheese as I laboriously recalled the previous day's sequence of events. As the cobwebs of sleep cleared, I realized that it had been a more-than-usually-eventful day. I ordered my thoughts while I munched on boiled eggs and fruit and finished off with a crust soaked in sweet wine. My father always told me I was a degenerate for eating breakfast in bed. Eating breakfast at all, for that matter. He thought it was an un-Roman practice and effete to boot. He was probably right, but I did it anyway. Just as I finished, Cato came back in.

"Master, there's some sort of commotion out front."

"Whatever might it be?" I said innocently. I had decided to keep quiet about finding the little wretch the previous night. "Where is Hermes?"

"Sick. Says he has a bellyache. I found his tunic soaking in a bucket this morning, so he must have fouled it last night."

"Tell that malingering little swine to get in here immediately," I said.

"He's not faking it, master," Cato insisted. "He's puked all over his room."

"How does that boy find so many ways to annoy me?" I said. I got up and went to his room. The reek of vomit was strong as I opened the door to his cubicle. The boy lay on his side on a pallet, his body curled around his fists, which in turn were pressed into his stomach. I squatted by him and felt his brow. He was not feverish and I sighed with relief. All I needed was pestilence in the house.

"When did this start?" I asked.

"In the middle of the night," he groaned. "I woke up with cramps." His scarlet face drained and turned pale. He sighed and sat up. "They come and go. I'm all right now, but it'll start again in a few minutes."

"Are the spasms getting worse?" I asked him.

He shook his head. "No. They're not as bad as they were a few hours ago, and they're farther apart."

"Did you eat at Milo's last night?"

"Yes. A couple of his men took me to the kitchen and I ate better than I do here."

"They probably slipped an emetic into your food. They have a rough sense of humor. Be careful around them. Milo may be my friend, but his men are all murderers and criminals of all kinds."

"Yes, sir," he said weakly. He didn't fool me. He yearned to be just like them.

"Listen, Hermes. I've decided to keep finding Nero's body last night secret. Say nothing to anyone about it."

"Yes, sir," he said meekly. Apparently he was too miserable to protest.

"Good. I'm leaving now. You'll probably have the runs next. If so, Cato will help you to the public jakes down the street. No sense making the smell in here worse than it already is."

"Yes, sir."

I left feeling relieved. It wasn't contagious, and he seemed to be recovering from whatever it was. In spite of everything, I had taken a liking to the boy. The world is full of humble, obedient slaves who rob you blind when you turn your back. Having one who didn't pretend to be anything but a villain was amusing.

I went out into the street and saw that a crowd had

gathered around the body. It now lay completely stripped, the clothes lying in a heap nearby. Apparently, somebody had come across it during the night and had removed all valuables. The clothes were too blood-soaked to bother with. In morning light the body just looked frail and rather pathetic. He might have tried to poison me, but he was just a boy who had got involved in matters too great and too dangerous for him.

My neighbors looked to me for instructions. I was, after all, the neighborhood Senator. I spotted a vigil who had apparently just got off duty. His bucket still dangled from his hand.

"Go to the *Praetor Urbanus*," I told him. "Report the murder of a patrician in the Subura." The thief had not taken the red sandals. Even the stupidest thief would know better than to try to sell those.

"What was he doing down here?" a man asked. The question had occurred to me as well. I knew that my mental faculties had been uncommonly slow of late, but I also knew it was no mere coincidence that Nero had been murdered a few steps from my door. Had he been sent to finish the job he had botched at the house of Capito two nights before? If so, why had he been murdered instead? It had to mean that the murder of Capito and the attempt on my own life were somehow connected.

"Neat bit of throat-slitting there," someone commented. There were connoisseurs of such things in my neighborhood.

My clients began to arrive and we retired within my house. There was one duty I knew I could not avoid. One of my clients had brought a slave boy with him, and I borrowed the youth.

"Do you know where the mansion of Clodius is?" I asked him. The boy nodded. "Then go there and tell him that he has a dead relative lying in the street here."

"Me? Talk to Clodius?" His eyes bugged with fear.

"You will probably only talk to his majordomo. If Clodius wants to question you, don't be afraid of him. He knows better than to harm another man's property. Now be off with you."

The boy ran out, and a few minutes later an official

arrived accompanied by a single lictor. I did not know him.

"I am Lucius Flavius," he said, "*iudex* of the Urban Praetor's court. Did you discover the body, Senator?"

"My neighbors found him this morning," I prevaricated. "But it looks as if a robber found him earlier."

"Do you know him?"

"Appius Claudius Nero. I met him at the house of Metellus Celer four days ago. He was with Publius Clodius, and I've sent a messenger to Clodius so that he can come to claim the body."

"That saves me a task, then. He seems to have been killed in the same fashion as Mamercus Aemilius Capito."

"He was at Capito's house the night of that murder. I don't know what the connection might be, if there is any."

Flavius shrugged. "Friends of Clodius often die violently. I imagine the lad just fell into bad company. If you'll forgive my saying so, this is a rough neighborhood. Probably he was looking for some of the low amusements available hereabout and ran into the killer by chance. It doesn't pay to be both well-dressed and alone in some parts of the city."

"All too true," I said. At Capito's house he had been accompanied by a pack of slaves, but if he'd come to kill me, he would not have wished to bring witnesses.

"I suppose I'd better wait for Clodius to come fetch the body," he said. I sent Cato for some food and wine and asked Flavius to join me in my study. He accepted gratefully. Apparently the murder of Nero did not interest him greatly, but I soon found out what did.

"I know we haven't met, Senator," he said, "but new friends are always valuable, even if met under unorthodox circumstances. You see, I am standing for a tribuneship for the coming year, and the support of the Metelli would not come amiss." This was an understatement. We controlled a tremendous voting bloc in the plebeian tribal assembly.

"I am not high in the family assemblies," I said, "but I am not totally ignored. What is your stand on the land for Pompey's veterans?"

"I intend to introduce an agrarian law in support of

the land distribution using a combination of public lands and land purchased from revenues. I've outline it to Cicero and he agrees it's workable."

"Good. Will you oppose Clodius's efforts to change his status to plebeian?"

"I'll interpose my veto to stop any such attempt. And it will be needed, because I happen to know that Clodius is pushing Caius Herennius for the tribuneship. The agreement is that Clodius will help Herennius get elected, and in return Herennius will propose a bill to transfer Clodius to the plebeians."

"I've heard that Clodius is using some unheard-of tactics to curry favor with the mob," I said.

"And very successfully. To hear the tavern-talk now, you'd think that Clodius was Romulus come again."

This sounded ominous. "If that's the case, you may count on my support." I had no idea whether I could trust his word, but I resolved to find out soon. We spoke of political matters for some time, until a client came to tell me that a party had come to retrieve the body. I rose and went to my front gate, my clients close behind me. I had little fear of a real fight with Clodius. Whatever his growing power in the slums, my district was strictly Milonian.

Outside, Clodius's crowd had brought a bier and waited by the body while the *Libitinarii* went through a perfunctory lustrum so that the body could be handled without contamination. The priest touched it with his hammer to claim it for the goddess, then went through the usual rigmarole with liquids and powders. Then he nodded to Clodius, who had been standing by, studiously ignoring me.

Clodius then performed his duties. The body was lifted onto the bier and he leaned over the dead boy's face, almost kissing him, miming the action of catching his last breath as it escaped the body. A little late for that, I thought, but it had to be done. He straightened, clapped his hands three times and shouted the *conclamatio*:

"Appius Claudius Nero! Appius Claudius Nero! Appius Claudius Nero!" After the last calling of the name, a crowd of female relatives and slaves set up the usual shrill lamentations and Clodius placed a coin under the boy's tongue, to pay the ferryman. As the bier was raised he turned to glare at me, but he said nothing until bier and body had been carried away and the mourning wails faded into the distance.

"Metellus! You murdered my cousin and I intend to bring charges against you in the Court for Assassins!" Obviously, he didn't really believe what he said. He preferred to kill his enemies without benefit of a trial.

"You're babbling even more dementedly than usual this morning, Clodius," I said. "Even if I wanted to murder the boy, I wouldn't do it in front of my own gate. Anyone can see that he was killed by the same murderer who killed Mamercus Capito, and I was in Capito's triclinium when that happened, as several of the most distinguished men in Rome will bear witness." I made no mention of the poisoning attempt. People might infer from it that I bore a grudge against the boy and had a motive to kill him.

"I didn't say you did it with your own hand!" Clodius yelled. "You're not that good with a dagger. The assassin was your hireling!" Behind him, a gang of his thugs growled, but all the rooftops were crowded with my neighbors, armed with enough stones to build a small city.

"If you want to make formal charges, you know how it's done," I said, "but a man under accusation of sacrilege cuts a poor figure in court." At this my supporters roared with laughter while Clodius grew scarlet in the face.

"Then perhaps we shouldn't bother the courts with this!"

I saw the glint of daggers being drawn among his mob, and behind me, my own followers gripped cudgels, stones and, no doubt, a few swords. I reached into my tunic and gripped my *caestus*. We had the makings of a full-scale riot here, and I was ready for one. The past few days had been frustrating, and a street brawl is a fine way to relieve tension, despite what the philosophers say. I have always held that excessive equanimity is unhealthy. We were about to come to blows when something unexpected happened.

The crowd in the street parted as if by magic as a herald came forward in his white robe, parting the mob with his ivy-wreathed staff. "Make way!" he shouted.

"Make way for the *Pontifex Maximus!*" The daggers disappeared as if they had never existed. I released my grip on my *caestus* and the crowd fell silent.

Caius Julius Caesar strode superbly into the space between the two hostile groups. He wore a magnificent formal toga, one fold of it drawn over his head as if he were engaged in one of his sacerdotal functions. He turned slowly in a full circle, and people fell back before his lordly eagle's frown. This was the first time I witnessed Caesar's easy mastery of crowds, and I was impressed. Now I could see why he was so influential before the huge public assemblies. In small gatherings, even before the Senate of his peers, Caesar's manner looked like bombastic posturing. In the midst of a great mob it was godlike. I began to have an inkling of what he would be like haranguing the troops before battle.

"Citizens!" he cried, at the precise moment when his speech would have the greatest dramatic effect. "This street has seen the murder of a noble youth of one of Rome's most ancient families, a patrician of the Claudii. Was this not enough? Would you anger the gods and bring their curse upon Rome by shedding civil blood before the *Pontifex Maximus?*" He ignored the minor lake of Nero's blood that spread over the cobbles. Maybe dried blood didn't count. People looked abashed, even Clodius's arena bait.

"Pontifex," Clodius said, "we would never offer you disrespect, but my kinsman has been foully murdered and I name *him*"—he jabbed a finger toward me—"as the guilty party."

"Rome is a republic of law," Caesar proclaimed. "Courts and magistrates and juries decide these questions, not mob action. I order that all here return to their houses. When your passions have calmed and you can behave as citizens should, then will be the time to try this matter publicly. Until that time, depart!" The last word snapped out like one of Jove's thunderbolts, and some of the Subura's most bloodstained ruffians fairly scurried to get out of his sight.

Clodius was so enraged that he was, for once, unable to speak. His face had darkened to crimson, and throbbing veins stood out on his brow. His eyeballs were red as a three-day hangover. If he had just stuck his tongue out, he would have been identical to those gorgons you see painted on old Greek shields. It was a most entertaining spectacle, but it could not last. Beneath Caesar's glare, Clodius's extravagant color began to fade. When he was self-possessed once more, he whirled and stalked off, followed by his uneasy entourage.

Within moments the street was empty except for Caesar. It was the most amazing thing I had seen in a good long while. He turned to where I stood in my gateway.

"How did this come about, Decius Caecilius?" he asked.

"Come inside and I'll tell you, Caius Julius," I said. Caesar came in. I didn't tell him everything, naturally, just about how I had met Nero and encountered him again at the herb-woman's booth and then at the house of Capito. I left out the parts about the attempted poisoning and coming upon the corpse the night before. Since I was as mystified as anyone else, I didn't need to fake it.

"None of this seems to make any sense," Caesar said.

"I could not agree with you more."

"Still, this is a disturbing thing," he mused. "Two murders, performed identically, and both victims patricians."

"Don't forget Capito's *janitor*," I reminded him. "He wasn't a patrician."

"He probably got a glimpse of the killer's face," Caesar said. "He must have been eliminated as a witness."

"I agree," I said. Then I told him what Asklepiodes had said about the wounds. Why was I speaking to Caesar so openly? Partly it was because I suspected him of being involved in some way and I hoped that he would betray complicity. Partly, also, it was because I had been ready for a mortal brawl with Clodius and Caesar had poured water on the fire. In a less frustrated state I might have been more cautious.

"This is strange indeed. Am I to understand that you have taken upon yourself one of your inimitable investigations?"

"It helps to pass the time," I said.

He grew very serious. "Decius, my friend, I have known many men who courted death for the sake of glory. Others do the same in pursuit of wealth, power or revenge.

You are the only man I know who does so as a sort of intellectual exercise."

"Every man finds his pleasures where he will," I said, quoting an old saying I had often seen carved on tombstones.

"You are an intriguing man, Decius Caecilius. I wish there were more like you in Rome. Most men are boring drudges. My niece told me of your visit yesterday. She was quite taken with you."

This surprised me. But I answered without prevarication. "As I was with her."

He nodded approvingly. "I am glad to hear it. We must discuss this further at a future date. Just now, though, I am called elsewhere. Good day, Decius."

His words rattled me somewhat. Was he suggesting a match? Or was he trying to distract me? If the latter, he did not shake from my head the question that had been there since his appearance.

"Caius Julius," I said.

He turned in the doorway. "Yes?"

"How did you happen to get here so quickly?"

He smiled. "Ever the inquirer, eh? As it happened, I was in the Temple of Libitina when Clodius's servant arrived to summon the undertakers."

"I see," I said. "Pontifical duties?"

"Arranging for some family obsequies," Caesar said. "The goddess is an aspect of the ancestress of my house." Caesar had just begun to stress the divine origins of the Julian clan. He omitted no opportunity to mention it. He left.

"That's a man to watch," said my old retainer Burrus. He had been waiting with the others in the atrium while Caesar and I conversed in my study. Burrus was a former centurion from the legion I had served with in Spain. He was gray as iron and had a face like a soldier's *dolabra*.

"Why do you say that, Burrus?" I knew why I was uneasy about Caesar, but I was curious to know how a man like Burrus would read him.

"I don't know the courts and the Senate like you, patron," he said, "but I know the legions. Give that man command of one or two good legions, and he'll work miracles."

This astonished me. "Why on earth do you say that?"

"I've heard him speak before the *Concilium Plebis*. You saw him out on the street just now? Well, he's always like that when addressing the plebs. Soldiers respond to a man who talks like that, sir. If he can soldier like he talks, they'll do anything for him."

I had thought that I knew Rome intimately, but here was something new to me. At the time I dismissed it. Talk was one thing, but the ability to endure the hard privations of a soldier's life? I knew how much I detested military life. Caesar's reputation for the love of ease and luxury exceeded my own by a wide margin, and my reputation in that area was by no means small. He could never amount to anything as a general. That was how much I knew.

Of far more interest to me were his cryptic words about Julia. Was he suggesting a union between our houses? I could think of it in no other terms. Marriages between the great families were always political, but there were gradations of meaning. We Caecilii were an immense *gens,* but the Julians were tiny. At any given time they had no more than one or two marriageable daughters. Such an offer was serious indeed. If it was an offer. More likely, I thought, it was a distraction. That would mean that Caesar was afraid I would find out something he wanted to remain concealed.

The whole matter, or rather matters, had grown too confusing. I decided to narrow my attention. I decided that if I were to regain any perspective at all, I would have to grasp my courage in both hands and confront the person in Rome I feared above all others. I would go and question Clodia.

I dismissed my clients. After the morning's delays, it would be futile for us all to troop off to attend Celer's morning call. I was especially courteous in my dismissal, though. These men had stood by me unflinchingly when I was about to go to battle with my mortal foe, even though many of them were too old for a street brawl. It was only a client's duty, and I was obligated to do the same for them, but an actual instance of fulfillment of the mutual obligation was special, and despite my life-long reputation for laxness, I have never been accused of ingratitude by my *clientela*.

It was a daunting prospect, but I did not need to nerve myself up to the task as I might have on ordinary days. I had faced a death-fight with her brother and bearded Caesar already since breakfast, so a bout with Clodia was not as daunting as it might have been.

By the time I arrived at Celer's house he had long since departed for the Curia on public business. The great house was quiet as his household staff busied themselves with their various domestic tasks. I told the majordomo to announce me to the lady Clodia and inform her that I requested an interview. He conducted me to a small waiting room off the atrium, and I stood about there for a few minutes until a barefoot slave girl appeared.

"Please come with me, sir," the girl said. "My mistress will see you now." I followed her. She was a slight but beautiful creature, with yellow Gallic hair. Clodia always surrounded herself with beautiful things: slave, freeborn, animal and inanimate.

She led me to a suite of rooms in a corner of the mansion. These rooms were plainly newer than the rest of the house, and Clodia's touch was visible everywhere. The walls were painted by masters, mostly landscapes and mythological scenes, and the floors were mosaics of equal quality. Every humblest furnishing was exquisite. The vases and statuary were worth a good-sized town.

"A private interview, Decius? How brave."

I turned from the lamp of Campanian bronze work I had been admiring. Clodia was as beautiful as any of the art in the room, and knew it. She stood in a doorway that opened onto a garden. It was a trick of hers with which I was all too familiar. It allowed light to pass through the sheer garments she favored. This day she had outdone herself. She wore a gown made of the famous, or rather infamous, Coan cloth. It was forbidden by every new pair of Censors, but that just meant that it was inadvisable to wear it in public. Her gown had been dyed purple, a further extravagance. She appeared to be surrounded by a fine violet mist.

"Why, Clodia," I said, "I am here on a mission assigned by your husband. I even have his permission to call on you."

"How unthinkably proper," she said. "You are always so dutiful."

"Attention to duty is what made Rome great," I said, quoting my second old saying of the day.

She smiled. "You know, Decius, every time I've counted you out of the game, you show up again with more friends, more influence and just a tiny bit more rank. I won't say power."

"Slowly and steadily," I said. "That's the best way to advance."

"The safe way."

"Safe is the best way to stay alive," I said. "At least, I've always thought so. Lately, someone has been trying to kill me for no reason I can imagine. It wouldn't be you, would it?"

"Just because I tried to have you killed before?" She looked truly hurt. "You were in my way then. I'm not frivolous. I don't try to kill people out of spite. Why do you suspect me?"

"Your little cousin Appius Nero tried to poison me a few nights back. Afterward he was seen coming here. You and Celer are the only people of consequence in this house, and that narrowed things somewhat."

"You're an idiot. He had no cause to poison you, and he came here because he'd had an argument with my brother and needed a place to stay. They must have patched things up, because I haven't seen him since yesterday morning."

"You won't be seeing him," I told her. "Someone killed him right in front of my house last night."

Her face froze in mid-smile. "Killed?" she said. Her control was great, but I was sure that she was shocked.

"Yes. Done in just like Capito."

She turned away from me so I couldn't read her expression. "Well. Poor Nero. I didn't know him well, but he was a kinsman and rather young."

"Old enough to try to poison me," I said.

"It's all distressing, but that isn't why you came here today, is it?" She turned back, and her mocking face was in place once more.

"No. What I came to ask about was your brother's indiscretion at the rites of Bona Dea. The city is shocked. There must be an accounting."

"Oh, you know Clodius. He loves to make fun of our religious guardians. He's never grown up and loves to make his elders angry."

This was an amazing thing to hear from Clodia because it was so perfectly true. Her adulation of her brother was legendary. She had even changed her name when he had changed his. She was often angry with him, but it was unlike her to belittle him in front of an enemy. I was already suspicious. Suspicion was a habit when dealing with Clodia. But this was intriguing. Could she be a bit upset with her beloved brother? Then someone called from another room.

"Clodia? Who is it?"

"Am I intruding?" I asked.

"Yes, but I forgive you. Come, Decius, you must meet Fulvia."

"Fulvia? Is she back in Rome?" I knew only one prominent woman of that name, but she had fled Rome after the Catilinarian debacle.

"No, this is a kinswoman of hers. She's just come to Rome from Baiae."

We went into a bedroom, this one betraying Clodia's taste for erotic art. It resembled the decor of a brothel in subject matter, but here as elsewhere everything was of highest quality. A young girl sat up in a silk-cushioned bed and I made a formal obeisance, careful to be impassive, because once again Clodia was trying to upset my equanimity.

The girl was exquisitely beautiful, her hair as blond as a German's. She was so slight and tiny that she might have been a child, but she wore another of the Coan gowns, and that dispelled any such illusion. Her eyes were huge, her mouth startlingly full-lipped. She appeared to be no more than sixteen, but her face, despite its purity, had that indescribable yet unmistakable stamp that bespoke depthless depravity.

"My dear," Clodia said, "this is Decius Caecilius Metellus the Younger, son of the Censor."

"I am terribly honored to meet such a distinguished man," Fulvia said. It was against such a voice that Ulysses had his men stuff their ears with wax. Unlike Ulysses, I was not lashed to a mast, but it required some effort not to leap onto the bed with her.

"All Rome rejoices to have so lovely a visitor among us," I said. "Is this just a visit, or can we hope you are here to stay?"

"Fulvia," Clodia said, "is betrothed to Clodius."

I looked at her with an eyebrow sardonically arched. I could not resist. "Aren't you jealous?"

She didn't flinch. "People such as we have a flexibility you cannot imagine, Decius."

She was underestimating my imagination, but I let it pass. "And was young Fulvia in Caesar's house on the now-infamous evening of the rites?" I asked, dragging her back to the subject at hand.

"The rites are only for married women, Decius," Clodia said. "Fulvia accompanied me there, but she could not take part in the rituals."

"And how did it come about that Clodius got in?" I demanded. "The mind boggles at the thought of him pretending to be a woman. Whom did he claim to be married to?"

"I'm sure I don't know," Clodia said. "He didn't tell me he was coming."

"I see. And just how was he found out?"

"Oh, that occurred during a . . ." She paused. "No, I'm afraid I am forbidden to tell you."

"Don't be absurd. When did you ever care about laws or rules, whether of human or divine origin? The cloak of piety doesn't fit you well, Clodia."

"Who speaks of piety?" she said. "This is a matter of law. Are you not sworn to uphold the laws of the Senate and People of Rome?"

"That is a debatable point," I said. On a sudden inspiration, I embroidered upon a recent conversation. "As a matter of fact, I recently was present at a debate involving some of the highest figures of government, where there was some question whether the cult of Bona Dea is of Roman origin at all. It may be that it is lawful to demand testimony concerning the rites." I had promoted our idle dinner chitchat to the status of senatorial debate, but she didn't have to know that. A look very much like fear flitted across Clodia's beautiful face.

"If that proves to be the case," Fulvia said, "then Clodius can scarcely face a charge of truly serious sacrilege."

I turned to her. "I see that you are a perspicacious as

you are lovely." You meddling little slut, I thought. It hadn't occurred to me. But when I turned back to Clodia, she still looked upset. Quickly, she composed herself.

"I believe dear Fulvia is correct. The Censors may frown upon offenses against foreign gods, but the courts surely could not exact stiff penalties in such cases. That is reserved for the gods of the state. I must consult with Cicero on this."

"I hadn't thought that Cicero was kindly disposed toward Clodius," I said.

"Oh, but Cicero and I have become great friends lately," she said, her smile back in place. This was bad news. At first I was not inclined to believe her, but then I remembered Cicero's recent rather hasty insistence that Clodia could not be involved in the scandal. Why would he say such a thing unless he, too, had fallen to her wiles? I was disappointed in Cicero, but I knew that I was in no position to judge. I had certainly been under Clodia's spell in the past.

"Can you go so far as to tell me who it was that discovered your brother?"

"It was a slave woman from the household of Lucullus. I think I can say that without risking divine wrath."

"Slaves attend the rites?" This was news to me.

"The musicians. I believe it was a harpist who betrayed him."

This seemed to me an odd choice of words.

"I wish I could have seen him," Fulvia said. She brought her legs from beneath the coverlet and sprawled belly-down on the bed. The Coan gown revealed her dorsal contours to be as shapely as her front. "Achilles was discovered in women's clothing, you know, and Hercules had to wear women's garments when he was enslaved to Omphale. She got to wear his lion's skin and carry his club. I've always found that exciting."

"You're very young for such recondite tastes," I observed.

"Some of us start earlier than others," she said. How very true, I thought. Her voice caused an uneasiness in the testicles. Clodia sat beside her and took her hand.

"Will that be all, Decius? Fulvia and I have things to discuss."

"And I would not think of interfering. I shall take my leave and let you ladies get back to ... whatever it was. My condolences, Clodia, for your recent loss."

"Thank you, Decius. Poor Nero. So many of us die untimely." And with that cryptic but ominous pronouncement in my ears, I left.

As I walked from Celer's house I passed someone going the other way. It was a woman swathed in veils, and something about her seemed oddly familiar. I restrained myself from looking at her, but when she was past me I turned in time to see her step through the door of Celer's house.

A short way down the street I found a wineshop with an open front. The barkeep dipped me a cup from one of the big jars recessed into the counter, and I carried it to a table near the front. There I could sit and ponder what I had learned while keeping an eye on Clodia's door.

It was always inadvisable to draw hasty conclusions when dealing with Clodia, but I thought I knew a few things now: Clodia had not known of Nero's death, and therefore was unlikely to have ordered it. She had been visibly upset when I suggested that there might be a legal way to subpoena testimony about Clodius's doings at the rites. Fulvia had queered my plan when she pointed out that in that case he could scarcely be charged with serious sacrilege. I had been annoyed at the time, but the randy little twit had unknowingly supplied me with further food for thought, because Clodia had *still* been upset at the thought of herself or someone else being forced to testify. The charge of sacrilege was not the one she feared her brother having to answer to. What else had he been up to that night? Dalliance with Caesar's wife, who must be above suspicion? That was laughable. As serious offenses went in Rome, adultery ranked right along with failing to wear one's toga to the games.

This opened whole new vistas to delight my vindictive spirit. I wanted nothing more than a chance to prosecute Clodius for something really serious. Up to now, I had been engaged on a rather frivolous investigation, the principal aim of which had been to keep Celer's wife out of it. Now this bare-bones project was gaining some real flesh. And if I was right about the woman who had just gone into Clodia's house, the sacrilege and the recent murders and the attempt on my own life were intimately connected.

She reemerged just as I finished my wine, a bit of timing I deem propitious. As she walked toward the wine-shop I turned away, then got up when she was past. It is never terribly difficult to follow someone through the streets of Rome in the daytime. The ways are narrow and the crowds prevent any fast movement. They also allow you to keep close without being detected.

Not far from the Forum Boarium, she went into a charming little public garden. Besides its plantings, it featured the usual image of Priapus and one of those quaint, miniature tombs we erect on ground where lightning has struck. She sat on a bench bearing a plaque that gave the name of the rich man who had donated the garden to the city, and another rich man who had undertaken its upkeep. I passed by that same garden not long ago. Now the plaque is gone and there is another, bearing the name and lineage of the First Citizen. He would claim that he founded Rome if he thought he could get away with it.

The woman started as I sat down beside her. "Well, Purpurea, we meet again!"

She got over her startlement quickly. "And not by accident, I'll bet."

"Yes, actually, I was wondering what you were doing in the house of Metellus Celer, which is also the house of his beloved wife, Clodia Pulcher."

"You were following me!" she said, indignant.

"Absolutely. Now tell me what you were doing with Clodia, or I'll cause all sorts of trouble for you."

"I'm just a poor, honest herb-woman. You've no call to be harassing me!" She shifted the basket in her lap. Something rustled inside it.

"I haven't the slightest interest in your honesty or lack of it," I told her. "But people are getting murdered all over the city, and I was almost one of them. I suspect you of involvement. Your best course is to implicate somebody else, so speak up."

"Murder! I am involved in no such thing. The lady Clodia sent for me to procure certain herbs and have her fortune told. Her and young lady Fulvia, that is, and isn't that one a hot little piece?"

"She is indeed," I agreed, "and no doubt Rome will suffer grievously because of her in years to come, but let's return to Clodia. Would whatever is rustling in that basket have anything to do with telling her fortune?"

"Oh, aye." She reached into the basket and hauled out a fat, torpid black snake at least three feet long. "Old Dis here is the best fortune-telling snake in Rome. He's not very lively this time of year, though."

"And the herbs?" I asked.

"Just the usual."

"The usual?"

"You know, aphrodisiacs. You ought to let me mix some up for you. Give you a cock like Priapus there."

"I don't suffer from the deficiency," I said, nettled.

"They all say that, except the ones old enough to be honest about it. I think her husband needs a bit of encouragement now and then."

"Are you sure that is all you delivered to her? No poisons, by any chance?"

"Now, sir, you've tried that one before," she chided. "Do you really think I'm going to admit to a capital offense?"

"I suppose not," I said, rising. Then I let fly an arrow at random, the sort that sometimes strikes an unexpected target. I do not know why I asked her, except that her craft was an ancient one, involving many arcane rituals. "Citizens are being murdered, Purpurea. Someone is stabbing them in the throat and then, after they are dead, smashing them on the forehead with a hammer. What do you know of that?" To my astonishment her face drained of color and her jaw dropped.

"You mean *they're* in the city?"

I was taken much aback. "Who? Who do you mean by 'they'?"

She jumped up, clutching her basket. "Nobody I want to be involved with. Take my advice and don't you fall afoul of them, either. Good day to you, sir." She shouldered past me and headed for the street.

"Stop!" I said. "I want to . . ." By that time, I was addressing her back, She was not just walking away. She was running. I began to chase her, but I quickly gave it up. The toga is a wretched garment for performing anything strenuous, and I did not dare throw it off. Someone would steal it for certain.

I shrugged, thinking that I could always find her in her booth. Then I trudged back home, where I found two notes waiting for me.

One was from my father, informing me that the following morning the Senate would go to Pompey's camp to give him formal permission for his triumph. I was to dress properly for the occasion.

The other was from Julia. It read: *I have important information. Meet me tomorrow evening at sunset on the portico of the Temple of Castor.*

IX

It was a fine morning, and we assembled in the Forum dressed in our best togas. It was not an official holiday, but there was a holiday spirit in the air, as there always is when routine is broken. Hortalus got up on the Rostra and proclaimed our mission, and the crowd cheered, praising the Senate's wisdom.

Of course, Pompey had known for days of the Senate's decision, but his flunkies had insisted that we revive the ancient custom of the entire Senate trooping in a body to the victorious general's camp to give him the good news personally. Since they had adequate historical precedent to cite, there was no way the rest of us could get out of it.

As we went down the Via Sacra to the city gate, we all kept good, impassive senatorial faces, but there was plenty of grumbling all around. I did a bit of it myself.

"It had better be the triumph to top all triumphs," somebody groused near me, "since he's putting us to all this trouble."

"Just like Pompey," said somebody else. "Not enough to get his triumph; he has to see the whole Senate come out to him to kiss his glorious backside." This was all to the good, to my way of thinking. In those days the Senate still had a great deal of pride and was an assemblage of peers. We did not like anyone who puffed himself up and gave himself kingly airs. A *triumphator* received semi-divine honors for a day, and that was thought to be enough for any man.

Pompey's lackeys had been petitioning the Senate to grant him the right to wear his triumphal regalia at all public functions, a piece of abject toadying that horrified all right-thinking Romans. Unfortunately, right-thinking Romans were getting fewer all the time.

Pompey's camp was laid out identically to a legionary camp, but without the customary fortifications. That would have been an intolerable provocation. His soldiers were still under arms, but they showed the lax discipline Pompey allowed between campaigns. Few bothered to wear armor or bear shields, and those detailed to guard the treasure merely belted on their swords and leaned on their spears, most of them passing the time with dice and knucklebones. There were some flaming faces as we made our way to his *praetorium*. Many felt mortally insulted that Pompey had not bothered to have his men turn out for an inspection parade to honor a visit by the massed Senate.

At the *praetorium* we found Pompey enthroned on a dais. We walked down the *via praetoria* between the ranks of his honor guard. These indeed were finely turned out, their mail newly cleaned and oiled, the sun flashing from the polished bronze of their helmets. Their cloaks and their horsehair crests were new and colorful. The damage had been done, though, when the Senate had seen the slovenly louts standing guard. I remembered what Cicero had said about Pompey, that he was a political imbecile. A man who neglected to flatter the most august body of men in the world had little future in Roman politics.

"Just like calling on the King of Kings, isn't it?" I turned to see Crassus standing close to me. "Look at him. That dais must be fifteen feet high, and that curule chair is ivory, unless my eyes deceive me."

Indeed, Pompey looked more like a king than a soldier, for all his gold-plated armor and scarlet cloak. His curule chair was draped with leopard skins, and his feet rested on a footstool cleverly wrought from the crowns of monarchs he had conquered.

"He certainly doesn't mind rubbing it in," I concurred. Behind him stood the eagle-bearers of his legions, their heads and shoulders draped with lion pelts above their old-fashioned scale shirts, and beside him stood some odd-looking men whose long, pointed beards echoed the shape of their tall caps. They were draped in rough brown cloaks. I asked Crassus about them.

"Those are the Etruscan soothsayers I told you about. He claims they bring him good fortune."

These were hard-faced, fanatical-looking men. But then, I thought, men who spent their days cutting open sacrificial animals and delving among their viscera for omens had not chosen the pleasantest of professions.

We stopped before the dais and stood there looking noble while Pompey tried to look regal. Hortalus stepped forward and spoke sonorously.

"Cnaeus Pompeius Magnus, we, the Senate of Rome, in exercise of our ancient right, do hereby grant you the honor of a triumph!" His grandiloquence was somewhat marred by the trumpeting of an elephant nearby.

Pompey stood. "Honorable conscript fathers," he began; then several more elephants blasted away. He waited for them to quiet down, then went on. "I accept this honor, to the glory of the gods of Rome and the ancestors of my house."

"What ancestors?" said some wag. "That flute-player four generations ago?" This raised some guffaws. Like many others, his family had been raised to prominence by Sulla. They had amounted to nothing before that.

Io triumphe!" shouted the honor guard, drowning out all the sly remarks being passed at Pompey's expense.

I heard Crassus say, in a low voice, "What an opportunity!" Something in his tone made me uneasy.

"What do you mean?" I asked.

"I mean, here we are, the whole Senate. And there he is, and all around us are his armed troops. He could massacre the lot of us right now and not a thing we could do about it."

"It would certainly be the crowning achievement of an extraordinary career," I said. I spoke flippantly, but the sweat began to spring out on my scalp. Surely, I thought, not even Pompey would be so bold. I would not feel safe until I was back within the walls of Rome. It taught me something else: that Crassus might very well seize such an opportunity, should it ever come his way. I determined that, should he ever be encamped outside the city awaiting a triumph, and should the Senate be summoned to go deliver him the good news, I would beg off on account of a sudden illness.

"The augurs," Hortalus went on when the soldiers were

quiet, "will take the omens and determine the will of the gods concerning a propitious day for the triumph."

"No need," Pompey said. He gestured toward his Etruscans. "My haruspices have already worked their art, and they have proclaimed the third day from today to be most pleasing to the gods."

I could see that Hortalus was furious, but he was a man of great experience and knew that he would cut a ridiculous figure trying to argue points of ritual in such a setting, where Pompey had arranged things to emphasize his own majesty. There was no dignified way to argue with such high-handedness, so Hortalus acceded gracefully.

"So shall it be proclaimed in the Forum," he said.

Now Pompey rose. "I give you all freedom of my camp, and I invite you to partake of some refreshment with me."

And so we ended up being Pompey's guests for lunch. He had laid out tables under an immense tent-roof, which also sheltered some of the more fragile items destined to grace his triumph: paintings and other works of art, fine furnishings, fabrics, brocades, even models of the besieged cities and forts carved from ivory and shell.

The food wasn't bad either. I got pleasantly tipsy since I saw no good reason not to. Happily stuffed, I got up from the table and wandered among the treasures, admiring as always our wonderful Roman talent for acquiring other people's property. Pompey had acquired a good many of the people as well. In one tent were enemy princes and nobles, tastefully fettered in golden chains. Another vast marquee sheltered some of the most beautiful women I had ever seen.

"Scandalous," clucked another senatorial inspector. It was Cato, naturally. "A triumph should not be made into a brothel."

"I don't know," I said. "These look like good stock. Who wants to be surrounded by ugly slaves?"

"Nonsense!" he retorted. "Within ten years half of them will be freed, living in the slums and spawning babies to be a further burden on the state." There was some justice to that. Reluctantly, I left the entrance of the tent. Several Senators were crowding in behind me.

"Come on," I said, "let's go see the elephants." Grumbling, Cato accompanied me. I disliked Cato greatly, but he was fun to have around on such occasions. He had no sense of humor whatever, and that made it easy to insult him without his noticing.

In a nearby field we found score upon score of the immense beasts, with their drivers putting them through their paces. Some were being trained to carry various trophies in procession. Others had platforms erected on their backs, bearing images of the gods. Still others carried small forts, and these were manned with slaves dressed to resemble the enemies Pompey had conquered.

There was another compound, heavily guarded, which held captive warriors. These were fierce men, too dangerous to leave at home and unsuitable for ordinary slave work. Most of them were destined for the arena, where a few of them might win their freedom at the whim of the crowd. Besides the legionaries, wooden towers at intervals around this compound were manned by expert Cretan archers with arrows fitted to their strings.

"Here, at least," Cato proclaimed, "Pompey hasn't let his men get too slack, even though he's had to employ those Cretan hirelings."

"He doesn't have much choice," I said. "Romans are swordsmen and spearmen, not archers."

"Did you see those idle louts as we entered the camp?" Cato all but hissed. "I cannot believe that those were Roman soldiers. I have heard of how slack his legions are, but I never guessed the extent of their indiscipline."

"All the more reason," I said, "that we should prevent him from ever getting command of Roman soldiers again."

Cato nodded. "You are right. In the future, I shall apply myself to blocking his attempts at further military commands." He mused for a while. "And those foreign soothsayers! What he did was an affront to the gods of our ancestors! I suppose it's what you might expect from a man whose father was killed by lightning." I did not argue with this.

As I walked back toward the camp entrance I passed the *praetorium* and heard voices speaking in a strange language. I thought it probably the conversation of Asiatic slaves and was about to pass on when some half-

forgotten familiarity in the sound of the language
stopped me. Slowly, I stepped nearer the great tent.

Just within one of the entrances I saw the soothsayers
huddled. Theirs was the voices I had heard. I suppose I
must have heard Etruscan spoken before, probably in
the form of prayers or chants. It was a dying language,
but was still spoken in some of the more remote parts
of Tuscia. One of the men looked up and caught sight
of me. He said something and they all fell silent and
glared at me.

I had no idea why they thought I was eavesdropping
on their conversation, since nobody on Earth except
Etruscans could understand their incomprehensible gibberish. Ill-mannered foreigners. If Pompey was cultivating such as these, he was welcome to them.

With a few other Senators as companions, I walked
back to the city. None of them were Pompey's supporters, so I was not constrained in my speech. Everyone
agreed that Pompey's arrogance had grown intolerable.
Nobody, however, had any good propositions as to what
to do about it. After listening to a number of futile sug-
gestions, I decided that our best course was probably
that put forth by Cicero: Let time, the absence of promising wars and Pompey's own political ineptitude bring
him down.

I had one major apprehension about this policy,
though. I feared that Pompey's downfall would probably
come about because he would be replaced by men more
unscrupulous than he.

It was barely midafternoon when I reached the Forum.
There were several hours left before sunset, when I would
meet Julia at the Temple of Castor. I wondered what she
might have discovered, but that was not the foremost
thing on my mind. I was more excited just to be meeting
Julia again. Too many women had inserted themselves
into my life in recent days: Clodia, Fulvia, even Purpurea. In the company of these mysterious and dangerous
women, Julia seemed positively wholesome, even if she
was Caesar's niece.

The Forum is always a good place to idle, so I idled. I
talked to friends and acquaintances, and got braced by
more *publicani* than I had known to exist. Most of these
were angling for public contracts out in the provinces,

because virtually all the builders in Rome were going to be engaged for the next couple of years on Pompey's new theater. Not only was the theater itself to be immense, but it was to be but the centerpiece of a veritable minor forum out on the Campus Martius. It would have galleries and gardens, a new voting-compound for the popular assemblies and a Senate house. It seemed that there was a sort of public-works rivalry between Pompey and Lucullus, and the city was doing well out of it. Lucullus, though, gave better parties.

As I ambled around the periphery of the Forum, I came upon one of those crowds that assemble wherever something ghastly has happened. With a sinking heart, I went to investigate. I could already see that they were gathered before a booth, one decorated with fortune-teller's symbols. I pushed my way through the gawkers and into the booth. Inside I found a man in a purple-bordered toga dictating to a pair of secretaries who stood with styluses and wax tablets poised.

All three were gazing down at the body of Purpurea, which was decorated with the now-familiar wounds on throat and brow. Her face was stretched into a mask of terror as exaggerated as those worn on the stage. Unlike the other victims, she had known what was coming.

"Good day, Senator," said the man in the *toga praetexta*. He was perhaps forty years old, with a serious face and reddish hair. "I am Lucius Domitius Ahenobarbus, curule aedile. This woman was murdered sometime this morning. Did you know her, or were you just curious to see what the fuss was about?"

I told him my name and enough of my lineage to let him know who I was. "I have questioned her in recent days concerning an investigation I am engaged upon."

"Under whose auspices?" he asked sharply.

"Metellus Celer," I said.

"He has no authority, but we both know he'll be one of next year's Consuls, and I'll be out of office then, so I won't dispute his right to appoint you."

"How was she discovered?" I asked.

"Several people entered this booth this morning but left thinking she was not here. A man who keeps a sausage-stand nearby came in to see if she had any garlic among her herbs, and he saw her foot sticking out from behind a pile of baskets. Whoever killed her covered the body."

"Is anything known about her?" I asked.

"Nothing but her name and occupation," Domitius said.

"I don't suppose she had a license to practice her trade here?"

"How could she?" he said. "It's illegal." He caught my reproving look. "All right, I know it's our duty to expel them from the Forums and markets, but the office of aedile was assigned when Rome was about one-tenth the size it is now. We have to test weights and measures, guard against usury and counterfeiting, put on the public games, keep all the public works in repair, clean and pave the streets—" He threw up his hands. "I could devote my whole year just to inspecting the wineshops and whorehouses, another of our duties, and never get to all of them!"

"The burdens of office are great," I agreed. "Any idea whether she was freeborn? If she was a freedwoman her former master may want to claim the body for burial."

"I intend to find out. One of my secretaries will go from here to the Archives."

"When you find out, could you send me word? I didn't get to finish questioning her, and there is a great deal I would like to know. I would esteem it a great personal favor."

He had been bored with the onerousness of office, but this brightened him. This meant he would be able to call on me for a favor someday, and that was not a small thing when the parties had names like Domitius and Metellus.

"I shall be most glad to, Senator."

"Thank you. My house is in the Subura. Your messenger can ask anyone there where to find me." I took my leave and went outside. I checked to make sure that my *caestus* was handy and my dagger was loose in its sheath. The way things were progressing, it couldn't be long before the man with the knife and the hammer came for me.

The Temple of Castor is the most beautiful in Rome. It had been built over four hundred years before, in gratitude for our victory at Lake Regillus. Actually, its full

name was the Temple of Castor and Pollux, but nobody
bothers with poor old Pollux, who, like Remus, is the
forgotten brother of the Twins.

I found Julia standing atop the steps, between two of
the tall, slender columns. She wore a belted gown of pale
saffron and a shawl of darker yellow. Her only jewelry
was a string of gold and amber beads. She was as different from Clodia as it was possible for a woman to be,
and that was the highest praise I could think of. She
smiled as I came up the steps toward her. She had wonderful teeth.

"You're early," she said. "The sun isn't quite down."

"I was anxious to see you again." I looked around the
portico, which seemed to be deserted. "No grandmoth-
ers lurking in the shadows?"

"We're safe," she said. "I'm supposed to be visiting an
aunt in the House of the Vestals."

"I have an aunt there myself," I said inanely.

"Actually, I went there," she said. "I wouldn't lie about
it. I just didn't stay as long as I hinted I might."

"That's nothing to anger the gods," I assured her. "Before I forget—when you said that Fulvia was at Caesar's
house on the night of the Mysteries, did you mean the
younger one, the one who is betrothed to Clodius?"

"Yes, that's the one. The elder Fulvia left the city in
disgrace last year. I met Fulvia that night, before the unmarried women had to withdraw. She's a beautiful creature. I've heard rumors about her, but I would not believe
them. Nobody that young can be that bad."

"Oh, yes, they can," I affirmed. "Some people are bad
from birth. Age merely confers experience and discretion upon their youthful promise. I met her yesterday,
and I couldn't have picked a better match for Clodius.
With luck, they'll kill each other, but I tremble for the
fate of Rome, should they produce children who live."

She laughed merrily. "I love the way you exaggerate,
Decius." Poor, simple girl. She thought I exaggerated.

"Just what is it that you unmarried women did that
night? Or is that another of those forbidden subjects?"

"Oh, no. There is a preliminary ceremony, an invo-
cation of the goddess. After that the Mysteries began,
and we had to leave. Mostly, we sat around gossiping in
the back of the house, and we would have been there all

night, but things broke up in the uproar over Clodius being there."

"I see."

"Well, don't you want to hear what I've found out?" she said impatiently.

"Certainly. Whatever makes you think otherwise?"

"Because you're acting just like a man!" As if that were some sort of condemnation.

"I should hope so. Now, what is it you've discovered?"

"I found out how Clodius got in!"

"Splendid. We already know he was dressed as a woman."

"Yes, yes, but he didn't arrive with the others. It was later, when the Mysteries were already well under way. He arrived with the woman who brought the laurel leaves."

"Laurel leaves?" I said. "You mean wreaths?"

"No, leaves steeped in something or other according to some ancient formula. The women chew them during the later phase of the rites. Things get rather ... abandoned, I understand."

"Imagine that," I said. "Respectable Roman matrons carrying on like a pack of maenads." Then the implication struck me. "This woman Clodius arrived with—you wouldn't have got her name, would you?"

Julia shrugged. "Just a peasant herb-woman. Is it important?"

I leaned against one of the fluted columns and rubbed my eyes. My head was beginning to throb.

"I could take you across the Forum and show you her corpse."

Julia's eyes widened and she gasped. She had led a sheltered life. "She was murdered?"

"The carnage is getting warlike," I said. "Four dead so far, slave, peasant and patrician. What next? A eunuch?"

"Then my information was of no use to you?" She looked so crestfallen that I was swift to reassure her.

"By no means. What you've told me is sure to be of the utmost importance. The murders tie in somehow with the sacrilege."

"Certainly it was scandalous," she said, "but worthy of multiple murder?"

"No. The profanation of the rites has been a real laugh-raiser. Romans aren't as pious as they used to be. Clodius was up to something else that night, and that is what he doesn't want discovered."

"Then you think Clodius has done all this?"

I shook my head. "He is involved, but I can't believe that he originated anything so devious. Direct action is his style. No, what we need to find out is who else was there that night."

"Who else? You mean you think Clodius was not the only man to profane the rites?"

"If not the rites themselves, then in another part of the house. Where better to meet for nefarious reasons than in a house where men are supposed to be banned for the night?"

"Conspiracy! This gets better all the time!" I could tell that her delight in winkling out plots matched my own.

"I suspect that Clodius attended whatever conference he and his co-conspirators had arranged, and then almost ruined everything because he couldn't resist sneaking back in to spy on the rituals. Serves them all right, whoever they are. Anyone who would trust Clodius deserves whatever happens to them." I glanced into the temple, where the priests were placing fires before the statues of the Twins. The moment the word "twins" entered my mind, the question that had plagued me was shaken loose.

"Julia, you said that Fausta was there that night. Yet she is not married. Was she with you unmarried ladies?"

Julia frowned in thought. "No, she wasn't. She arrived with Claudia the wife of Lucullus. She wore a veil, but it was almost transparent and I knew her by sight. I didn't notice if she withdrew when the rest of us did. Are you sure she isn't widowed?"

"She has never married. So what was *she* up to? All sorts of anomalies keep cropping up in that night's doings. You will find that it is the anomalies that are truly important, when investigating the deeds of infamous men."

"I suspected as much," she said rather coolly. Apparently, I was pointing out the obvious again.

"I think it might be time to concentrate on Fausta," I said. "It should not be difficult to get other ladies to gossip about her—she's the center of much gossip as it is. Try to find out if anyone else remembers her doing anything suspicious that night."

Julia smiled again. "I shall do that."

"But carefully, mind you. Someone is killing people without regard to sex or social standing. I would hate for you to be the next victim. Or even the one after, for that matter."

"I shall be discreet. What will you be doing?"

"Dangerous and foolish things," I assured her. "Stalking violent and ambitious men, searching for murderers who employ a singular technique for dispatching their victims, that sort of thing." I was beginning to feel quite heroic.

"Then do take care yourself. You are unique, and the Republic can scarcely afford to lose you."

I could not but agree with this, but I modestly forbore to acknowledge the fact. She took her leave and descended the steps of the temple. I waited in the shadow of the portico until she was out of sight. I now realized, belatedly, that it was perilous for her to be seen in my company. I scanned the surrounding area for surreptitious watchers, but that was futile. Rome provides from every prospect more alleys, windows, warrens, rooftops and other lurking spots than the human eye can readily discern.

When Julia was gone I left the temple and walked through the city's rapidly darkening streets. I tucked my hands beneath my tunic as if warming them, but actually to grip my weapons. As I walked I pondered, trying to fit the new anomalies into some sort of order.

As I had told Julia, the anomalies are important. So are correspondences, linkages, kinships, anything that ties the facts together in some fashion, however bizarre they might seem at first. My problem was that, when thinking of Clodius, I found it difficult to think of anything else. I decided to concentrate on other things and see if they led back to Clodius, or somewhere else.

Fausta had some odd part to play in this. She was the daughter of the late Dictator, Sulla. What else was she? She was the ward of Lucullus, who had been named Sulla's executor. Her twin brother, Faustus, was Pompey's loyal henchman. That was another scent that could easily distract me. I longed to pull Pompey down almost as much as Clodius. In Pompey's case because he was a prospective tyrant and king of Rome. With Clodius it was personal. So Fausta had that connection with Pompey. She lived in the household of Lucullus, who hated Pompey, but she would be more likely to side with her beloved twin than with her protector. She had arrived at the house of Caesar on the night of the rites in company with the wife of Lucullus. And his wife was Claudia, elder sister of Clodius and Clodia. The other Claudian brother, Appius, was out there in Pompey's camp someplace, but he did not concern me. To the best of my knowledge, he had found legionary life to his taste and settled on a military career, taking little interest in politics.

This might prove embarrassing. I had already told my friend Milo that I would aid him in his courtship of the woman. He would not take it kindly if she were to be exiled because of me. Between Celer's insistence that I keep Clodia out of the scandal and Milo's infatuation with Fausta, I was placed in something of a quandary. Trouble with women was nothing new in my life, but this was a novel variant of it.

Who else might have been in that house on the night of the rites? And for what purpose? The fact that they had gone to such extremes to keep their doings secret, and were murdering people to cover themselves, meant that whatever it was was very, very bad indeed. And what could Capito have had to do with it?

I reached my house without any attempts being made on my life.

X

The next morning I found that Hermes was mostly recovered from his malady, pale but upright and rubbing his belly from time to time.

"Can't guess what it might have been," he said. He had a furtively guilty look but he usually looked that way, so I could not tell whether that signified anything. "Maybe an enemy put a curse on me," he said.

"More likely you broke into my wine closet and drained a jug or two," I said. "I'll look into it later."

I greeted my clients, and in the midst of it a man arrived with a note. I recognized the fellow as one of Asklepiodes's slaves.

Please come visit me at your earliest opportunity, it read. Below the message was the whimsical seal the Greek used: a sword and caduceus. This looked promising. Perhaps he had discovered something.

We all trooped to Celer's house, and at the first opportunity I took him aside.

"Have you determined anything?" he asked.

"Just a great deal of confusion," I said. "But I must ask you something. A few days ago I spoke to Caesar in this house. He said that he had come to ask you for a night's lodgings while he was banned from his own roof."

"So he did."

"Was he here all night?" I asked.

"Well, no. About midnight he went out. He said that he had to go take the omens. He was wearing his *trabea* and carried his crooked staff. Why? Is this significant?"

"It may be," I said. "Did you see him after that?"

"Yes. He came in shortly after I got up. He said he'd been up on the Quirinal, but that the night had been too cloudy for decent omen-taking. Why?"

"Oh," I said, trying to sound casual, "I am just trying to account for everybody's location that night. It all happened at his house."

"Stick to Clodius, my boy. Don't go trifling with Caius Julius."

"I'll keep that in mind," I said. I did not tell him that I suspected more powerful men than Caius Julius were involved.

I dismissed my clients and told Hermes to follow me. We walked back through the Subura and trudged up the Quirinal to the ancient Colline Gate. Like all the gates, it was a holy place and had seen many battles. Hannibal is supposed to have heaved a spear over it as a gesture of defiance, and just twenty-one years before Sulla had smashed the Samnite supporters of the younger Marius outside the gate, a battle the Romans had watched from atop the walls as at an amphitheater. After the rigors of the previous years, I am told that it was something of a relief seeing blood shed *outside* the walls.

Since Rome had no military or police within the walls, the guardianship of the gates was parceled out among various guilds, brotherhoods and temples. The Colline Gate was the responsibility of the *collegium* of the nearby Temple of Quirinus. These were the Quirinal *Salii*, who danced each October before all the most important shrines of the city. The young patricians did not pull night guard themselves, of course, but their servants did.

In the temple I went to the wardroom, where the gate guards stayed. Then I requested to be shown the tablet of the night when the rites had been profaned. The slave who kept the wardroom rummaged among the tablets while I looked over the small facility. There was no one else there. The gates were only watched at night.

"Here you are, sir," the slave said. I looked at the scratchings on the wax. Several freight wagons had entered the city during the night. All had left the same way before first light. There was no record of the *Pontifex Maximus* going out to take the omens. I asked the slave if he knew anything about it.

"The augurs are always supposed to check here at the temple before they go out the gate after dark, sir. The pontifex Spinther came here about ten days ago, with his striped robe and *lituus*. None since then." I thanked him and left.

"Why are you asking these questions?" Hermes asked me as we descended the hill. "Is it something to do with the patrician who tried to poison you and ended up dead instead?"

"I don't know, but I suspect that it is all connected. Why do you want to know?"

Hermes shrugged. "If you get killed, I'll just get passed on to somebody who's not as agreeable."

"I am touched. Yes, there's something very strange going on. Somebody tried to murder me, and Capito was murdered on the same night. The next night the rites of Bona Dea were profaned in Caesar's house. Caesar told Celer that he was going out to look for omens on the Quirinal that night, but he didn't. The boy who tried to poison me was murdered. The woman I suspect of selling him the poison was murdered. The boy was staying with Clodius, my worst enemy. The murdered woman was with Clodius when he sneaked into Caesar's house dressed as a woman. Doesn't it strike you that there is some common thread running through all this?"

Hermes shrugged. "Free people are mostly crazy. Noble ones are the worst."

"Stay a slave," I advised him. "That way your problems will always be simple."

We crossed the city and went over the bridge to the Island, then over the other bridge to the Trans-Tiber.

"Where are we going now?" Hermes asked.

"The *ludus* of Statilius Taurus, to visit a friend."

He brightened at that. "The gladiator school? You must know everybody!" He was always impressed with my familiarity with the lowest strata of Roman life.

At the school I left him in the training yard, gaping at the netmen as they went through their drills and practice fights. For some reason the netmen had caught the fancy of the slaves and lowest classes. Probably because sword and shield were the honorable weapons of citizens. Like many boys his age, he probably thought of gaining fame as a gladiator. He was too inexperienced to realize that it was just a delayed death sentence. Luckily, he was old enough to understand the whip and the cross.

Asklepiodes greeted me and insisted on going through

the usual amenities with wine and cakes before he would
enlighten me. Eventually, we sat by a wide window and
looked down upon the men practicing below.

"Since we last spoke," he said, "I have been flogging
my brain to remember where I had seen that hammer
wound. Yesterday I was sitting here, idly watching the
men at practice, when I saw some new men arrive. They
were to have direction of the *munera* Pompey will give
after his triumph. Some were old champions paid enor-
mously to come out of retirement to grace the games,
but among them were some Etruscan priests. Have you
ever seen the fights as they are conducted in the more
traditional areas of Tuscia?"

My scalp prickled. "No, I have not."

He beamed with satisfaction. "Well, the sight of these
Etruscans reminded me. Some years ago, I accompanied
a troupe to some funeral games near Tarquinia. There I
witnessed something I had not seen before. Now, in the
munera, what happens after a defeated man has received
the death-blow, before the *Libitinarii* come to drag the
body away?"

"The Charon touches the corpse with his hammer to
claim it for the death-goddess, Libitina," I said.

"Exactly. Have you ever wondered where he got his
attributes? The long nose and the pointed ears, the boots
and the hammer? These are not the attributes of the
ferryman of the Styx who bears the same name."

I shifted uncomfortably. "They are said to be Etruscan
in origin, like the games themselves."

"That is correct. In reality, he is the Etruscan death-
demon, Charun, who claims the dead for the deity of the
underworld, whom you call Pluto and we call Hades.
Well, in Tuscia, he does not simply touch the corpse. He
stands over the head and smashes the brow with his
hammer."

"And these men came from Pompey's camp, you say?"

"That is an unhealthy and unseasonal sweat I see shining upon your forehead," he observed.

"As long as you see no hammer mark there, I am satisfied," I said. I took a long drink from my wine cup and
he refilled it. Then I took a long drink from that one.
"Something else falls into place," I said. "Murders with
an Etruscan stamp, just when Pompey has a collection of

Etruscan priests outside the walls. And Crassus told me that Pompey has lent some of them to Clodius."

"Ah! Pompey and Clodius. An unsavory pairing. What might all this portend?"

I told him what I knew, and he nodded sagely as he listened. He had that trick of nodding sagely when he had not the slightest idea what you were talking about. It was a faculty I, too, learned in time. When I described Caesar's dispersal of the crowd before my door and our subsequent discussion in my house, he interrupted me.

"Just a moment. Caesar said that the goddess Libitina is the ancestress of his house? I have gone to hear him orate many times, and he has often named the goddess Aphrodite as his ancestress."

"Venus," I corrected him. "Yes, he's taken to doing that a lot lately. That's because you practically have to go back to the time of the gods to find a Julian who ever amounted to anything. But our Venus is a more complex goddess than your Aphrodite. Libitina is our goddess of death and funerals, but she is also a goddess of fields and vineyards and of voluptuous pleasures, in which aspect she becomes the dual goddess Venus Libitina. Thus Caesar can call either of them his ancestress without contradiction."

"Religion is a thing of marvel," Asklepiodes said.

I spun the rest of the tale, not gloating over my acuity but rather telling of my perplexity. When I had finished, he refilled our cups and we thought in silence for a while.

"So this investigation of yours, which was to seek out the guilt of Clodius, now involves Pompey and Caesar?"

"And Crassus," I said. "Let's not forget him. If the other two are involved, so is he."

"What if the purpose of their plotting is to destroy Crassus?"

"That's involvement, isn't it?" I demanded.

"Excellent point," he conceded.

I rose hastily. "I thank you. I see someone down there I should speak with."

Asklepiodes followed my gaze and saw the young man who had just entered the exercise yard. "A handsome youth! And what striking coloring, almost like a German."

"Fairness like that is extremely rare among Romans,"

I told him. "It's common only in a single patrician family, the *gens* Cornelia."

"I forgive your hasty leave-taking. I might be so precipitous myself to greet a youth so comely." He was, after all, a Greek.

The young man looked up when I approached him. His eyes were like Egyptian lapis. "I don't believe we've met since we were children, but I saw you yesterday in Pompey's camp. I am Decius Caecilius Metellus the Younger. Are you not Faustus Cornelius Sulla?"

He smiled. "I am. I believe we rode together in the Trojan Game when we were boys."

"I remember. I fell off my horse." Faustus was a small, almost delicate-looking man, but I knew that was deceptive. He had made a name for himself as a soldier in Pompey's service, and had even won the *corona muralis* for being first over the wall at Jerusalem when Pompey had taken that ever-troublesome city.

"Are you here concerning Pompey's upcoming *munera*?" I asked him.

"Yes, and to begin arrangements for my own. My father enjoined a *munera* upon me in his will. Since I've been old enough to celebrate them, I've been away from Rome. This is the first time I've had a chance to discharge the obligation, and I mean to get it out of the way before I'm sent off to another war someplace." He was another of those men who had chosen foreign soldiering as a career and considered domestic civil service an onerous duty. I was precisely the opposite. My Greek friend had mistaken him for a youth because of his exquisite, almost feminine Cornelian features. Actually, he was no more than a year younger than I.

"I understand Pompey is adding an Etruscan element to his *munera*," I said. Faustus had been watching the fighters practice, but now he glanced toward me sharply.

"What do you mean by that?"

"A friend saw some of his Etruscan priests here yesterday."

"They are just soothsayers," he said quickly. "They'll have nothing to do with the fights. They said they could ensure a better show by rejecting unlucky swordsmen."

"It seems to me," I said, "that some of them will have to be unlucky, or it won't be much of a show."

"I don't think that's what they meant," Faustus said.

We were interrupted when Statilius Taurus himself arrived to take charge of his distinguished visitor. I took my leave of them and retrieved Hermes.

"Who's that?" the boy said, jerking his chin toward Faustus.

"Faustus Cornelius Sulla, only living son of the Dictator," I informed him.

"Oh," Hermes said, disappointed. Doubtless he would have preferred some illustrious criminal. Well, there were plenty of those to go around, too. I decided to call on one of them.

It took some asking, but I finally tracked Milo down in a massive warehouse near the river. His guard at the door let me pass the instant he recognized me. I was one of perhaps five or six men who had access to Titus Annius Milo at any hour of the day or night.

Inside the warehouse, the scene was not greatly different from the one I had left at the *ludus.* Milo was drilling his men in some of the finer points of street-brawling. He had shed toga and dignity, and stood in his tunic while men circled him warily with clubs and knives. Hermes gasped when a man darted in and swung a club at Milo's head. Milo didn't duck the weapon like any ordinary man. He caught it instead and it made a noisy clack hitting his palm. I think Milo could have caught a sword that way. His years at the oar had given him palms as hard as the brazen shield of Achilles, and somehow they stayed that way all his life. His other hand grasped the front of the man's tunic and with a fierce wrench sent him careening into another who was approaching with a knife. Both men collapsed in a heap. Milo never carried a weapon and never needed one.

"That was good," he said. "Let's try another."

"No fair, Chief," said a gap-toothed Gaul. "The rest of us can't catch weapons like that."

"Then I'll teach you something you can use," Milo said, grinning. "Line up in two teams, facing one another." The men did so. "Now, the idea is, you just defend yourself against the man directly in front of you, but keep aware of the man fighting your comrade on the right or left. The moment he leaves himself open, turn and get him. You'll usually have your chance when he attacks the man before him. Move quickly. He won't see you coming, and the man you're engaged with won't be expecting the move. Come back to guard instantly, and he won't be able to take advantage of it. Now let's see you try it."

The two groups went at it with relish, and Hermes cheered every smack of wood against flesh. These men were inveterate brawlers and they actually enjoyed the exercise. Ever since the Gracchi, mob violence had been a common fact of Roman political life. With his usual cold-blooded realism, Milo was polishing his men's technique the way Caesar or Cicero would polish a speech. When he was satisfied with their performance, he came over to me.

"They're shaping up," he said grudgingly.

"They look fierce enough," I acknowledged.

"Ferocity is common. Clodius's gang is plenty fierce. It's concerted action that wins big fights. The gladiators only know single combat and the brawlers never think past their own knuckles. I need a street army and I intend to have one."

"You had better be careful, Titus," I cautioned. "A few words in the wrong ears could get you charged with insurrection."

"I have Cicero and a good many others working on my behalf," he said. "For every Senator who wants to see me brought down, there's an enemy of Clodius who sees me as the savior of Rome."

"Cicero is not in high favor just now," I warned, "and when Pompey comes back into the city in a couple of days, he'll be the power in Rome until new alliances can be formed."

"Thanks for your concern," Milo said, "but I've been working hard for years to arrange the sort of support I need. I feel secure for the time being."

"As you will," I said. "Titus, I need to know what sort of naughtiness Mamercus Capito might have been up to. I—"

"I can tell you right now," he interrupted. "Nothing. I looked into it as soon as I learned he was murdered. He had no meaningful contacts among the Roman underworld, which is to say, my own colleagues. As far as I was able to learn, he wasn't taking bribes beyond the acceptable limits. He had a few silent partners, mostly his freedmen, running businesses for him, since as a patrician he couldn't be officially involved. They insist that he had no business enemies with cause to kill him. He must have been murdered for personal or political reasons. Your Senate contacts will know more about how he voted in the Senate than I."

"You've saved me a great deal of time," I told him.

"Then perhaps you can employ it in my behalf. Have you spoken with the lady yet?"

"No, but I go from here to the house of Lucullus. With luck, I'll get there in time for lunch."

"Enjoy yourself, but be eloquent."

"I'll do my best, which if I may say so is considerable. By an odd coincidence, I've just met with her brother at the Statilian School. The resemblance is striking, and I'm told they both greatly resemble the old Dictator. I'm afraid he's Pompey's man, though."

"That's unfortunate. I hope I don't fall afoul of him, since I intend to be his brother-in-law."

"Matrimony is often a perilous enterprise," I told him.

Hermes and I left, stepping over the writhing or inert bodies of thugs who had been practicing all too seriously. My slave was inordinately excited by the whole experience.

"Why don't you sell me to him, master?" he said. "I think I'd enjoy belonging to Milo."

"If he ever offends me mortally, I'll give you to him as a gift," I assured the boy.

I arrived at the house of Lucullus a little late for the full lunch ceremony, but a place was made for me at the table as the last course arrived, and that was far more than I could possibly eat even with the aid of the gods. I moderated my wine intake since I was to be doing some important negotiating later on.

Because I was not an invited guest, I did not feel that I could rightfully impose myself on Lucullus, but I lagged behind while the others took their leave, which all did very shortly after the meal. Luncheon was still so new that a routine for socializing afterward had not yet been developed. Before long, I was sitting with Lucullus in his garden while his slaves dug in the huge planting-beds, readying them for the spring.

"Does this involve the investigation Celer is being so

sly about?" Lucullus asked. "If so, I fear I would be of
little help. My wife is a Claudian first, like the rest of her
family. She would never tell me anything that might get
her dear little brother into trouble."

A server poured us wine from a golden pitcher. I
sipped at it. It was Caecuban, of a vintage most men
would have saved for the celebration of a victory, and
only faintly cut with rose-scented water.

"No; for a change I come on an amatory mission."

His eyebrows went up. "On your own behalf?"

"On behalf of a friend. Titus Annius Milo."

Lucullus sat back and stroked his chin. "Milo. A rising
man, sure to be a power in Rome in the future, if he
doesn't find an early grave first."

"That grave awaits us all," I said.

"How true. And just who might be the object of that
formidable man's affections?"

"Your ward, Fausta. He met her here a few days ago
and was immediately felled by Cupid." I sipped again at
the excellent wine. This was a new activity for me.

"I am amazed that anything can fell Milo. He is of
doubtful birth," Lucullus pointed out, "and his activities
are little more than criminal."

"As to his birth, he has been from birth a Roman citizen, and there is no higher birth than that."

Lucullus clapped his hands. "Bravo. If this were one
of the popular assemblies, I should rise to my feet and
cheer."

"If his activities lack a certain gentility, is it more respectable to slaughter foreigners than to brawl in the
streets of Rome? Besides, once he has come to great
prominence in the state, his youthful excesses will be
forgotten, as is always the case. Look at Crassus. At Sulla,
even. Both of them were abhorred as degenerate young
reprobates, but the highest elements in Rome were kissing their backsides soon enough. Just wait. Soon all Rome
will be puckering up for Titus Milo."

"I'll admit he couldn't have sent a better man to press
his suit. I almost want to marry the rogue myself now."

"Then you will allow him to pay court to Fausta?" I
said.

"There is a small but significant difficulty," he said.

"What might that be?"

"A frog croaking in my fishpond has as much influence with her as I have. I am the executor of her father's will, but she doesn't think that extends to her person, whatever the law might say. She is a Cornelia, and a daughter of Sulla, and she is not about to submit herself to a mere Licinius like me. We get along well enough, but that's about all. She gets on better with Claudia, and that's a bad sign. But if Milo is willing to risk his future happiness with a haughty demigoddess of a Cornelia, he has my permission to chance it."

"Might I speak with her?" I asked.

"I'll send for her, but I can promise you nothing beyond that." He raised a hand so slightly that it might have been mistaken for an involuntary twitch. But his slaves were sensitive enough to detect his slightest wish. One came running and all but prostrated himself. "Tell the lady Fausta she has a visitor in the garden," Lucullus murmured. The man dashed off with winged heels.

Lucullus rose. "I wish you the best of fortune, Decius. The woman is self-willed, but not without a certain intelligence. She regards the sort of men I favor as too dull to hold her interest. If any man could strike her fancy, I suppose it would have to be someone like Milo."

He left me in the garden, leaving likewise the golden pitcher. I helped myself to another cup. Caecuban like that didn't come my way every day. While I waited for Fausta I lazed back in my chair, trying to imagine what it would be like living as Lucullus did. Without turning my head very far, I could see at least fifty slaves working in the garden. This, I knew, was only a fraction of his household staff. The table was fine porphyry, and the pitcher that sat on it was solid gold. It looked as if it would weigh more empty than a common pitcher when full. I determined to empty it and find out.

What must it be like, I thought, to pass a particularly lovely spot when traveling between, say, Rome and Brundisium, decide that you fancy the place, turn to your steward and say: "Buy all the land for ten miles around and build me a villa there." And then pass by a year later and see a mansion the size of a middling town, fully landscaped, decorated with the pick of the loot of Greece and Asia, and ready for you to move in if you should feel like resting from your trip. I thought this seemed

like an extremely pleasant way to live. The problem was
that the only way to amass such wealth was to conquer
some extremely rich kings, as Lucullus had.

By the time Fausta arrived, a warm, fuzzy mantle had
settled over the world. It was truly excellent Caecuban.

"I am terribly sorry to have kept you waiting so long,
Decius Caecilius." She was no less beautiful than when I
had seen her before, dressed in a gown of saffron linen
over which she had thrown a brief pallium of fine white
wool.

"I came unannounced," I said as I rose, "and to wait
in the house of Lucullus is to live like a king. Who can
complain of that?" A slave hovered nearby with a tray,
from which I seized a goblet which I filled for her. The
old rules against women drinking with men were fast
fading, especially for informal occasions such as this. Ordinary rules never applied to women like Fausta in any
case.

"Thank you," she said, taking the cup but not drinking. "Word is spreading that you are investigating the
profanation of the rites. Is that why you are here?"

"I am hurt," I said. "Everyone thinks that all I do is
snoop. Actually, nothing could be further from my
thoughts at this moment." This was not strictly true. "Actually, I come in the guise of Cupid."

"A marriage proposal?" she said coolly. "I had heard
that you were not married." The idea seemed to interest
her about as much as looking for toads under rocks.

"Not at all. If that had been the case, my father would
have called upon your guardian. No, I come on behalf
of my good friend, Titus Annius Milo Papianus. He met
you here a few days ago and was smitten, as might any
man have been."

Instantly, she grew more animated. "Milo! He is no
ordinary man, to be sure. I found him fascinating. But
his family is unknown to me. He has an adoptive name.
How did that come about?"

"His father was Caius Papius Celsus, a landholder from
the south. When he came to Rome he had himself
adopted by his maternal grandfather, Titus Annius Lus-
cus. This was strictly for political reasons, so that he
would have city residency and membership in an urban

tribe." At least this was simple. A patrician pedigree might have forced me to drone on for an hour.

"But the rural tribes are more respectable," she pointed out. "All the best families belong to rural tribes."

"That was the old days, my lady. Power in Rome now resides in the urban mob, which Milo intends to lead. Forget names and lineages. Milo intends to make his own name and he is well on his way. Many men with fine old patrician names live in near-beggary. Marry respectability and that is all you get. With Milo you would lead what can only be described as an interesting life."

"That does sound intriguing. I suppose he has a city house of suitable magnificence?"

"One of the largest and best-staffed in Rome," I assured her. I suppose I should have told her that it was a fortress and its staff consisted of thugs, arena-bait and cutthroats such as one rarely encounters, but why deprive her of a unique surprise?

"I get so many suitors," she said, "and they are all so boring. I am twenty-seven years old, you know. I had all but decided to remain unmarried, even if that meant remaining a legal child under the care of Lucullus. This is the first interesting offer to come my way. You may inform Milo that I am willing to entertain his suit. He may call upon me informally, but he is to understand that any agreement must be between the two of us. I have sworn to open my veins rather than submit to an arranged marriage."

"Perfectly understandable. You could end up married to Cato otherwise. I am sure that this news will give Milo the greatest joy. Would you care for some more of this excellent Caecuban?" She shook her head. I do not believe she had so much as sipped at her own cup. I refilled mine. "Now that that is settled, I don't suppose you would like to enlighten me concerning the scandalous evening that has become the delight of all Rome?"

"I'm afraid that I can't," she said.

"Ah. Forbidden by ritual law, like everyone else?"

"Not a bit of it. I didn't go to Caesar's house that night."

The cup stopped halfway to my mouth. "You did not? But you were seen there."

Her eyes didn't flicker. "Then someone was mistaken

or else lying. Only married women take part, and I wasn't about to waste an evening gossiping with a pack of well-born girls half my age."

"Then I must have been misinformed," I said. "Please forgive me."

"Why? I haven't been offended. Tell Milo I shall look forward to hearing from him." She rose and extended her hand, which I took. "Good day, Decius Caecilius." I watched her walk away. That was pleasant, but it told me nothing of her truthfulness. Either she was lying, or Julia was. I knew which one I preferred to believe.

I found Hermes waiting on a bench in the atrium. He looked up, annoyed, when I gestured for him to join me.

"You look like you ducked out and went to a tavern," he said. "Are you going to have to lean on me all the way home?"

"Nonsense," I said. "No one gets drunk on vintage as fine as I've been drinking." We left the house and walked toward the Forum.

"I've attended at banquets in houses as fine as this," he said. "I never realized the guests were puking from sheer joy."

"You are a vulgar little rascal," I chided. "You should not speak about your betters in such a fashion."

"You ought to hear how we slaves talk about you when there are no freemen about."

"You aren't earning yourself any favors this way," I warned him.

"Hah. You probably won't remember—uh-oh." His eyes went wide and so, I confess, did mine. A crowd of brutal-looking men swaggered toward us, blocking the narrow street. In center front was the ugliest of the lot: Publius Clodius Pulcher.

"Uh-oh, indeed," I muttered. "Hermes, be ready to back my play."

"Back you? What can you do against that lot?" The boy's voice quivered with terror.

"Just watch and keep your wits about you," I said re-assuringly. I picked a level spot. To my left, a flight of steps led between two buildings to a higher street. Behind us, the street was relatively clear, but it ascended steeply. While I was by no means drunk, I wished belat-edly that I had been more moderate with the Caecuban.

"Metellus! I have the feeling that you have been avoiding me! I am hurt!" He grinned his ugly, oily grin. Clodius had been making no formal calls and was dressed only in tunic and sandals. These latter were ordinary brown leather, although he was entitled to the thick-soled red buskins with the ivory crescent at the ankle. Even his tunic was the workingman's *exomis,* the Greek type that leaves the right shoulder and half the chest bare. Clodius, man of the people.

"You know how dearly I cherish your company, Publius," I said. "You have but to call at my house during my morning reception."

His laugh was loud and false. "When did a Claudian ever come calling on a Metellan?"

I waggled a finger at him. "Careful, Publius, your patricianship is showing. People might think you were wellborn, and you'll have wasted all that slumming and hanging around with low company."

"He's drunk," said one of the thugs.

"Drunk is as good a way to die as any," Clodius said. "Get him."

"Just a moment," I said, holding out a palm. "You have the advantage. Give me a moment." Ceremoniously, I removed my toga and folded it.

"He wants to make a fight of it," Clodius said. "I wouldn't have given him credit. Go ahead, Decius. Afterward we'll wrap you up in it, and you won't look so bad when your servants come to carry you home. You'll look better than poor Appius Nero did after you murdered him."

"I didn't kill him, Publius, you did, or maybe it was Clodia."

He went into his vein-popping routine again. "Enough of this! Kill him!"

As I have already said, running in a toga is futile. Since I was no longer encumbered with mine, I bounded like a deer up the steps to my left. When I reached the street at the top of the steps, I turned right, downhill. I survived the next few seconds only because Clodius and his men were temporarily surprised by my bolting. Only a fool could have expected me to stand and fight against such odds, but men are capable of endless folly, and Publius Clodius of more than most men.

Nonetheless, I could almost feel their breath on my heels as I dashed down the street, with startled pedestrians dodging out of my way. Romans were all too familiar with the sight of a man running for his life and knew how to behave accordingly. I mentally vowed a goat to Jove, asking him to cloud the eyes of the people before me. My greatest fear was that someone would recognize Clodius behind me and would try to stop me to curry favor with him.

I was far from Milo's territory and I did not know what Clodius's strength might be in this area. If I could make it to the Subura, I would be safe. Clodius and his men would probably not make it back out alive. Unfortunately, to make it all the way to the Subura I would have to be as swift and enduring as that Greek who ran with the news from Marathon to Athens. I cannot recall his name just now.

Our fine new colonial cities have beautiful, wide boulevards, flat as a pond and straight as a javelin. Rome has none. The streets I ran on rose and dipped, bent in serpentine curves or sharp angles, narrowed without warning and transformed into steps with no order or reason. This worked to my advantage, because I was recently returned from military service and Celer had insisted that his officers train as hard as the legionaries, to include broken-field running in armor. This stood me in good stead as I dodged, hopped, turned and leapt over the occasional recumbent drunk.

Clodius had no athletes in his following, and most of his ex-gladiators were well-drilled in arms but not in running. When I risked a glance over my shoulder, I saw that Clodius was close behind, but he had lost all but three or four of his men. The odds were getting better all the time.

I came to a warren of low wineshops and whores' cribs. The road had narrowed to an alley and took a right-angled turn to the right. On both sides rows of low doorways gave access to tiny cubicles and the services of their inhabitants. I ducked into one, and such was my state of heightened awareness that I still remember the sign above the doorway. It read: *Phoebe: Skilled in Greek, Spanish, Libyan and Phoenician* (this did not refer to languages). *Price: 3 sesterces. 2 denarii for Phoenician.* The smell within was rank, and from the back of the room came heavy breathing and the sound of flesh slapping rhythmically against flesh. I had my dagger and *caestus* out, and when a shadow crossed the doorway I lunged. There was a sharp indrawing of breath and the man toppled, clutching his belly. The face was bearded. Not Clodius, worse luck. Another man tripped over the one I had stabbed, and I kicked him in the jaw as he fell. I barged out the doorway, swinging at the first face I saw, and felt a jawbone crack under the bronze spikes of my *caestus*. Someone swung a curved short sword at me and I felt it draw a cold line along my shoulder, missing my throat by a finger's breadth. Before the man with the broken jaw had a chance to fall, I got my unwounded shoulder into him and sent him crashing into Clodius.

With a single leap I cleared the tangle of bodies and flailing limbs and was running at top speed down the alley. I passed a crowd seated in the open front of a wineshop, and they whistled and clapped in appreciation. In the years since, I have sometimes had cause to wonder what the Phoenician style might be. It must have been complicated. Two denarii was awfully expensive for a girl in that part of town.

My shoulder began to sting, but the fire in my lungs was worse. The alley opened onto a small plaza in front of a temple of Vertumnus. This gave me my bearings, and I ran toward the temple with the sound of sandals slapping close behind me. A few more of Clodius's men must have caught up with him. I veered to the right and went down the narrow street that ran between the temple and a towering tenement. Unwillingly, I had to slow down and tread carefully. The pavement before a tenement is often slick, because the wretches who inhabit such places are often too lazy to carry their chamberpots to the nearest sewer opening and just dump them into the street. Squawks and thuds behind me told me I was correct in being cautious.

The road began to level out, and I began to feel a bit of hope that I might get out of this alive. The great, hulking building just ahead of me was the Basilica Aemilia. I was looking at its unornamented rear, and I knew that if I could just get past it, I would be in the Forum, where even Publius Clodius might hesitate to murder

me. My sides were cramping and my lungs were working
so hard that I felt as if blood were about to burst forth
from them.

Then I was past the basilica and down its steps and
onto one of the wooden trial platforms in front of it.
And, just my luck, there was a trial in progress. I knew
that because it was crowded with men and a barrister
was in mid-gesture, his beringed hands raised dramati-
cally as he made the crowning point of his argument. I
will never forget the look of horror on his face when I
ran into him. We went sprawling across the platform, his
snowy toga billowing about us like the sail of a ship carried away in a storm.

I came up in time to see Clodius bearing down on me,
his face distorted with transcendent rage, purple as a
triumphator's robe. In one hand he brandished a curved
short sword. So he was the one who had cut me. I was
swept up with the urge to do the same to him, only worse.
The sword came down at me with a wild slash, which I
managed to deflect with my *caestus*. I stabbed straight for
his throat, but he lunged forward and ducked, throwing
a shoulder into my belly and wrapping his arms around
my waist. I went over backward, and this time we both
rolled over the unfortunate lawyer. I struggled to keep
Clodius from getting his sword arm free while he concentrated on biting my face off. I kneed him in the balls
and that, at least, made him open his mouth, freeing my
nose. Another good one to the cods and he squealed like
a gelded pig. I broke his hold and scrambled out from
beneath him, dealing a weak, backhanded blow to the
side of his neck as I did so. It was enough to half-stun
him and send him sprawling on his belly. I clambered
onto his back and seized a handful of his thick, curly,
greasy, goatlike hair and yanked his head back. I placed
my dagger beneath his neck and was poised to cut his
throat from larynx to spine when both my arms were
grabbed and all but wrenched from their sockets. A lictor's fasces was placed across my throat and locked there
by the official's arm in a unique variant of the common
wrestling hold. The bundle of rods nestled into the crook
of his elbow while his hand, on the back of my head,
pressed my throat against the rods until the breath whis-

tled in my nostrils. Another team of lictors applied the same treatment to Clodius.

The jury and spectators whistled and stamped at this rare entertainment. The lictors hauled us before the praetor like reluctant sacrifices.

"Who dares offend the majesty of a Roman court in this fashion?" The man in the curule chair wore an expression of cold fury. It was the distinguished praetor Caius Octavius, famed jurist and soldier and, incidentally, the true father of our esteemed First Citizen, who was still a burping baby in that year.

We croaked our names, the pressure of the fasces making it very difficult to articulate the simplest sounds. This raised a good laugh. I must admit that my voice sounded rather comical.

"And what prominent person has died," Octavius said, "that we have funeral games in the Forum?"

"Clodius and his thugs attacked me!" I said. "I was running for my life! Do you think I would seek a fight with a dozen armed men?"

"Just going about your business, eh?" said Octavius. "Just like any other citizen, with a *caestus* on one hand and a *pugio* in the other? Bearing arms within the *pomerium* is another punishable offense."

"At least they're respectable weapons," I pointed out. "He was carrying a *sica*!"

"A pertinent point!" said one of the lawyers, unable to help himself. The distinction between honorable and dishonorable weapons was a strict one in Roman law. The glare Octavius gave the lawyer boded ill for the progress of the trial.

"What have you say for yourself, Publius Clodius?" the praetor demanded.

"I am a serving Roman official and cannot be charged with a criminal offense!" he said, gloating.

Octavius gestured with his baton toward a white-gowned figure seated near him. It was one of the Vestals.

"You realize," he said, "that had one of you killed the other in this lady's presence, the survivor would have been taken outside the walls to the execution ground and there flogged to death with rods. There are few capital offenses left on the tables, but that is one of them."

"In that case," I said, nodding to the lictors, "I wish to thank these fine citizens for preventing me from killing that loathsome and deranged reptile over there."

"It is lucky for you," Octavius said, "that you intruded upon a court for extortion. Had this been the court for crimes of violence, I might have had you charged, tried and judged on the spot." He exaggerated. Actually, there was a good deal of oath-taking and posting of sureties before a trial could begin. "This is not the first time the two of you have been charged with public riot. You are a menace to the safety of all citizens."

"I protest!" I cried. "I was just minding my own—"

"Silence!" Octavius barked. He raised his eyes and gazed out over the Forum. "Where is the Censor Metellus?" He gestured to a lictor. "There he is, over by Sulla's monument. Fetch him." The man ran off and a few minutes later returned with my father. I could tell by the way he was glaring at me that the lictor had been giving him a colorful account of recent events.

"Noble praetor, what is your wish?" Father said.

"Cut-Nose, I am going to charge your son with public riot and bearing arms within the *pomerium*. I am also going to check the law books and see if a charge of crime against *Maiestas* is appropriate. I would like to do the same for Publius Clodius, but there is some question whether his quaestorship protects him. Will you stand surety for Decius the Younger if I release him to you?"

"I will," Father said.

"Then take him away. I will send to Pompey's camp for Clodius's elder brother, Appius. Perhaps if we can keep these two separated, we need not fear for the destruction of Rome and the sanctity of her courts." He truly had a gift for sarcasm.

"I will see to it that my son arrives for trial on the appointed day. No Roman is above the law."

"These two least of all," Octavius said wryly.

The lictors released me and I stooped to pick up my weapons. The charge had been made, so it didn't matter if I had them in my possession now. Clodius and I exchanged a final, mutual glare, and I turned to walk away with my father.

"You have always been an idiot," my father began as we walked across the Forum, "but this surpasses your previous enormities by a wide margin. Whatever possessed you to try to murder Clodius in a Roman court under the nose of the senior praetor?"

"I thought I might never get another chance!" I said.

"You were specifically instructed to keep away from him."

"I've done my best," I protested. "He sought me out. He set a dozen men on me. I had to run and I had to fight."

"Am I to take it, then, that the blood on your dagger is neither yours nor Clodius's? I thought it best not to ask in front of the praetor."

I shrugged, sending a dart of fire through my wounded shoulder. "Oh, there may be a body or two in the streets back there. Nobody who amounts to anything, just Clodius's hired scum."

"Good. I would hate to think I had raised a coward as well as a fool. How bad is that shoulder?"

"Kind of you to ask. It's painful and bleeding freely. I think it will need stitching. I'll go see Asklepiodes in the Trans-Tiber. He's sewed me up before."

"The question is, can I trust you to go there without getting into more trouble?" Of course, it never occurred to him to accompany me there.

"One fight a day is enough even for my glory-lusting spirit, Father." We were out of the Forum by this time, and passersby ogled at my wild appearance.

"I think you should leave the city for a while," Father said.

"But I just got back!"

"Rome can take only so much of your presence. A stint managing the estate at Beneventum might settle you a bit. The realities of farm work could only improve you."

There is a belief among us that the only respectable life is agriculture. Probably because it is the dullest life imaginable. Of course, there is no virtue in working the land. The virtue lies in *owning* the land. How instructing an overseer to boss a gang of slaves returns a man to the realities of tilling the soil escapes me, but many swear by it.

"I have an investigation to conduct, Father," I said. "I can't just break it off to go watch slaves spread manure under grape vines."

"Your wishes are of no importance," he said.

One of the most infuriating provisions of Roman law is the one conferring lifetime authority upon the paterfamilias. You can be the gray-haired commander of legions and conqueror of provinces, but if your father is still alive, you are still, legally, a child.

"It's a matter of state security," I insisted.

He gave a short, humorless laugh. "That business about the rites of that foreign goddess?"

"There is far more to it that that," I said with some urgency.

"Go on," he said, still walking from long habit at the standard legionary pace.

I gave him a somewhat truncated account of my findings to date, along with some speculations as to their significance. I did not identify Julia. He would assume that any woman who shared my taste for snooping must be unworthy.

"So you suspect Pompey is behind it, eh?" He said this grudgingly, but I could tell that his interest was piqued. Like the rest of the aristocratic party, he hated Pompey and feared that the man would crown himself king of Rome.

"No one else is so bold. He is the one who has a pack of tame Etruscan priests."

"And," Father mused, "he wants to settle his veterans on public lands in Tuscia."

"He does?" I said. This was new to me.

"Yes, as you would know if you ever paid any attention to important public business instead of crawling through every sewer in the city."

"I've only been in the Senate for a few days," I said.

"That does not excuse you. And you realize that your vaporings are built upon the words of some of the most degenerate people in Rome?"

"I always take that into account," I said. A sudden inspiration struck me.

"Tell me, how did Capito stand on the question of settling Pompey's veterans?" At this question Father actually stopped in his tracks and stared at me as if at some wonderful apparition sent by the gods. I wiped blood from my upper lip with the back of my *caestus*. My nose was bleeding inside and out from Clodius's bite.

"There may be something in your mad sophistry after all. Capito opposed the settlements most violently."

"So does more than half the Senate. What was Capito's particular objection?" We were nearing Father's house by this time. We presented an odd spectacle, I must admit: the dignified Censor in his *toga praetexta* and I, who looked like the receiver of the second-place award in a *munera*. And the subject was politics, as always.

"He claimed it would upset the public order and give Pompey a power base near Rome and so forth; everyone says that. But the real reason was that his family leases a huge tract of the *ager publicus* in Tuscia, an area that will be cut up into farm plots for Pompey's veterans if the legislation goes through."

I grinned, but it made my mouth hurt. "So Capito's family has been farming and grazing that land for several generations, paying the state at a nominal rate set a hundred or more years ago?"

"Closer to two hundred."

"Oh, the elevated and patriotic motives of our Senators," I said.

"You'll see worse than that in the Senate, if you live," Father said. By this time we were at his gate.

"Could you send a slave to my house?" I asked. "My boy, Hermes, should be there by now with my toga. Have him meet me at the surgery of Asklepiodes. He knows where it is and bring me a tunic."

Father popped his fingers and a slave came to take my instructions. The man ran off and we continued with every Roman's favorite subject.

"Where does Caesar stand on these questions?" I asked.

"As a *popular*, he is for giving the land to the veterans, but he favors the *ager publicus* in Campania. A bit farther from Rome, but the best farmland in Italy."

"They don't seem connected, do they? What have those two concocted between them? I think it must be behind all this."

"They both argue that their settlements will strengthen the state," Father said while I dripped on the tiles of his atrium. "Be a reservoir from which to draw soldiers for future generations. All that sort of talk."

In spite of everything, I managed a short laugh. "What pap! We all talk about the fine old times of the founding fathers and the virtues of the Italian peasant, backbone of the state. Does anyone really believe we can conjure those times back, like some necromancer raising the dead to prophesy? How long will those stalwart veterans last on their idyllic little farm plots, Father? How long before they sell up and leave the land to join the urban mob here in Rome? What peasant, however hard-working, can compete with *latifundia* the size of small countries and worked by thousands of slaves?"

"They might last for Pompey's lifetime," Father said. "That's long enough for his purposes."

"How very true."

"And what would you do?" he asked, his face getting red. "How would you change things?"

"Break up the *latifundia* for a start," I said. "Forbid the importation of new slaves and the selling of Italians into slavery. Tax those plantations until the owners have to sell off land."

"Tax Roman citizens?" Father bellowed. "You're mad!"

"We're dying by inches as it is," I insisted. I usually didn't talk like this, but I was very tired and had lost a lot of blood. "I'd pay the owners a small, very small, indemnity and repatriate those slaves right out of Italy. They're the root of most of our problems. The fact is, we Romans have grown too damned lazy to do our own work. All we do anymore is fight and steal. We have slaves to do all the rest."

"This is wild talk," Father said. "You sound worse than Clodius and Caesar combined, far worse."

I laughed again, this time quietly and a little shakily. "I'm no radical, Father," I said. "You know that. And I'm not going out into the streets to rabble-rouse, if only because I know how futile it would be. Reform or reaction, all they mean is Roman blood in Roman streets. We see enough of that as it is."

"See that you curb your tongue, then. Talk gets you killed as efficiently as action, these days."

"I don't suppose," I said, "that I could talk you out of a litter and some bearers to take me to my physician?"

"All that bad, is it? Oh, very well." He called to another slave and there was some scurrying about. The old man was mellowing with age. Time was when he would have lectured me half the day about how he had marched for fifty miles in full armor with wounds far worse. Maybe he had. I never claimed to be especially rugged.

The ride to the Statilian *ludus* was a bit hazy. The sun kept getting brighter, then dimmer. I think only the fortification of that excellent Caecuban kept me from passing out. As it was, the gods sent me visions. I thought I saw the goddess Diana, in her brief hunting tunic, bow and quiver, but then she became Clodia, and she was laughing at me. Clodia had laughed at me before, with good reason. I was about to tell her what a scheming slut she was when I realized that it was not Clodia but Fausta. She said something that I could not understand, and I tried to ask her to repeat it, but then I saw that it was not Fausta but her brother, Faustus. The metamorphosis had been subtle because the twins were so alike. He was reaching something out to me in a beringed hand, but that did not seem right, because soldiers rarely wear a great many rings, especially large poison rings. Another transformation had occurred. Now it was Appius Claudius Nero, and he was holding something, something he urgently wanted me to take, trying to speak despite the puncture in his throat and the dent in his brow.

Then a huge shadow reared up behind Nero. It was a four-footed beast towering over him, and its great paw descended, crushing him before he could give me whatever it was. I looked up and saw that the beast was Cerberus, the guard-dog of the underworld. I knew this because, unlike ordinary dogs, he was gigantic and had three heads. They were not dog heads, though, but human heads, like one of those hybrid Egyptian deities. The head on the right was that of Crassus, regarding me with those cold blue eyes. That on the left was the jovial head of Pompey. The one in the center was in shadow and I could not recognize it, but I knew that this one was the master of the other two, else why was he in the center? Then someone else was in front of Cerberus. This was Julia, and she, too, was reaching out for me. Her hand touched my shoulder.

"Decius?" Asklepiodes gripped my unwounded shoulder lightly and shook me. His face wavered in my vision, then solidified.

"I really would have preferred Julia," I said.

"What?" His elegantly bearded Greek face showed

concern. "I was not expecting to see you again quite so soon, Decius." He turned and shouted something over his shoulder. A pair of gladiators came and lifted me out of the litter as lightly as if I had been an infant and carried me to the physician's quarters, where his servants efficiently stripped and washed me as he examined my wounds.

"Up to your old activities again, eh? Are those human teeth marks I see on your face?"

"Actually, they belong to a rodent, a species of weasel, or perhaps a stoat." His poking and prodding elicited the usual flares of agony. This was the part he liked.

"Well, I can stitch and patch you up enough to keep you alive and relatively mobile, but the ladies will shun your company for a few days. Speaking of ladies, who is Julia?"

I averted my eyes as the silent slaves brought in horse-hair sutures, wickedly curved needles and ornate bronze pliers.

"I was confused. I had a vision on the way here, and the last thing I saw was a lady of my acquaintance named Julia."

"She must be exceptional, since you seem to prefer her company to mine despite your manifest need for my attentions. What sort of vision? I am not especially skilled in the interpretation of dreams, but I know of some skilled practitioners not far from here."

"It wasn't a real dream, but a sort of waking vision. I was aware of what was going on around me while it happened." I spoke mainly to take my mind off his activities. I am not among those person who believe that all their dreams are of great significance, and wish to tell you all about them, at great length. I rarely remember them, those I do remember are usually duller than my waking life, and such visions as the gods have given me have usually come to me under just such circumstances as these: wounds, blood loss or severe blows to the head.

I related my vision to Asklepiodes, and he sat facing me with chin in hand, murmuring occasional wise noises. When I had finished, he resumed his horrid labors.

"The appearance of persons with whom you have recently been involved is not at all unusual, even in the common or nonportentous dream," he said. "But the appearance of a mythical beast is always of the highest significance. Does Cerberus have a significance among you that he does not have among Greeks?"

"None that I know of," I said. "He is the watchdog of Pluto, who keeps the dead from leaving the underworld or the living from entering."

"Pluto, then: How does he differ from Hades?"

"Well, besides being lord of the dead, he is also the god of wealth."

"He is so among us, too, and by the same name, Pluto. That may be from confusion with Plutus, the son of Demeter, who is also a personification of wealth. But then, this may be because the name of both is derived from the very word for 'wealth,' which is—" He broke off when I squealed almost as Clodius had recently. In his pedantic reverie, he had dug a needle in too deep. "Oh, please forgive me."

"You're enjoying this," I said.

"I always enjoy learned discourse," he said, deliberately obtuse. "But it may be that wealth is behind all this."

"It usually is, when men plot villainy," I said. "But I think it may be more significant that Cerberus has three heads. One body, three heads; that is important."

"You saw the heads of Pompey and Crassus, enemies you have come up against in the past. But the third was unclear?"

"Unclear, and the greatest of the three. How can that be? Who could be greater than Pompey and Crassus?" This, truly, seemed an impossibility.

"I don't suppose it could be Clodius? You are rather obsessive about him."

I almost laughed, but I knew how it would pull at the stitches. "No, not Clodius. He is a flunky and a criminal, nothing more."

"Then what of the boy Appius Claudius Nero? What was he trying to give to you, and why did the three-part beast crush him?"

"That," I said, "I would give a great deal to know."

XI

I woke up and immediately wished I hadn't. Not only were my wounds screaming at me, but the night before, I had sought to promote sleep by draining a good-sized pitcher of cheap wine. I was now suffering the effects of both.

"Serves you right," Hermes said. "Leaving me there like that, holding your toga while you ran like a mountain goat up those stairs."

"You should have seen me on the flats," I croaked. "Faster than a racehorse then. Silverwing on his best day couldn't have touched me."

"Those men might have killed me!" he said indignantly. Slaves like Hermes take things so seriously.

"Why would they have done that?" I said. "It was me they were after. I'm just glad that none of them thought to snatch my toga and you didn't think to sell it."

"You certainly have a low opinion of me!" he huffed.

"Yes, I know I'm probably wronging you, but just now I am not a friend to humanity. I feel like going out and upending a chamberpot all over a Vestal." I got some breakfast in me and felt a tiny bit better. My morning calls went by in a fog, and I was about to leave for Celer's when a new man arrived. It was the gap-toothed Gaul I had seen at the warehouse with Milo.

"The chief wants to see you at the baths, Senator," the man said without preamble.

"The baths? At this hour?" I said.

"He doesn't keep most people's hours," the Gaul said.

When I thought of it, a long, hot soak sounded like a good idea. I told Hermes to get my bath things and followed the Gaul through the streets. Celer was a busy man and probably wouldn't even notice that I was absent. The

154

bathhouse we went to was a modest one, but it adjoined the building that served as Milo's home and headquarters.

Leaving Hermes to watch my belongings, I followed the Gaul into a steam room, where Milo sat with a group of his cronies. He looked up and grinned when I walked in.

"It's true!" he crowed. "All Rome says you fought a pitched battle with Clodius and his men and ended up right in front of Octavius while he was holding court!" He laughed his huge, infectious laugh. I would have joined in, but it would have hurt too much.

"Come back from the army without a scratch," Milo went on, "then cut to ribbons in the streets of Rome! What irony!"

"Oh," I said, sitting down stiffly, "one expects the occasional scar when in service to Senate and People." Indeed, in this company it was easy to be modest about a few little scars. Some of the men were arena veterans with more scar tissue than skin showing when they were stripped. One of them leaned forward and studied my shoulder.

"Neat bit of stitching there. Asklepiodes, eh?" I confirmed that he was correct.

"Seems unmanly to me, all this Greek seamstress work," said another veteran. He gestured to a hideous trough of puckered flesh that slanted from his right shoulder to his left hip. "A red-hot searing-iron, that's the way to stop a cut bleeding. Atlas gave me this one, a left-handed Samnite."

"Got to watch out for those lefties," said a companion.

Milo turned to me, and the others turned away from him. They were a well-drilled band, and we might as well have been alone.

"How did it go with Fausta?" he asked bluntly.

"Extremely well," I assured him. "I conversed with her for some time, and she seems most sympathetic to your suit. She is bored with the men of her own class, as well she might be, and finds you exciting and interesting. I think that if you call on her, she will welcome you most warmly."

"Very good," he said.

"Always glad to be of service," I told him.

"And I'll be of service to you as well. I've passed the word that any assault against you by any of Clodius's men earns instant death. My people will watch out for you in the streets. As long as you stay in plain view, that is. When you go sneaking around, as you have a habit of doing, I can't guarantee your safety."

"I can take care of myself," I said, slightly miffed.

He leaned close. "Are those teeth marks on your face? I thought you fancied yourself a swordsman, not a *bestiarius.*"

"I do appreciate your help, Titus. My real problem now is that I am at a loss to understand what is going on. With each new bit of evidence that comes my way, I think I have the key that will make all else fit, but it never does."

"Bring me up to date," Milo said. I told him of the various oddments of information I had picked up. He raised an eyebrow slightly when I spoke of Julia, and frowned when I mentioned Fausta's words.

"I do not like the idea that she is involved," he said ominously. Keeping the sundry women out of the matter was getting difficult.

"Oddly, I think that both she and Julia are speaking the truth. How this can be so I can't say yet."

"Then here is another bit of information for you to exercise upon: The day after the sacrilege, Crassus posted surety for all of Caesar's greatest debts. He is free to leave Rome now. All that keeps him here now is Pompey's upcoming triumph."

"This is significant," I said. "But why should he hang around for the triumph, other than that it is sure to be a fine show? I would think that the only triumph that could interest Caesar would be his own, and the very prospect of that is laughable."

"That's another little question for you to ponder, isn't it?"

"How does this happen, Titus?" I said, a little of my long-held disgust coming to the surface. "Here in Rome we've built the only viable Republic in history, and now it's falling to the shadowy machinations of shadowy men like these. I mean, it all worked so well. We had the popular assemblies, the Centuriate Assembly, the Senate and the Consuls. No kings. We could have the occasional Dictator when the times called for one, but only on a time-limited basis, the power to be handed back to Senate and People as soon as the emergency was over. Now it's all falling to military adventurers like Pompey, plutocrats like Crassus and demagogues like Clodius. Why?"

He stretched and leaned his head back against his folded arms. "Because the times have changed irrevocably, Decius. What you describe is a system that was perfect for a little city-state that had recently thrown off its foreign kings. It even worked well enough for a rather powerful city-state that dominated much of Italy. But the city-state days are over. Rome governs an empire that extends from the Pillars of Hercules to Asia. Spain, large chunks of Gaul, Greece, the islands, most of the southern Mediterranean lands: Africa, Numidia, Carthage, Mauretania. And what governs all this? The Senate!" He loosed his huge laugh again.

"The greatest governing body known to man," I said with great dignity. I was, after all, a new-minted Senator myself.

"Nonsense," Milo said without rancor. "They are, for the most part, a pack of time-serving nobodies. They've won office because their forefathers won the same offices. Decius, these men have been handed an empire to govern, and what is their qualification? That their great-great-great-grandfathers were wealthy farmers! At least these schemers you detest have worked and fought and, yes, schemed to get what they want."

"Can Rome be handed over to the likes of Clodius?" I said.

"No, but not for constitutional reasons. I plan to kill him first. But you, what is your protection from him? Besides my friendship, I mean."

"There are still plenty of people in Rome who have no use for his sort of demagoguery. My neighbors in the Subura will keep his men from my door."

"Forgive me, Decius, but you hold their esteem as much by your colorful, brawling habits as by your Republican rectitude. How long do you think you will keep their loyalty if Clodius should succeed in transferring to the plebs and gets elected tribune, as surely he will? He promises every Roman citizen a perpetual grain dole. That is a powerful inducement, my friend."

"It is not worthy of a free people," I said grudgingly, knowing that I sounded like my father.

"They may be free in the technical sense, but they're poor, and that's a sort of slavery. The day of the free-holder is past, Decius, and it won't come back. They've become a mob, and politically they will act like a mob."

"And you intend to control Rome as a mob leader," I said. I wasn't asking a question.

"Better me than Clodius."

"I won't argue that." There seemed to be no more to say on the subject. I studied the austere but tasteful bath-house. "This is convenient, having a place like this so handy."

"I own it," Milo reported. "I own the whole block now, and all the buildings on the facing streets."

"That's better than convenient," I commended, "it's tactically sound."

"I try to look ahead. When you're through soaking here, why don't you let my masseur work you over?" He pointed to a low doorway. "The table room's through there."

I winced at the very thought. "The last thing I want is someone pounding my body."

"Try him anyway," Milo said. "Handling wounded men is his specialty."

Mile could be a hard man to refuse, so I tried his masseur. To my amazement, the man was exactly what I needed. He was a huge Cretan, and in his way his knowledge was as profound as that of Asklepiodes. His powerful hands were brutal where the flesh was merely bruised and contused, gentle where I was cut. By the time he was finished, I actually felt not far from normal. My muscles and joints flexed with their usual ease, and only the areas around my wounds were painfully tight. I was almost ready to take on another fight, as long as it was not too strenuous.

There was still a question left unanswered but answerable, and I went to resolve it. The walk from Milo's citadel to the Aventine let me loosen my newly massaged muscles, and I was pleasantly winded at the end of the brief climb.

I stood on the steps of the lovely Temple of Ceres. It overlooked the open end of the Circus Maximus and commanded one of Rome's more breathtaking views, and Rome is a city of numerous splendid views. Aside from its religious function, serving the all-important goddess of grain, the temple was the ancient headquarters of the aediles. It was the special province of the plebeian aediles, since they were the judges of the grain market, but the curule aediles, though higher ranking, also had their offices here.

There was a great, rushing deal of coming and going as I climbed the steps, for the early plowing and planting ceremonies were about to commence. Wellborn Roman women were everywhere in evidence, since this was overwhelmingly a woman's temple. Children by the hundreds, dressed in spotless white tunics, were practicing their roles in the upcoming ceremonies. Despite my deadly serious mission, I paused to watch the little ones as they solemnly went through the intricacies of their part in the devotions to the goddess.

Despite Milo's cynical words, which I knew in my heart to be substantially true, I still felt myself to be at the heart of Roman life at such times and such places. Seeing these ladies and their children preparing for the ancient rites so innocently and with such perfect benevolence, I found it hard to believe that men of evil intent were using the equally ancient and honorable institutions of the Senate and the legions to bring about their own selfish gains.

In the warren of basements and outbuildings, I located the cramped quarters of the curule aediles. In a room full of tablets, old papyruses, decayed money-sacks and rancid rushlights, I found the aedile Lucius Domitius Ahenobarbus. He glanced up from his pile of tiresome ledgers when I entered, and hastily rose and took my arm.

"I cannot tell you how relieved I am. Anything that gets me away from these stacks of bills and records. I was about to send a man around to your house. Just today I found out about the woman who was murdered."

"Splendid!" I said. "Who was she?"

"She was from an estate not far from the city, born a slave but manumitted six years ago."

"Whose estate?" I asked. "Who manumitted her?"

"Caius Julius Caesar," he said.

Somehow, I was not surprised. It always came back to Caesar. Caesar's house, Caesar's debts, Caesar's ambitions. Now, Caesar's freedwoman. One might as well throw in Caesar's unfortunate wife, who must be above suspicion. Her husband was not. I had been so distracted by Pompey and Clodius that I had not given Caius Julius the attention he deserved. And, I confess, I had been reluctant to make him a primary suspect because of his connection to Julia.

It was not that I was besotted with Julia, as once I had been with Clodia, but I sensed in her one who shared my peculiar leanings. I also sensed a goodness and decency of a sort growing rare among Roman women, at least among the intelligent ones. Caesar's seeming proposal of a match had distracted me from my duties. There was no excuse for exempting anyone involved from suspicion save evidence of innocence. My personal wishes and feelings should play no part in it.

So much for the idealized, iron-willed servant of the Republic. What I was stuck with was Decius Caecilius Metellus the Younger, a man whose susceptibility to feminine charms was all but legendary. And Julia had mentioned that her uncle took a more-than-passing interest in me and my activities.

As I walked from the Temple of Ceres, my head ached. Why did all this have to be so complicated? Worse yet, I seemed to have reached a blind alley in my investigation. I had questioned everyone except Pompey himself, and he was one man I was not about to annoy. Then I remembered that there was one person involved with whom I had yet to speak. And this one was hardly in a position to cause me any grief, which suited my mood. I was not up to any major challenges. I began to walk toward the house of Lucullus.

The majordomo came up to me as I entered the atrium.

"May I help you, Senator? The master and mistress are not at home just now."

"No matter. I've been commissioned to investigate the late unpleasantness at the house of the *Pontifex Maximus.*"

"Yes, sir, the master has informed us and instructed

us to cooperate in any way you desire." That was helpful of Lucullus.

"Excellent. I have been informed that among your staff you have a slave woman who plays the harp, and that this woman actually discovered the interloper. I would like to question this woman."

"I shall fetch her at once, Senator." The majordomo showed me to a small waiting room off the garden and hurried off. It seemed odd to me that so lofty a personage as the majordomo of a great house would attend to such a task personally, rather than employ one of the legion of slaves who lounged about with far too little to do. When he returned I understood. He was accompanied by not one but two women. One was a lovely young Greek in a simple shift. The other was a middle-aged woman in a rich gown, whose facial features resembled those of Lucullus.

"I am Licinia," said the older woman, "eldest sister of General Lucullus. My brother has instructed that you are to receive all the aid we can give, but I must attend this interrogation to ensure that this girl does not reveal anything forbidden."

"I fully understand, my lady," I said. What a way to conduct an investigation, I thought. I sat in one of the chairs and the two women sat on a bench facing me. The Greek girl looked nervous, as slaves usually do when then are being questioned by someone in authority.

"Now, my dear, I want you to have no apprehension whatsoever. I merely wish to establish the exact sequence of events as they occurred that night. No one suspects you of any sort of wrongdoing. Now, first, your name?"

"Phyllis, sir." She smiled shyly.

"And you are a musician?"

"Yes, sir, a harpist."

"And you were employed in that capacity on the night of the rites of Bona Dea? These questions may seem simple-minded, but this is how they would be asked at a trial."

"I understand, sir. Yes, I was there to play the harp."

"Good. And just when did you make the discovery that a man had intruded upon the rites?"

"It was when—" She glanced at the older woman, who gave her a sharp look. "Well, it was at a time when we musicians were not playing. I glanced at a hallway entrance and I saw the herb-woman and the one with her. The herb-woman hung back in the hall, but the other came into the atrium. The herb-woman reached out and took his arm, as if to stop him, but he pulled loose and walked into the atrium. That was when I recognized him."

"I see. I've heard from others that he was veiled. Was the light sufficient for you to see that it was a man's face?"

"No, sir. It was more the way he walked. You see, I have seen Clodius many times in this house, when he has come to visit his sister, my mistress Claudia. I felt sure it was him; then I recognized a ring on his hand and I yelled that a man was in the room. The mother of the *Pontifex Maximus* rushed over and tore off the veil. There was a great deal of screaming after that."

"I should imagine. And I understand that they had just arrived?"

She shook her head. "Oh, no, sir. They must have been there for quite some time. I saw them arrive early in the evening, when most of the other ladies were arriving."

"What? Are you certain?"

"Oh, absolutely, sir. This was the third year that I've played my harp at the rites, and I knew the herb-woman from that purple dress she wore."

I tried to keep a self-condemning curse behind my teeth. This was what came of giving too much credence to secondhand information. Somebody makes a mistaken assumption, and for lack of contradiction it gains the stature of fact. If I had come to question this girl first, I would have got my facts straight and perhaps the herb-woman would be alive. It struck me that the purple dress was her professional trademark, since her name was Purpurea. Then something else struck me.

"You recognized the herb-woman from her dress, not her face?"

"She also wore a veil, Senator."

"There seem to have been a number of veils that night. Clodius, naturally enough, now Purpurea. I've also heard that Fausta was veiled."

"Then you heard wrong, Senator," said Licinia. "The lady Fausta"—she gave the little sniff that highborn women perform when they mention their scandalous sisters—"was here in the home of Lucullus that night."

"I see," I said. "And you did not attend the rites?"

"I was unwell that night. As for Fausta, she has no respect for religion and did not wish to attend the preliminary ceremonies, as unmarried women should."

So now the argument as to Fausta's presence stood at one for, two against. But the vote for was Julia's, and I was still reluctant to discount her words. I rose.

"Thank you. I think that this will prove useful to my investigation."

"Good," said Licinia. "There must be a trial. What will become of Rome if we allow our sacred rituals to be violated? The gods will take a terrible vengeance."

"We certainly can't have that," I said. I no longer had the slightest interest in the sacrilege. I was burning to find out what else had been going on that night. I was about to leave, but I turned back. "Phyllis?"

"Yes, sir?"

"You've said that Clodius and the herb-woman were standing in a hallway entrance. Do you know where that hall leads?"

"It's one of the ones that lead to the rear of the house, Senator."

"Where the unmarried women retire at a certain stage of the rites?"

The girl thought for a moment. "No, that is on the other side of the house. The hall where I saw the two of them leads back to the living quarters of the *Pontifex Maximus*. Some years, we slaves were sent to wait there when we were not needed."

"But not this year," I said.

"No, Senator."

I thanked the two women and left the house. I was still thoroughly mystified, but now I was excited as well. I felt sure that I now had the crucial piece of evidence that would resolve the puzzle of what had happened on that very odd evening, if I could just figure out where it fit. There had been too many anomalous women present, and too damned many veils.

Hermes was waiting outside the gate. He had taken the opportunity to return my bath gear to my house. He fell in beside me, and after a few minutes of walking I noticed that he was imitating me, walking along with his head down and his hands clasped behind his back. I stopped.

"Are you mocking me?" I demanded.

"Who, me?" His eyes went wide with innocence. "They say that slaves always come to look like their masters, sir. That must be what it is."

"That had better be the case," I warned him. "I will not be treated with disrespect."

"Certainly not, sir!" he cried. We resumed walking. "But I was wondering, sir. All this questioning and people trying to kill you and all—what's it all about?"

"That is exactly the sort of thing that I am famed for detecting," I said.

"And have you figured it out?"

"No, but I expect to have everything sorted out soon. A little time for peaceful reflection is all it takes."

"I don't know about you, sir," he said with heavy insinuation, "but I never think my best on an empty stomach."

"Now that you mention it, it's been a while since breakfast. Let's see what the district offers." Luckily, you never have to go far in Rome to find someone selling food. Before long, we had acquired bread, sausages, pickled fish, olives and a jug of wine and retired to a public garden to restore the mental faculties. We sat on a bench and watched the passing show for a while as we attacked the food and drained the jug. The streets were unusually crowded and many vendors were setting up, although it was an odd hour for it.

"Jupiter!" I said. "Tomorrow is Pompey's triumph! I'd all but forgotten. They're setting up now to have good spots in the morning."

"I hear it's going to be a great show," Hermes said, munching and nodding eagerly.

"It ought to be," I said. "He's robbed half the world to finance it."

"That's what the world's for, isn't it? To make things good for Romans?" He did not say this bitterly, as a foreign-born slave might. Like most native domestics, he expected to be manumitted and made a citizen someday. We are far more easygoing about such things than most nations.

"I'm not sure that was the original intention of the gods, but that is how things turned out," I said.

"Then it ought to be a good show," he maintained. "I mean, who cares about a bunch of barbarians?"

"Spoken like a true Roman," I said. "You have real citizen material in you, Hermes, even if you were given a Greek name."

Men in blue tunics were running down the streets with paint pots and brushes in their hands, posting the schedule of events, writing with incredible speed upon walls already thick with such writings. Other graffitists had been through earlier in the day, whitewashing patches on the walls to carry the glorious news. I called a painter over and tossed him a coin.

"What's the lineup?" I asked.

"The games will go on for days, Senator," he said. "Just now, we're posting the schedule for tomorrow. We'll be posting each day for the following day's entertainments. The big *munera* won't be for three days. That's what everybody's waiting for."

"What's on for tomorrow?" I asked him.

"To begin with, there'll be plays. Italian mime in the two old wooden theaters, but a full-dress Greek drama with masks in Pompey's new theater on the Campus Martius. The theater's still under construction, but there's enough finished to hold the highest classes."

"That's unfortunate," I said. "I'd prefer the mimes to Greek drama, but I suppose the Senate will have to go to Pompey's theater. What's the play?"

"*Trojan Women,* sir."

"Sophocles, isn't it?" I said. "Or was it Aeschylus?"

"Euripides, Senator," he said, with a slightly pitying expression.

"I knew it was one of those Greeks. May we hope for something more lively later in the day?"

"After the plays there will be *lusiones.* All the men to fight in the great *munera* will be fighting demonstration bouts with mock weapons."

"That's better," I said. "Not as exciting as the real death-fights, but fine swordplay is always a joy to watch. When will the great triumphal procession be?"

"The day after tomorrow, Senator, and it will be a ceremony of unsurpassed magnificence. Leading off will be the beasts General Pompey has collected in his travels, all to fight in the morning shows before the gladiators. Besides the usual lions, bears and bulls, he has collected leopards, Hyrcanian tigers, the biggest wild boar ever seen, a white bear from the far north . . ."

"It all sounds inspiring," I said. "There's nothing like a triumph to stir the blood and remind people what Rome is all about. And what embodies Rome these days better than Cnaeus Pompeius Magnus himself?"

"Quite right, Senator," said the sign painter a little hesitantly. He left and went back to his task.

"Uh, master, maybe you'd better be more careful how you talk, right out in public." Hermes looked around, distinctly ill at ease.

"Why?" I demanded. "Have we reached such a pass that a Roman citizen—a Senator, no less—can't publicly express his opinion of the likes of jumped-up would-be monarchs like Pompey and Crassus and even Julius Caesar?"

"I take no more than a slave's interest in political matters," the boy said, "but as I understand it, we've reached exactly such a pass."

"It's intolerable!" I said, out-Catoing Cato. "I tried to behead Clodius right in front of the senior praetor and I'll probably have to pay a fine for it. But say the wrong thing in public about a lowbred military adventurer, and I'm supposed to worry that he will try to kill me."

"Maybe he already has," Hermes said. "Tried to, I mean."

"What's that?" I said.

"Well, *somebody* tried to poison you. Haven't you had run-ins with Pompey before?"

"Yes, I have." Somehow, I had neglected to suspect Pompey of that particular crime, perhaps because of the relative abundance of other suspects. "To be brutally honest, I never believed I was important enough to attract his hostility. Some rather important men have told me exactly that, in fact."

"Master, I may be only a slave, while Pompey's the greatest conqueror since Alexander, but even I know that there's no such thing as an enemy who's too small to kill."

"This will bear some thinking," I said. "You may turn

out to be not such a burden after all, Hermes. Keep thinking like this. After he tried to poison me, you saw Nero go to the house of Celer. I'd thought only of Clodia, since she's the sister of Clodius and has tried to do away with me before, but she's acted as cat's-paw for Pompey in the past. But he has those lethal Etruscans with him. Why not send one of them?"

We thought about that for a while, passing the jug back and forth.

"How about this?" Hermes said. "Maybe he didn't want people to think you'd been murdered at all. You can't always tell with poison. People die all the time from bad food or simply unknown causes."

"Right. I was just back in Rome. I might have picked up some horrid disease in Gaul. And since he was already having poor old Capito murdered that night, perhaps he didn't want to overdo it."

"So you think he had Capito done away with?" Hermes was enjoying this talk of murder far too much.

"He certainly had reason to." I told him about Capito's interference with Pompey's land settlements. The boy gave a low whistle.

"And I thought Clodius and Milo were dangerous men to deal with! These leaders of the Republic are even worse!"

I nodded. "Very true. Clodius and Milo are small-scale gangsters, with purely urban ambitions. These men are criminals of world stature. Do try to moderate your admiration."

"Well, what do you propose to do about it? Clodius you can always fight. Milo is your friend and his gang is as big and as powerful as Clodius's. You can't fight Pompey, if the whole aristocratic party in the Senate can't do anything about him."

For a slave, the boy was learning political nuance quickly. Suddenly, the family farm at Beneventum seemed like a good place to be.

"I think you'd better make your peace with him, master," Hermes advised.

"The problem is, I don't even what I've done to offend him, if he truly is the one who tried to have me poisoned. I could never prove anything against him in the past. Why should he care about me now?"

"You have a reputation for finding things out about people, don't you? Things they'd rather keep hidden? Well, maybe he's done something, or plans to do something, that he'd just as soon nobody found out about."

"Hermes, you amaze me," I said. "That is very astute."

"I told you I thought better on a full stomach."

There are stages in the investigation of a crime, conspiracy or other mystery that involves many people acting from many motives. At first, all is confusion. Then, as you gather evidence, things get even more complicated and confusing. But eventually there comes a point when each new fact unearthed fits into place with a satisfying click and things become simpler instead of more complex. Things begin to make sense. I now felt that things had reached that stage. It seemed to me that my guardian *genius*, my ferret-muse, hovered near and was aiding me to untie this knot of murder and intrigue.

Or perhaps it was just the wine.

XII

Rome was decked out in full holiday attire, with garlands and wreaths and fresh gilding everywhere. Statues of heroes had been given fresh victory crowns so that they could share in the triumph. Incense burned before the shrine of every smallest god, and the greatest deities of the state were carried through the streets in solemn processions, seated in ornate litters borne on the shoulders of attendants.

It always did my heart god to see the city like this, even when it was to celebrate the triumph of someone I detested. Everywhere one looked, people were reeling through the streets, singing triumphal songs and giving the wineshops a tremendous business. Labor had ceased and the farmers had poured in from the countryside, along with what appeared to be the entire populations of several nearby towns. Children dashed about, freed from the tyranny of their schoolmasters for a few precious days.

All was gaiety, but my spirits were depressed by the thought that I would have to spend the morning at Pompey's theater, watching some tedious old Greek's contribution to Athenian culture. I would far rather have gone to see the mimes in the old wooden theaters, or to the Circuses, where *lusiones* and animal shows would be going on all day. But that was out of the question. The Senate, the *equites* and the Vestals would have to attend the theatrical display in the new theater. To fail to do so would insult not only Pompey, a prospect many of us would have relished, but also the gods of the state.

We marshalled in the Forum, and the state freedmen got us into the proper order, with the Consuls in front, followed by the Censors, the praetors, the Vestals, the pontifixes led by Caesar, the *flamines*, then the main body of the Senate with the Hortalus as *Princeps* in front, followed by the consulars and all the rest in order of their enrollment in the Senate. The result was that I was at the very end of the procession. Ahead of me were some men very nearly as undistinguished as I. It was a long march out to the Campus Martius and the complex of buildings surrounding the new theater.

Off we trooped, amid shouts of "*Io triomphe!*", showered with flower petals. It might be wondered that there were such petals available at that time of year, but Pompey was not about to let his triumph be marred by the season. Against just such an eventuality, he had collected vast quantities of them and had them dried, supplementing them with shiploads of petals brought in from Egypt at intervals to assure that there would be a leavening of fresh flowers for throwing and making wreaths. Huge baskets of them stood along all the streets.

"The whole city's going to smell like a whorehouse for weeks," groused a young Senator in front of me.

"It didn't smell all that good before," someone pointed out.

Because of the huge new building project, half the Campus Martius was a jumble of building materials, with heaps of cut stone and rubble fill everywhere, along with mountains of concrete and great stacks of wood for scaffolding. Half-built walls stood, abandoned for the holiday by the workmen.

"You know," I remarked, "if you aged things a bit and added a few lurking animals, this gives an excellent idea of what Rome would look like in a state of ruin."

"You're in a fanciful mood this morning, Metellus," said a Senator who had been a quaestor in the same year as I.

"Fancy is in the air," I said. "Take Pompey: that theater over there." I pointed to the squat hulk of white marble that had just begun to rise from its supporting platform. "I've heard that when it's finished, it will hold ten thousand spectators. Pompey has a most unrealistic idea of the Roman capacity for Greek drama."

"I don't think that's what he intends it for," said a Senator named Tusculus, who was rumored to be the great-grandson of a freedman. "I've spoken with his spectacle-planner. He says that the inaugural games for the theater when it's finished are to include a whole city sacking onstage, complete with cavalry and infantry and catapults."

"That would give old Euripides fits," I said. "Roman tastes in entertainment are a bit more robust than those of the effete Greeks."

All this conversation with accomplished with rigid faces, barely moving our mouths, coupled with the most rigid bearing. It would not have done to allow our *gravitas* to slip before the eyes of the citizenry. Once we were within the nascent theater we could relax, because there was no seating for the lower orders, all of whom went off to see livelier entertainments. I wished I could go with them.

The more lordly personages took their seats nearest the orchestra, just in front of the stage. Only these seats had been completed, and were made of white marble. The rest were temporary bleachers of wood. The stage itself was also of wood, as was the immense, three-tiered proscenium that rose behind the *scaena*. Eventually, this would all be rebuilt in stone, but no effort had been spared to make the temporary structure sumptuous, and all was bright with new paint and colorful hangings. Fountains sprayed perfumed water in high arcs, helping to dull the odor of fresh paint and new-cut pine.

"If I get pinesap on my new toga," said an *eques* behind me, "I'll bill Pompey for it." This raised a laugh. Now that the mob had hied away, we could revert to our natural state, which is to say, a pack of outspoken Italians.

"Here comes Pompey!" someone shouted. We all stood up and applauded dutifully as the great man made his appearance. He was wearing a golden wreath and a *triumphator*'s voluminous purple *toga picta* covered all over with golden stars.

"Well, that's a pit premature, isn't it?" said Tusculus. "The procession's not until tomorrow."

"No," I said. "As giver of the games, he's entitled to the *picta*, worse luck. He just wants to get us used to seeing him wearing it. He intends to make it his full-time dress." There were a lot of boos from the anti-Pompeian faction, together with some of the ruder noises possible with the imaginative employment of lips and tongue. He did not deign to hear.

With Pompey's party I saw young Faustus Sulla, and they all took their places in the front row with Caesar, Crassus, Hortalus and the rest of the great men.

After a lengthy exchange of greetings, good wishes and insults, we all settled down to be bored into a state of deathlike stupefaction. As the chorus came out to begin their intolerable chanting, we surreptitiously rummaged through the contents of our togas. One of the few advantages of the great ceremonial toga is that it provides innumerable stashing-places for snacks and drink. I had brought along a skin of decent Vatican. It would have been criminal to store really good wine in a skin.

Of course, it was strictly forbidden to eat or drink during a performance, but who was going to bother us? All the important men were down in front, pretending to understand what was going on on the stage, where a troupe of men was mincing across the *scaena,* masked and dressed as women.

"Disgusting," I grumbled. "At least in the Italian mime, women's roles are still played by women."

"And none of those ridiculous masks, either," said a Senator. "Wigs and face paint are good enough. All a lot of Greek degeneracy, if you ask me."

"Everybody knows playgoing is bad for the public morals," I said. "Just ask Cato." I tossed a handful of parched nuts and peas into my mouth.

Caesar turned around and glared at the rear rows of Senators.

"Uh-oh," said an *eques,* "there's old Caesar, giving us the holy look."

"Good thing *his* wife must be above suspicion," said Tusculus. "Mine certainly isn't." We all tried not to laugh too loudly.

Some actors began screeching in horrid falsettos. One of them, Hecuba, I think, or perhaps it was Andromache, began to wail something about the gods and how they had made a fine old mess of Troy. I had to admit that the man had a fine command of feminine gestures. Every movement made his long gown sway gracefully.

Suddenly, I was absorbed in the performance and I took no note of my neighbor's rude comments. It was not that I had precipitously acquired an appreciation for Greek tragedy; rather, I felt that I stood on the verge of something. As the actor continued to intone I scanned the stage lineup of men in women's garments, then the front row of seats where sat Caesar and Crassus, Faustus and Pompey. Pompey, in his purple robe.

I was overcome by a blinding revelation from the gods, forgetting, in the exultation of the moment, that the gods always mean trouble when they send you a revelation like that. I felt as if surrounded by a golden nimbus as I leapt to my feet, abruptly caught up in the Greek spirit of things.

"Eureka!" I shouted.

"Who do you think you are, Metellus?" hissed somebody. "Bloody Archimedes? Sit down or you'll be arrested!" I ignored everything but my own brilliance.

"They were all there!" I said, not quite shouting. "All dressed as women!"

Now the whole front row had turned around, staring at me. My father looked close to apoplexy. Nobody looked pleased. A praetor pointed toward me, and a crowd of lictors began to march up an aisle between the seats, the axes gleaming in their fasces. My exultation evaporated as swiftly as it had come upon me, and I realized with dread what a terrible blunder I had made. I stumbled into an aisle and began to dash toward a gap in the barely begun outer wall.

"Must be a case of the runs," I heard somebody say as I got clear of the bleachers. Amid hooting and clapping, I dashed out as fast as my toga would allow. I glanced back over my shoulder to see if any lictors were in pursuit, but they were not. It would have been beneath their dignity. I slowed to a fast walk. Not only was running awkward, but heat built up beneath the heavy woolen toga at a tremendous rate.

A bit of my god-visited mood returned as I reentered the city, and the city itself was like something seen in a dream. It was all but deserted, with the whole populace packed into the two huge Circuses and the theaters. Adding to the dreamlike quality was the profusion of triumphal decorations, the heaps of flower petals that lay everywhere. The Forum was like a city of gods, populated by statues. I glanced up toward the Temple of Jupiter Capitolinus. Within its dimness, through the smoke of the incense burning to the god's honor, I could just descry the great statue of Jupiter, the one that was supposed to give us warning of plots against the state. I threw the god a salute. If I could manage it, Pompey would not sacrifice in that temple on the morrow.

My slave Cato gaped as I came in through my front gate.

"Senator! We'd not expected you until this afternoon! There's a lady here to see you, but we told her—"

"Where's Hermes?" I said, brushing past him. Then his words sunk in and I turned. "What lady?"

"A lady Julia, one of the Caesars. She insisted on waiting for you to return. She's in the atrium."

I entered the atrium and Julia was there indeed, rising from a chair with a look of unutterable relief.

"Decius! How glad I am to see you alive. You're in terrible danger!"

"I know that," I said. "But how did you find out so fast?"

"So fast? But I only learned late last night."

"This is all too confusing," I said. "Just a moment. I must speak with my slave."

"No, you must speak with *me*!" She grabbed both my arms with surprising strength and swung me around to face her. "Decius, Clodius came to see my uncle last night. He wants to kill you. He was raving like a madman!"

"Of course he was," I said. "He *is* a madman. What had Caius Julius to say to that?"

"He was terribly angry. He shouted that you were not to be killed for any reason whatsoever, but Clodius wouldn't listen. My uncle said: 'If I learn that you have the blood of Decius Metellus on your hands, I will solemnly pronounce the curse of Jove Optimus Maximus upon you before the whole Roman people.'"

This was a serious threat. It would mean that no Roman citizen anywhere in the world could so much as speak to him or give him any aid. No allied king could take him in. He would become a rootless wanderer among barbarians.

"And what did Clodius answer?"

"He laughed. He said: 'Jove need not concern himself.

Charun will have him.' I don't know what he meant by that."

I felt as if I had fallen into the cold pool at the baths. "He means that he has set his Etruscan priests on me."

"I wish I could have stayed to hear more, but I'd had to tiptoe from my own quarters when I heard the shouting, and I might have been discovered at any moment. I couldn't leave the house until my uncle left for the theater, and I had no way of getting word to you earlier."

"I don't know how I can thank you," I said, my mind whirling. "But you dare not be seen with me. Just coming to my house put you at terrible risk." Further implications hit me. "They could be out there already. There's no place to hide in these deserted streets. You have to stay here until dark."

"Would they dare attack me?" she asked, all patrician haughtiness.

"Ordinarily, no," I answered her. "Clodius fears Caius Julius. But now his derangement has entered a particularly lurid stage, and he is liable to do anything. And the Etruscans are fanatics. Only Pompey can call them off, and he's not about to do that. Not after the theater this morning."

"What?"

She was not the only one with questions. Just then I was wondering why Caius Julius was so determined to keep me alive. It was a relief to know that there was someone who was not out for my blood, but I could think of no reason why in Caesar's case. Doubtless all would be made clear in time, when more pressing matters were settled.

"Oh, I made a bit of a scene this morning. A great revelation came to me while we were watching *Trojan Women.*"

"A vision from Apollo!" she cried, clapping her hands. "But of course! Euripides is the most sublime of playwrights, and *Trojan Women* was the most inspired of his plays. I love Euripides."

"Indeed?" I said. Women are difficult to fathom. "Well, in any case, I was suddenly vouchsafed a glimpse of the meaning of a number of anomalies. It was the sight of all those Greek men in women's clothing, and Pompey sitting there like a puffed-up bullfrog in his *triumphator*'s robe. And do you know what my first thought was? Without even knowing why it came to me, I thought, 'Milo will be pleased.' "

"You make no sense whatever," she said with considerable restraint.

"Made no sense to me at first, either. That's the way it is with divine revelations. You see, my friend Milo wants to marry Fausta. He was very displeased when he heard that you saw her there that night when she had no right to attend the Mysteries but didn't join you unmarried women. He hinted that he might be quite unhappy with me should I implicate her in any wrongdoing, and Milo is not a man I would want to fall afoul of. So imagine my relief when I understood that she was not there that night!"

"But I saw her," Julia said coolly. "Do you think I am a liar, or merely a fool?"

"No, no, nothing of the sort," I said, laughing and shaking my head. I must have looked and sounded truly demented. "You see, that wasn't Fausta you recognized. It was her twin brother, Faustus, dressed as a woman!"

Her jaw dropped gratifyingly. "Dressed as a woman? Like Clodius?"

"Yes, like Clodius. And Pompey, and your uncle, Caius Julius. I suspect that Crassus was there as well. Pompey was wearing the dress of the peasant herb-woman, a purple dress. He does so love to wear purple."

"But Uncle Caius? Can you be sure?"

"He was supposed to spend that night at the house of Metellus Celer, but he went out, ostensibly to look for omens on the Quirinal. I checked at the Temple of Quirinus and found out that he did not go out through the Colline Gate that night. I think he, too, must have donned women's clothing and went into his own house thus disguised. And if Caesar, Pompey, Clodius and Faustus were there, then Crassus was most likely involved as well."

"Oh, dear," she said weakly. "But why? Why meet together in such a bizarre fashion?"

"That is what I am about to find out," I said. "Come along. Let's have a few words with my slave boy, Hermes."

"Your slave?" she said as she followed me to the rear of my house, Cato close behind us.

"Exactly." I threw open the door to his cubicle, and the boy backed against a wall, white-faced. "Where is it, you thieving little swine?" I shouted.

"What do you mean, master? I don't know what you're talking about!" At least he had the grace to look as guilty as Mars in Vulcan's net.

"I mean the things you stole from the body of Appius Claudius Nero, you disgusting creature!" I slapped his face twice, forehand and backhand.

"Under my bed!" he cried, all but bawling.

I threw back his pallet, revealing a cache of rings, bracelets and coins in a hollow scooped into the dirt floor. Among the glittering loot was a plain bronze cylinder as long as my palm and as big around as my thumb.

"You couldn't resist, could you?" I said. "You went back out there that night and stripped the body. That's pretty low, Hermes, robbing a corpse!"

"Of course it's low!" he yelled. "I'm a slave! What do you expect! You noblemen can murder each other in the streets, and the praetor sends you out of town for a year or two. We get sent to the cross! I couldn't just leave him lying there with all that gold on him. Anyway, I sacrificed to Mercury, and he's the god of thieves."

"Admirable piety. Well, you may have cleared things with the gods, but not with me. You made a mistake, Hermes. You came back here with your ill-gained loot and you had to gloat, didn't you? It was still dark, but you couldn't resist trying the quality of the gold." I held the poison ring before his nose. There were teeth marks on its capsule.

"You didn't know this was a poison ring and you bit into it. You didn't suck out all the poison, but you got enough to give you a bellyache all the next day."

"So poor old Nero had his revenge after all," he said, wincing at the memory.

"He deserves more!" I shouted. "Cato, bring the whip!"

"You don't own a whip, master," Cato said. I turned to face him.

"Yes, I do. A great, nasty-looking *flagrum* with bronze studs along all the thongs. My father gave it to me when I set up in my own house. Where is it?"

"You lost it in a dice game years ago," Cato said.

His wife, Cassandra, appeared in the doorway. "Will you all stop yelling? The neighbors will think we're disorderly. I'm trying to get dinner together. Nobody's going to whip any slaves in this house, master. Cato's too old and you're too softhearted."

"Oh, let's go back out to the atrium," I said, disgusted. "It's too crowded in here." I could swear that I saw Julia masking a smile. I examined the bronze tube. The wax seal over its cap was broken. Back in the atrium, Julia and I took chairs while Hermes, temporarily reprieved, stood nervously shifting from one foot to the other.

"You've been into this, I see," I said, holding up the tube.

"I thought there might be something valuable in it," Hermes said. "But it was just a roll of paper."

"That is because this is a message tube. And did you read the message?"

"How could I? I can't read."

"And did it not occur to you that Nero might not have come to kill me, but rather to bring me a message?"

"Did it occur to you?" he said insolently.

I sighed. "I really must purchase another *flagrum* and a strong, stupid, stony-hearted slave to wield it."

"If I'd know it was for you, I'd have brought it immediately, master," Hermes mumbled.

"What does it say?" Julia urged impatiently.

I slipped the paper from the tube and unrolled it. The letter was written in a fine, aristocratic hand, the sort that our schoolmasters whip into us at an early age, but the formation of some of the letters was a trifle shaky, the sign of a writer in a state of emotional distress. The grammar was impeccable, but the phrasing was a bit awkward. One did not expect literary elegance from a Claudian. I began to read aloud.

[To the Senator Decimus]: a misspelling, but a common one, since my *praenomen* is extremely rare, while Decimus is not: [*Caecilius Metellus the Younger:*

[I dare not set my name to this, but you will know who I am. When I came to Rome to live, I sought only the support and patronage of my family to begin and pursue my career. Instead, I have become involved in matters that terrify me; matters involving murder, conspiracy and, I think, treason.

*Upon my arrival, my kinsman Publius Clodius made much
of me, and much of his own glowing future, persuading me to
take service as one of his followers. Greatly flattered, I agreed.
He entrusted me with matters of some sensitivity, some of them
of questionable legality. He continually assured me that this
was the way things were done in modern Roman political life.*

*For more than a month, Clodius hinted about a crucially
important meeting he was arranging. All month, he met many
times with Caius Julius Caesar, with Marcus Licinius Crassus
Dives, and on several occasions I accompanied him to the camp
of Cnaeus Pompeius Magnus to confer with the general.*

*All this time, Clodius showed the greatest signs of merriment,
and behaved as if he were maneuvering these powerful men at
his own will, into his own power. "I'll control them all," he
told me on more than one occasion. How he was to accomplish
this I could not imagine.*

*After his last meeting with Pompey, Clodius came away
greatly agitated. When I asked him why he was so upset, he
said that the general had required of him that he kill the son
of the Censor Metellus, who had just returned to Rome. I had
heard him speak many times, very bitterly, of this man and
asked why he was so displeased with the commission. He said
it was because it was at Pompey's behest rather than for his
own satisfaction, and that Pompey had required that the deed
be accomplished with poison so that it might appear that his
enemy died of natural causes.]*

"I told you," said Hermes.

"Quiet," I said, and continued reading.

*[Clodius sent me to the herb-woman Purpurea to procure the
poison. I had been sent to her before, to borrow from her a
purple gown, for an unexplained reason. You encountered me
just as I left her booth with the poison. Dutifully, I took the
poison to Clodius. Then he horrified me by telling me that I
was to administer the poison myself! He had discovered that
you were to have dinner at the house of Mamercus Capito, and
had managed to secure an invitation to the same dinner. I was
to take his place, giving the excuse that he could not eat at the
same table as you, his mortal enemy.*

*I protested, and he grew enraged. Then he all but knelt to
beg me to perform this deed. He said that all his plans hinged
upon keeping the goodwill of Pompey for this little time, and if
I would do this for him I would have his eternal gratitude, and*

*he would make me second only to himself in Rome. At last I
agreed. Nobody could be more relieved than I that I failed.]*

"That was my doing," Hermes said to Julia. "I saved
his life."

"I'm keeping that in mind, Hermes," I said. "Perhaps
I'll get a *flagrum* without the bronze studs."

[After the assemblage broke up upon the death of Capito,] I
continued reading, *[in which I swear before all the gods I had
no involvement, I called for my slaves and left. Thinking I had
murdered you, I could not bear to face Clodius, and fled instead
to my kinswoman Clodia, at the house of Metellus Celer.*

*The next day I spent in the temples and the Forum, con-
sumed with guilty agitation. You cannot imagine the relief I
felt when I saw you before the Curia, very much alive and
conferring with Cicero and Lucullus. I resolved to have nothing
further to do with Clodius and went to his house to tell him
so. He was displeased that I had failed, but merely said that
we would have to try another time. He was far too preoccupied
with the meeting planned for that night to concern himself with
you. I told him that I did not wish to engage in further dealings
with him, but he merely brushed my protestations aside, saying
that I would overcome such childish scruples as I gained so-
phistication in Roman politics. At last I agreed, but I would
do nothing unlawful.*

*Clodius laughed and called me his friend, and assured me
that the night's doings would be more in the nature of a lark.
I was to take the purple dress and another woman's gown and
veil to the camp of Pompey, where, to my amazement, the general and Faustus Sulla were to don them and return with me
to the city after sunset. I was to tell the watch at the gate that
these were two ladies from a country estate coming to the city
for the rites of the Good Goddess. My patrician insignia would
assure compliance.*

*I did as instructed, although the experience was most bizarre.
In the Forum we were joined by Clodius, also in women's attire,
and two other men similarly clad. They mingled with the crowd
of highborn ladies entering the house of the Pontifex Maximus and went inside.*

*I loitered about the Forum for several hours, until I heard a
great commotion from inside. Clodius came running out of the
house, stripped almost naked and pursued by a mob of women,
screaming like furies. I threw my toga over him and we ducked*

down an alley and ran back to his house. All the way, Clodius
was laughing like a madman, with tears of glee streaming from
his eyes.

At the house he called for wine and began to drink heavily,
without watering the wine. Soon he was quite drunk and boast-
ing so loudly that I dismissed the household staff, lest they over-
hear. He said that now all his ambitions would be realized, and
I asked him to explain, still under the impression that the
night's doings had been no more than a prank.

He said that the three men who were to rule Rome had met
at the house of Caesar and had determined upon the future
course of the empire and that he, Clodius, had arranged all
this. The two most powerful, Pompey and Crassus, could never
work together and their rivalry would plunge the empire into
civil war. Clodius believed that Caesar was greater than the
other two, and had urged him to agree to this meeting, where
their rivalries could be hammered out to the profit of all.

This seemed fantastic to me, and I asked him what he meant
by it. He replied that he, Clodius, had perceived that Crassus
and Pompey were too unimaginative to settle their differences
save through battle; that Caesar, while brilliant and masterful,
was too lazy to set a reconciliation in motion, and that all three
were too bound by traditional forms to do as Sulla did, and set
aside the constitution.

At the meeting in Caesar's house, Clodius said, the Pontifex
Maximus *bound them all by the most solemn oaths to abide by*
the conditions of their covenant, and the agreement they made
was this:]

"Now we get to the heart of the matter," I said.

"Stop commenting and read!" Julia said, obviously in
a state of considerable agitation, which I humored.

[To begin, since Caesar must be away in Spain for his pro-
praetorship, and would not be in Rome to moderate between
the other two, they were to comport themselves as friendly col-
leagues in his absence. Upon his return, their three-man coali-
tion would begin to work in earnest to further the ambitions of
all three. In token of his support, Crassus was to stand surety
for Caesar's debts so that Caesar could leave Rome to assume
his magistracy. Pompey required, apparently in fulfillment of
an earlier, less formal agreement, that the other two be seen
prominently in his triumph so that all might know that he
enjoyed their wholehearted support.

Caesar's reward was to be a Consulship upon his return from

Spain, and following it an extraordinary magistracy over all of Gaul. All would work to secure Crassus the war with Parthia that he desires. Pompey was to have whatever command he desires aside from Gaul and Parthia.

Since these projects would require that all three be absent from Rome for extended periods, Clodius was to be their representative in the city. They would support his suit for transferral to plebeian status, and thereafter support his campaign for the tribuneship. As tribune, he would introduce laws in furtherance of their own ambitions. As popular leader, he would reign as virtual uncrowned king of the city, and they would protect him from action by the Senate. Pompey, regarding himself as the greatest of the three, insisted that Faustus Sulla act as the colleague of Clodius to assure that Pompey's interests were properly looked after in his absence. Although reluctant, Clodius assented. With these agreements made, the meeting broke up.

As they were leaving, Clodius went into the main part of the house to spy on the Mysteries, although Pompey tried to restrain him. When he was detected, the others made their way out amid the ensuing uproar.

Clodius related all this in highest humor, apparently expecting that I would admire his cunning. Horrified, I asked him, What of the constitution? What of the Senate? Scornfully, he said that the Senate was an outdated pack of nonentities and the constitution was what the strongest man said it was.

Understanding that I was involved in a treasonous conspiracy to overthrow the state, I fled the house of Clodius. I found lodgings in a small tavern and spent all the next day and all of this fearing that, sober, Clodius will understand that he said far too much to me and will seek me out. All his men know me by sight, and I dare do nothing until after dark. I have written this letter, which I propose to affix to the door of your house. Then I shall flee Rome and never return. It is now dark, and I shall leave my lodgings as soon as I seal the message tube. Do with these words as you see fit. The Senate must take action. Long live Rome.]

"That poor boy!" Julia said when I had finished reading.

"Yes," I agreed, "he was guilty of no more than bad company and owning a wretched prose style. But he has given me exactly what I need."

"How will you use this?" she asked.

"With this," I said, holding the letter aloft, "I can bring them all down. First, it will hold them all up to ridicule, as undoubtedly Clodius intended when he concocted this bizarre plan. Can you imagine it? The great conqueror, the richest man in the world and the very *Pontifex Maximus* all skulking about the city dressed as women! They could never survive the ridicule! Even more important, though, is the fact that Pompey was there at all."

"What do you mean?" Julia asked.

"He entered the city, crossing the *pomerium*. At that instant he laid down his imperium and forfeited his right to celebrate a triumph!"

"I don't understand," Julia said. "The Senate had already granted him permission for his triumph."

"It makes no difference. They could have given him permission a year ago, when he was still in Asia. No Roman with imperium may enter the city save as *triumphator* on the day of his triumph. This will be a humiliation he cannot endure."

"I don't believe it!" Julia said, jumping to her feet. "Caius Julius is not a traitor, and he would have no part in such a loathsome conspiracy!"

"Julia," I said, holding the scroll before her face, "do you really think that naive boy made all this up?"

"No, of course not," she said, relenting a little. "But Clodius might have. We all know what a villain he is. Pompey and Crassus, of course, but Clodius may have added Caesar's name to make his scheme sound greater than it is."

"Julia, I *know* that Caesar was not in Celer's house that night, and all Rome knows that Clodius was discovered in the house of Caesar. He was there."

She wrung her hands, seeking any way she could to extricate her uncle from treasonous charges. "But even Clodius said that he enjoined the other two to do nothing while he is away from Rome. Perhaps he just meant to keep them from committing civil mischief in his absence."

"Perhaps you are right," I said, knowing that she was not. Because it had come to me, while reading the letter, that every bit of this scheme was Caesar's doing. Oh, maybe the business of dressing as women had been Clodius's, it was the sort of madcap whimsy that would appeal to him, but the rest was Caesar's. Tricking Pompey into crossing the *pomerium* before his triumph put him, the most powerful of the three, firmly into the grasp of the other conspirators. That was Caesar's brand of subtlety. Getting Crassus to stand surety for his debts neatly accomplished a number of his ends at one stroke, another favorite technique of his.

Most of all, though, Caesar had tied the two most powerful men in the world to him, had solved his own debt problems, assured that Rome would be tranquil in his absence, secured a Consulship upon his return and a rich province to govern afterward and even his co-conspirators' patronage for his flunky Clodius. And he had accomplished all this while providing *absolutely nothing* of his own. This was another quality of Caesar's with which I was familiar. He could persuade men to give him what he wanted as if he were doing them a favor. It seemed that now he wanted to be given the world, just for being Caesar.

For I had no doubt of what this signified. These three men (Clodius and Faustus did not count) had met in conspiracy to divide the world among them. And over bullheaded, overgrown juvenile thugs like Pompey and Crassus, Caesar would rule, shining like a god. Caesar was an actor, and this was the ultimate actor's role. If the Senate allowed this to happen, the Senate would deserve whatever might befall it.

"I shall make this public," I vowed. "I shall take this before the Senate and People, and I shall bring them down."

"Excuse me, master," Hermes said, "but do you really expect to live that long?"

XIII

It was a long wait until nightfall. Several times I went out on my roof and crawled on my belly to peer over the parapet. The deserted street before my house made it easy to spot the shadows lurking in nearby doorways. At least two were visible each time: men in long brown Etruscan robes, with pointed beards.

"Still out there," I said after the last scout. "But people are coming back from the festivities now. We'll have crowded, darkening streets soon, and then I can make my move. Hermes, I want you to go to Milo's house."

"Through those streets?" he squealed.

"Of course not. What Roman boy needs streets when there are perfectly good rooftops? Choose your route carefully, and you can get from here to Milo's without your feet touching ground. There aren't three streets in Rome too wide to jump across. I want you to tell Milo that I need a strong bodyguard to escort me across the city and the lady Julia to her home. This is most serious and there are armed murderers after us. Now, be off with you." Pale-faced, he went up the stairs to do my bidding. For a wretched corpse-robber of a slave, the boy had promise.

Julia sat shaking her head, the picture of despondency. It grieved me to see her so, but my duty to the Senate and People outweighed her loyalty to her uncle.

"Oh, don't feel so bad, Julia," I said. "If I know Caius Julius, he'll get out of this as he does everything else. It's Pompey whose hide I want to nail to the Curia door."

"And what of Crassus?" she said dully.

"He'll buy off his jury. Remember, they haven't really *done* anything yet. The laws concerning conspiracy, even the treasonous sort, are notoriously vague. Only Cicero could bring a strong prosecution against them, and he won't dare, since he faces exile over his handling of the Catilinarians.

"No, for Caesar and Crassus, the best I can hope for is public ridicule. The picture of them meeting in women's dress will catch the public's fancy like nothing else in history. The comic playwrights will put the scene on every stage in Italy for years to come. But Pompey tried to have me poisoned, and I want him."

"Not to mention his plotting against the state," she said dryly.

I shrugged. "He hasn't a chance. For whatever reason, he's already forgone the opportunity to make himself Dictator by force of arms, when he could easily have done so as recently as last year. Now he wants to play politics, and I must agree with Cicero that he's too stupid and inept politically to accomplish anything that way. If he survives at all, it could only be with Caesar's expertise and Crassus's wealth. Without his army, he couldn't even carry out one trifling little assassination."

"And to what do you attribute your extraordinary good fortune?" she asked.

"Conspirators like to keep their own hands clean by entrusting their dirty work to subordinates. Unworthy or inept subordinates can ruin almost any conspiracy. Pompey wanted me out of the way because he knew that I was the one man in Rome most likely to uncover and expose what he and the others were up to. He wanted to make it look natural, so he opted for poison. He gave the job to Clodius, but among infamous crimes, poisoning is second only to arson, so Clodius farmed it out to Nero. That was no task for an amateur, and Nero bungled it.

"When Clodius came to his senses after his sacrilege, he knew that Nero would try to warn me, so he sent his Etruscan assassins to keep an eye on my house. When Nero showed up, they killed him."

"Why didn't they find the message-tube?" she asked.

"It was the inept-subordinate problem again. Clodius, like the others, is a conspirator of long experience. Such men know that the first rule of conspiracy is never to put anything in writing. It never occurred to him that the little twit would bring me a letter instead of delivering his message personally. He told his goons to kill the boy, but not to search him for an incriminating document."

"And the herb-woman?"

"A bit of track-covering. She knew about the poison; she knew that her dress had been borrowed so that someone could take her place at the Mysteries. That was too much for her to know with an investigation going on, so she was eliminated."

Julia shuddered. "Such ruthless people."

"I assure you, this is a small-scale naughtiness by these men's standards. They routinely depopulate countries to further their aims. Not that I mind kicking the barbarians around a bit when the good of Rome calls for it, but it's not right to make war on people just to give one man's career a boost."

During this time, I had been going over my weapons. My *gladius* was legionary size, a bit large for concealed carry, but I was no longer concerned with niceties. I assured myself that its edge would still slice a straw without effort and belted it on. I tucked my dagger into its usual place, and this time, just in case, I concealed *both caesti* instead of my usual one.

"Stay away from the river," Julia warned. "If you should fall in, you're sure to drown, carrying all that metal."

"Thank you for your concern," I said, distracted by my own thoughts.

"I would like to remind you," Julia said, red spots appearing on her cheeks most fetchingly, "that I came here for the express purpose of warning you that your life was in danger, at no little peril to myself. I might add that I am doing my reputation no good by coming, unescorted, to the house of an unmarried man, and staying here until who knows what hour, under the eyes of spies. If I should get back to my uncle's house alive, my grandmother will undoubtedly be waiting like a dragon. She will undoubtedly order me flogged, and believe me, *she* knows where the family whip is. After that, I shall be exiled to one of those barren little islands in the Aegean to atone for bringing dishonor upon the family name, something that, apparently, no man can do."

"Oh. I do apologize, and I cannot adequately express

how grateful I am, and I shall surely set things straight
with your father ..." This woman had the unerring capacity to make me babble.

"My *father*?" she all but shrieked. "You are going to
talk to my father? It will amaze me if you are still drawing breath by the time you reach the end of the street
out there!"

I just knew she was going to burst into tears.

"Oh, never fear. With a few of Milo's bullies behind
me, I'm not worried about a few contemptible Etruscans
with their little sticking-knives and hammers."

"You idiot!" she yelled, sounding very much like my
father. "Clodius knows Milo is your friend. He'll have
his whole mob out looking for you. He'll get reinforcements from Pompey if he has to! You are doomed and
so am I!" Then she did cry.

"Please try not to get too emotional about this," I
pleaded. Then she fell into my arms, bawling. I shall draw
the veil of well-bred decency over the events of the next
little while, except to say that we lacked the opportunity
to get down to anything really serious.

"Master," said Cato a little while later. "Your friend is
here."

We went out to find my atrium crowded. Milo was
there, big as a house and backed by twenty others just as
big and far, far uglier. I made introductions, and he
looked Julia over with his usual frankness.

"I've never admired your taste in women before, Decius," he said. "I'm glad to see that you improve with
age." Julia stiffened, but he smiled his huge, infectious
smile and she joined him. No one could resist Milo when
he turned on the charm.

"Come with me, Titus," I said. "We need to talk."

I took him into my study and gave him an abbreviated
account of what had transpired and what I had learned.
He listened with his usual intense concentration and he
read Nero's letter when I got to that part. He had that
odd trick of being able to read without speaking the
words aloud, something I was never able to master. When
he finished he handed the letter back to me, smiling once
more.

"You see? I told you she could not be involved."

"And I rejoice with you that the lady Fausta is innocent of wrongdoing. But there is still the little matter of treason."

"Oh, that. Decius, the Senate can look out for itself. But this might be a good opportunity to get rid of Clodius."

"Believe me, I will not stand in your way. I need to accomplish two things: I have to get Julia back to Caesar's house, and I need to present my findings to the Senate."

"The Senate exists as a body only when a meeting is summoned," he pointed out. "The rest of the time, there are about five hundred Senators scattered all over Rome and the empire. There won't be another session called until well after the triumph."

"That's true," I said. "But tomorrow evening, after the great procession, there will be a banquet of the entire Senate in the Temple of Jupiter Capitolinus. I will get up before them and present my case. I intend to see Pompey stripped of his triumphal regalia and disgraced right in front of the statue of Jupiter!"

He shook his head in wonderment. "Decius, if you can accomplish all that with a lot of talk and an unsigned letter from an obscure boy, you'll be the greatest Roman who ever lived. But I'll back you, whatever you want to do."

"That's all I ask," I said.

"Where do we start?" he asked.

"We take Julia home."

Rarely has a patrician lady been escorted home in quite the way Julia was that night. She and I strolled hand in hand down the middle of some of Rome's most disreputable thoroughfares. The moonlight was bright and sounds of revelry came from all around as Rome celebrated a triumphal holiday. There were other sounds as well. We were closely surrounded by a tight-packed crowd of Milo's thugs, and from its periphery came strangled yells, the sound of blows, the clink of metal striking metal and the unmistakable wood-cracking sound of Milo's bronzelike palms slapping somebody. Sometimes the cobbles we walked over were a little slippery, but we made it to the Forum and the house of the *Pontifex Maximus.*

I told the *janitor* to fetch the master and he went off.

The person who appeared was not Caius Julius, though. It was his mother. She glared with astonishment, first at Julia, then at the men with her. Milo and I were among Rome's more presentable young men, but the same could not be said of his feral-looking followers.

"My son, the distinguished *Pontifex Maximus,* is at the Temple of Jupiter Capitolinus, preparing the triumphal rites. I am his mother."

I bowed. "All Rome knows the august patrician matron Aurelia."

"I do not know you, but you have the look of *gens* Caecilia. Since you are wellborn and a Senator, I will allow you the opportunity to explain how you happen to be with my granddaughter, who has been missing from this house most of the day."

"The lady has assisted me with certain services on behalf of the Republic which have unavoidably detained her. As you can see, I have been careful to provide the lady with a proper escort." The thugs grinned and nodded, a sight to frighten demons. "Please inform Caius Julius that these matters involve not only his august self but the glorious Pompey and the wealthy Crassus. I am sure he will inform you that he fully approves of his niece's actions today."

She nodded fractionally. "Very well. I shall take no action against Julia until I have spoken with my sons, both of them. If her honor has been compromised in any fashion, I shall take measures to have the Censors expel you from the Senate for moral turpitude." She nodded toward Julia and, with a sideways glance at me, Julia disappeared into the house.

"I think we have no further business, Senator," she said, and stalked back into the house.

"Come on, Decius," Milo said. "Getting back won't be so easy. There'll be reinforcements now. Come to my house. It's closer and far stronger."

As we walked back across the Forum, somebody behind us said: "Does Caesar's niece have to be above suspicion, too?" and everybody laughed uproariously until we were attacked by a crowd armed with every manner of weapon, some of them carrying torches. An Etruscan, all eyes and teeth and pointed beard, came for me with a knife in one hand and a hammer in the other. I had the great satisfaction of cutting him down with my sword. The knife-and-hammer business was only good for killing unprepared men. I picked up the fallen hammer and dropped it inside my tunic.

"That one's for Capito," I said to Milo. "I want two more for Nero and Purpurea."

"They were no friends of yours," he said through his grin.

"They were Romans, and foreigners shouldn't be allowed to kill Romans. I take it very ill of Pompey that he should use his barbarians thus."

We made it to Milo's house with only minor casualties. With the massive door bolted behind us, Milo called for food and bandages and sent sentries up to the roof. With the excitement over, I began to ache in a hundred places. Apprehensively, I opened my tunic and examined my cut. So excellent was Asklepiodes's sewing that I had not sprung a single stitch, and only a bit of blood oozed from the wound's edges.

"Decius," Milo said, "eat something, have a little wine and get some sleep. I'm not sure how you propose to survive until tomorrow night even with my help. I can ask a great deal of my men, but even I can't demand that free men miss a triumph just to preserve the hide of Rome's maddest Senator."

This was odd phrasing, but in later conversation with Milo's men I learned that I was, indeed, gaining this reputation for eccentricity. They regarded me as a sort of mascot, rather as soldiers in foreign parts will adopt some exotic beast and invest it with spurious, luck-bestowing qualities. I thought it rather presumptuous that such lowborn scum should regard a noble Senator thus, but it is always a good idea to stay on fine terms with men like those.

I did as Milo suggested. I ate well, had just a little wine, then went to one of his guest rooms and slept gloriously. I would wager that I slept better that night than Pompey, Caesar, Crassus or Clodius.

XIV

It was a beautiful morning. I rose just before sunrise and went up to the roof of Milo's house to watch the first light strike the gilded rooftops of the Capitol. Since it was likely to be my last such sight, I took it in with uncommon relish. All my frustrated agitation of the past few days was gone. I knew exactly what I had to do, and I was at peace.

This is not to say that I was not excited. It would be an eventful day, whatever its outcome. I spoke with the sentries and they said that Clodius's men had hung around for several hours, but then had gone away. They also said that there had been a good many unfamiliar faces among the enemy. Pompey's reinforcements, I thought.

At intervals along the roof, between the fire buckets full of water, stood bins of fist-sized rocks. The city had no laws against possession of rocks, but few things are more effective when launched from a roof. The guards boasted that they had left some sore heads among the besiegers.

Milo came onto the roof, active and alert as always. He never seemed to sleep.

"What's the plan?" he asked. "The triumphal procession will be forming up soon."

"As a Senator," I said, "I will have to take part, so first we must go to the Circus Flaminius. Just get me there safely and I will do the rest."

He was incredulous. "You really propose to march in Pompey's triumph?"

"As a Senator, I consider it my duty," I assured him.

He leaned back and roared with laughter. "You may be a fool, Decius, but you have real style. To the Circus, then."

Hermes had delivered my formal toga to Milo's house so that I would be properly dressed. Awkward though the garment was, it was so voluminous that it gave adequate concealment for my weapons.

"I wonder if Pompey will be bold enough to have you attacked during the procession," Milo mused as we walked toward the Campus Matrius.

"With luck, he won't know I'm there for a while," I said. "The Senate and magistrates march in front, with the gods. Pompey can't even come into the city until his soldiers have marched through the whole route and had the gates shut behind them afterward. As for Clodius"—I patted the handle of my sword to reassure myself—"we shall just have to see how rash he is."

All Rome was flocking to get a good position to see the triumph. The greater part would be in the two great Circuses, but a window or rooftop along the route would afford a better and closer view. Along the Via Sacra, some people had camped out for the past two or three nights on especially favorable rooftops, and landlords had rented out the best windows for tidy sums. The Roman need to gape at glory was insatiable.

At the Circus I had to leave the comforting proximity of Milo and his thugs. Circus officials, accustomed to sorting out huge crowds, were ordering matters. Near the gate where the chariots enter for the races, I was hustled toward the rear of the senatorial procession.

"By Jupiter!" said a junior Senator. "It's Decius! I can't believe you'd show your face in public."

"Duty calls," I said. "How could I forgo my very first opportunity to participate in a triumph?"

"Don't get us laughing in front of the citizens, Metellus," said another.

Atop the *spina*, a sheep was sacrificed and its entrails examined. To nobody's surprise, the priests announced that the gods were favorable to the celebration of a triumph on that day. I have never known them to be unfavorable at such a time. I squinted at the priests, but they were just ordinary Etruscan haruspices, not the strange hammer specialists Pompey had brought to the city.

With a blast of trumpets, we stepped out and entered the Circus, walking up one side, rounding the *spina* and then back down the other side. The populace applauded respectfully, although the Senate certainly wasn't what they had come to see. And so it went, all the long triumphal route, finally down the Via Sacra to the Forum, then up the Capitol. It was exhilarating, although my mind was elsewhere much of the time.

After a formal salute to the image of Jupiter Capitolinus, we Senators scattered to get good vantage points for the main part of the show. I began to walk down the hill toward the Forum and the Rostra, which was a fine vantage point from which to view a spectacle. And from which to be seen.

A hand gripped my arm and I reached for my sword. I hadn't expected to be attacked on the Capitol. Men have died for less foolish assumptions.

"Draw that and I'll have you sentenced to the Sicilian sulfur mines."

"Why, Caius Julius Caesar, you do me great honor." He smiled widely, nodding and acknowledging greetings and well-wishers. I smiled back as gaily. We were two distinguished Romans, walking down the hill on this great day of Rome's triumph.

"Pompey wants you dead, and by all the gods, I never saw a man cooperate so wholeheartedly in his own assassination! How did a family of plodding drudges like the Metellans ever produce a specimen like you?"

"Oh, come now, Caius Julius, we may be a bit conservative, but we are scarcely—"

"Shut up and listen!" he hissed. "You might, just might, live to draw breath tomorrow if you will heed me. Pompey will be far too busy to concern himself with you for the next few days, what with his triumph and his games. Clodius thirsts for your blood, but while the celebrations are going on, he won't be able to get his men to do anything."

"Good," I said. "Just Clodius and me. That's the way I want it."

"Venus, my ancestress, deliver me from such fools!" Caesar cried, in one of his better theatrical gestures. "He has those Etruscans Pompey loaned him, and they don't care about Roman holidays."

"And I killed one of them last night," I said with satisfaction.

"Worse. Now it's personal. Decius, I will stand beside you on the Rostra for the great procession, and maybe they won't try to attack you. But when Pompey goes up to the Capitol, I will have to be there to preside over the sacrifice and then the banquet. Do Rome a favor and sneak away. Come back in a month or two, when Pompey has more immediate enemies to concern him."

We were almost to the Rostra by this time, and to all outward appearances we were conversing in greatest conviviality.

"I know what you were up to, Caius Julius," I said. "You and Pompey and Crassus. I wish I had been there. The sight of you three in women's gowns must have been a rare spectacle."

I had expected him to be embarrassed. "Political expediency is not always consistent with one's highest vision of one's own dignity. But even that particular indignity is not to be despised. Glorious foreign conquest usually means months of lying on a verminous pallet, fever-ridden, covered with one's own blood and bodily effluvia, yet it can result in a triumph such as this." By this time we stood at the railing of the Rostra, and Caesar gestured toward the marching soldiers bearing standards and trophies, his golden bracelet flashing. I understood then that men such as I was up against had no more concept of shame than of conscience.

"Why are you so solicitous, Caius Julius?" I asked. "Why try to preserve me when your friends want me dead?"

He looked at me with open puzzlement. "Why do you call them my friends?"

"Cohorts, then. I know what you plotted, dividing the world among you, setting aside the constitution and the Senate, and I intend to destroy all three of you!" I never made such a reckless speech sober.

"How did you figure it all out?" Caesar said, smiling gently and obviously interested. I almost told him about Nero's letter, but decided that it might make me look less astute. I still had a young man's vanity, but more importantly, I had learned that it was best to maintain a sense of mystery about one's own capabilities. That was something Caesar had long known.

"To a logical mind," I said, "to one who knows how to see with clarity and think with penetration, the evidence was all there." That, I thought, was rather good.

"You are a truly remarkable man, Decius Caecilius," he said. "And that is why I go to so much trouble to preserve you from your own suicidal stupidity. I shall have work for you to do, in the future."

"What?" I said incredulously. "You won't *have* a future after this evening!"

"Look!" he said, pointing. "Here come the animals!"

So we watched the procession: the floats bearing treasures, the exotic beasts, the chained prisoners, the unthinkable booty Pompey had assembled in three separate conquests. And Pompey himself, of course. He stood like a statue in his *toga picta* and red paint. Getting a little pudgy, it seemed to me.

"Love your purple *dress!*" I shouted as he went past. Under the red paint I couldn't tell if he turned truly red. In the uproar, I doubt if he or anyone else heard me.

As the crowd broke up, I noticed that Caesar was gone. It struck me, with a chill, that I was now on my own. I saw other Senators making their way up the Capitol, toward the banquet in Pompey's honor. I began to go that way myself. It was time to confront the three would-be tyrants before the assembled Senate and bring them low. Besides, I was hungry.

It was getting dark fast. I was perhaps halfway up the hill when I saw the first Etruscan. He lurked in a space between two buildings, and the last beams of the setting sun struck glimmers from his bronze hammer and steel dagger. One was no problem. I glanced at the other side of the street. Two more. Then I saw a small crowd behind the two. These were Romans, most likely followers of Clodius, taking a few minutes from the festivities to eliminate an enemy. I looked up toward the temple, which suddenly seemed to be very far away. I was already in plenty of trouble with the Roman courts, and the gods seemed to have deserted me, so I drew my sword.

"Two more!" I yelled. "I want two more of you pointy-bearded Tuscian slaves to pay for the blood of two Romans. The one I got last night wasn't enough!" No sooner asked for than received. The Etruscans attacked, howling. Even in the excitement of the moment I noted that the others weren't so eager. I would like to think that they were overawed by my heroics, but more likely they thought it unworthy to assist wretched foreigners in killing a Senator.

One came in, swinging a hammer. I ducked the blow and ran him through and then jumped on the next one before he had a chance to understand that it was I who was on the offensive. With a sense of the very finest irony, I poked him in the throat with the point of my *gladius*, just as my instructor had taught me years before, in the old Statilian *ludus*. I only wished that I had a hammer to whack him between the eyes with.

The others began to close in. I'd had my two. Rome was avenged. I turned and fled downhill, scattering citizens right and left. The pack baying at my heels caused further alarm. The press of celebrating citizenry got too dense to push through, and I turned to confront my pursuers. At that moment, something large and solid bowled into me, shoving me through a dense pack of ivy-wreathed celebrators and into an alley, down a flight of stairs and through a low doorway.

"Keeping you alive could call for the full-time attentions of a legion," said Titus Milo. People looked up from their tables. I smiled at them and sheathed my sword. They returned their attention to their food and wine.

"I have to get to the temple," I said.

"You won't. At least, not for a while. Let's wait here until things are quiet outside. I don't think they saw where we went."

"Good idea," I said. The tavern was like a hundred others in the city. By law they were not supposed to stay open to the public after sunset, but this was a holiday, and besides, nobody paid any attention to that law anyway. We found a table and within minutes were tearing into roast duck with fruit and white bread, which we helped down with rough local wine. I told Milo about the odd interlude with Caesar.

"He's a strange one, Caesar," he said. "But he's like one of those horses in the Circus that surprises you by coming out of nowhere to win, when you'd put your money on the flashy, quick ones."

"I think you're right," I said, helping myself to a handful of figs. "Until now, I'd dismissed him as a posturing buffoon. Everyone has. But he's been behind it all."

"Behind what all?" Milo said alertly.

I told him what I had learned from Nero's letter. "Clodius thinks it was his own doing, and doubtless Pompey and Crassus each thinks himself the dominant member of this—this *triumvirate*, but it is Caesar who holds the reins. He is the near trace horse." The familiar chariot-race image seemed the best way to describe Caesar's place in the arrangement.

Milo sat back, and I could see the machinery working in his head as he sorted through this information and analyzed it for political content.

"Perhaps his niece is right," Milo said at last. "He may be trying to keep the peace between the others while he is away."

"That's part of it, I have no doubt. But when he returns, the three of them will be at each other's throats. Three such men cannot last as peaceful, cooperating colleagues: a general, a financier, and a . . . whatever Caesar is."

"A politician," Milo said. It was a new word. I think Milo made it up. "He is a man whose sole qualification for office is that he knows how to manipulate people. As you have remarked, he brings nothing to the bargain but shattering debts and inexperience. It does not matter. He is using the system itself to propel himself into prominence."

"He underestimates the Senate," I said.

"Does he?" Milo's bland, understated contempt for the wisdom and power of the Senate did more than anything in my recent experience to shake my faith in it.

I reached within my clothes and took out the message tube. "When I reveal this, they will have to take action. The Senate has grown lax and corrupt, but even so, they cannot allow such men as these to wield power. As for Caesar and Pompey and Crassus, their ambitions could never survive such ignominy."

"Let us hope so," he said.

We ate for a while in silence. "Speaking of the Senate," Milo said, "If you are truly foolish enough to go up there and confront Pompey, you had better do it while they're sober enough to understand you."

"You're right," I said. "It is getting late."

We rose and went outside. To my surprise, the streets were still jammed. We forced our way with difficulty through the Forum and began to ascend the Capitol. Above, we could see a great lurid glare of torchlight and could hear a raucous bellowing, some of it human.

"What's happening?" I said. "The procession ended hours ago." I had a dreadful premonition that there had been a change in procedure.

"Let's ask somebody," Milo said, with his accustomed good sense. He took a citizen by the arm and made the relevant inquiry.

"Pompey is coming back down," the man said. "Word spread an hour ago that he is planning something extraordinary!"

"He's cut the banquet short!" I said. "It should go on until midnight!"

Milo grinned. "But then most of the citizens would be asleep and unable to admire their idol."

"I have to get up there!" I shouted. "If I can't get to the temple before the Senate breaks up, it will be days before they meet again!"

"And you don't have days to live, at this rate," Milo said. "Let's see what we can do." What Milo could do was considerable. He shouldered his way through the tight-packed mob almost as if it weren't there, and I followed his broad back.

Feverishly, I thought about the usual triumphal honors enjoyed by a victorious general. Ordinarily, the day culminated with the banquet on the Capitol, at the end of which the *triumphator* descended the hill, escorted by the Senate, bearing torches to light his way. Lucullus, at the time of his triumph, had thrown his own banquet in his new garden, but I had not heard that Pompey had asked permission for a change of routine. Pompey, it seemed, was fond of his little surprises.

Halfway to the Capitol, we broke through the crowd. A mass of lictors held it back, holding their fasces obliquely, the way soldiers carry spears when they are controlling a mob.

"I must get to the temple!" I shouted at them.

"You may pass, Senator," said a lictor, "but not your friend." There is no one more officious than a lictor who has been given a little authority.

"You're on your own," Milo said cheerfully. "Try not to die foolishly."

I began to trot up the hill. There was a great deal of milling about going on up there. The heat built up rapidly beneath my heavy toga, but I dared not throw it off. Running heavily armed into the massed Senate could mean real trouble. I stopped to catch my breath and brush the sweat from my face; then I saw what I had feared the most: a double line of torches coming toward me. I cursed mightily and resumed running toward the lights, so agitated that I didn't notice that they moved rather oddly. As I neared them, I snatched the message tube from within my tunic and held it aloft.

"Noble Senators!" I screamed. "I must address you! Stop! Cnaeus Pompeius has no right to—" Then I stopped and gaped. The torches were not held by Senators wearing wreaths. The were carried by elephants, at least fifty of them.

Pompey had assembled his monsters atop the Capitol so that he could come down the hill in real style. Each elephant had a mahout straddling his neck, and behind each mahout was a wooden castle manned with youths and girls who were armed with baskets of flowers and trinkets to scatter among the onlookers.

The mahout on the lead elephant pointed at me with his goad and gabbled something. I stood transfixed by the bizarre spectacle, at risk of imminent trampling.

"Metellus, I knew you'd show up!" Broken from my trance, I looked up to see that the lead elephant's castle wasn't manned by any youths and maidens. It held Publius Clodius and some of his thugs. Whooping like a hunter who has started a hare, he snatched up a javelin and hurled it at me. I leapt nimbly aside, and the iron-shod point struck sparks from the pavement.

Toga flapping, I whirled and ran back down the hill. It seemed that I was spending a great deal of time running from Clodius these days, but an elephant gives a man an unfair advantage.

Another javelin sailed past me by a good margin. Clodius was always a wretched spearman. Of course, his swaying platform and the uncertain light could not have helped much. Ahead of me, the crowd of citizens and lictors gaped and pointed, at me and at the elephants. I couldn't pick out Milo's face among the mob.

I plowed through the lictors like a ship ramming through an enemy's battle line. They stumbled trying to get out of my way as the crowd heaved back, instinctively wanting to avoid the path of the trumpeting, torchbearing monsters. Another javelin missed me, but I heard a scream as it impaled some unfortunate citizen.

The uproar grew deafening as half the mob tried to

run away from the oncoming beasts while the other half
surged forward to get a closer look. It was like one of
those circus riots where a panic starts and hundreds of
people get trampled. I looked back over my shoulder
and saw the huge gray beast towering above the mob as
Clodius poised his arm for another throw. Behind him,
cheerful young people mounted on other elephants
waved and threw their flowers and trinkets into the mob.
He missed again.

I got all the way down to the Forum in this hallucinatory
fashion. The mob and the elephants spilled into the great
plaza close behind me, and despite the best efforts of the
mahouts, the animals lost all cohesion and began to scatter
amid the confusion. People screamed or laughed. All Rome
loves an event like this. There was much fleeing from before the beasts, unnecessarily. Terrifying as they are to behold, elephants are actually quite careful where they step
and rarely inflict more than a crushed toe. War elephants
have to be trained to trample enemies, as it is not their
natural behavior. Needless to say, this was not common
knowledge in the Roman streets.

An elephant passed by me, and its inhabitants showered things all around me. This turned out to be almost
as deadly as the javelins Clodius was hurling, for it transpired that Pompey was not scattering mere trinkets this
night. In the torchlight I saw gold coins, carved gem-
stones, vials of perfume amid the flowers, and wherever
they landed, fights broke out over possession.

I looked for Clodius and saw him standing in his little
castle, looking all over for me. I saw that his beast was
about to pass close by the Rostra. I got to the fringes of
the mob and ran toward the old monument and dashed
up its back steps. There I threw off my toga, consigning
the expensive thing to unavoidable oblivion, crossed the
base and stepped out onto one of the bronze ship's rams
that decorated the marble front of the platform.

As the elephant jostled by, I jumped into its castle, my
sword bare in one hand and a *caestus* on the other. The
men whirled around with looks of shock and I smashed
my bronze-spiked left fist into the jaw of one, in the next
instant slashing another across the face. Both men tum-
bled screaming to the pavement fifteen feet below. Now
it was just Clodius and me.

Screaming, he leapt on me before I could rebrace myself. I had not anticipated the rocking of the platform beneath my feet and I swung my arms wide to regain balance. That gave him the chance to grasp both my wrists as he closed, trying to knee me in the crotch. I spent several seconds jockeying to protect myself. He tried to bite my nose off again, but I tucked in my chin and butted him in the face instead.

As he staggered back, the platform began to rock violently. I spared a glance down and saw that scores of Clodius's thugs had rallied to him and were trying to scramble up the sides of the elephant to rescue their master. The poor beast trumpeted with alarm, waving its torch-laden trunk about and scorching several bystanders.

At last, the strain proved to be too much for the unstable castle. The elephant stumbled sideways and the girth parted. The tower lurched and fell, landing on a set of steps amid a great splintering of wood and rending of wicker. We were thrown violently apart, and I somehow managed to retain my grip on my weapons. I lurched to my feet to see Clodius's whole mob a few steps away, but they had the look of abashed schoolboys and did not climb the stair as they helped Clodius, shaking his head groggily, to regain his feet. I looked to see who had cowed them and saw, standing in the doorway behind me, the lady Aurelia, Caesar's mother, livid with rage.

"Who dares to bring bloodied weapons to the house of the *Pontifex Maximus*?" she screeched. Hastily, I resheathed my sword and thrust my smeared *caestus* beneath my tunic.

"If you will excuse me, my lady," I said, "these men are trying to kill me. May I come inside?" I could see Julia standing behind her.

"If you enter this house, I will demand your public flogging!" said the old bat.

"Let him in, Grandmother!" Julia pleaded.

"Never!"

Clodius grinned and came for me again, and I was about to draw when a clopping of hooves interrupted us. From a courtyard beside the house came Caius Julius and a sizable retinue, all mounted. This was a rare sight in the city, especially after nightfall. Well, it was a night for strange sights.

"What is this?" Caesar shouted. He wore a military tunic and boots.

"This man," his mother said, pointing at me, "has violated your house. Have him executed at once, my son!"

Caesar smiled. "Now, Mother, calm yourself. This is Decius Caecilius Metellus the Younger, and the gods keep special watch over such as he. I, the *Pontifex Maximus,* have said so." He turned to Clodius. "Publius, call off your dogs."

But Clodius had gone into his gorgonlike rage. "Not this time, Caesar! He is mine!"

"Decius, come here," Caesar said. I stepped over to him, keeping a wary eye on Clodius. Caesar leaned from his saddle, an eyebrow sardonically arched. In a low voice, he said: "Decius, just how badly do you want to get out of Rome alive tonight?"

"Rather badly," I admitted.

"The only way you are going to do it is to ride out with me. I am on my way to Spain, and my men are all veterans of long experience. Clodius won't dare attack. But I want something from you first."

"Is that what you do these days, Caius Julius?" I said bitterly. "Make bargains, like some *publicanus* angling for a government contract?"

"It's the way of the new Rome," he said. "Be quick about it."

"What do you want?"

"Many things, but right now what you must give me is your evidence." He held forth his hand.

I looked at the enraged Clodius and his murderous men. Nowhere could I see Milo or his thugs. I was alone and I could measure my life expectancy in seconds. I took the message tube from my tunic and placed it in Caesar's hand.

"Is this all?" he demanded.

"It is," I said, sick at heart. He snapped his fingers, and a man led up one of the remounts and helped me scramble onto its back. He had a hard, scarred, veteran's face.

"Attack if you will, Clodius," Caesar said, radiating contempt. Clodius and his men fell back as we rode through them. I looked back at the doorway and Julia waved shyly. I waved back, rejoicing in my survival, sickened at my defeat. It was an odd sensation, and the situation was rather like one of those tedious Greek dramas.

We passed through the Forum, which was still alive with its surging mobs and its miniature elephant stampede. This night would be remembered for some time to come. I didn't see Pompey. As we rode through the streets, Caesar read the letter by the light of a torch held by one of his men. When he was finished, he stuffed it into a saddlebag.

"What a young fool, to put something like that in writing," Caesar said. "Just as well he's dead. He certainly had no future in Rome."

We moved out through the Ostian Gate and it closed behind us. After a mile or so, we halted.

"Come with me to Spain, Decius," Caesar said. "I shall attach you to my staff."

I shook my head. "My father tells me the family estate in Beneventum is in urgent need of my attention."

"As you will. You can return to the city in a month or two and all will be forgotten, temporarily. It will be interesting times when we are all back in Rome together again." He smiled. "As I said, I shall have work for you."

"I will never do your work, Caius Julius," I promised.

"You'll change your mind. And I want you to marry my niece, Julia Minor."

I gaped, unable to think of anything to say.

"Farewell, Decius," Caesar said. He wheeled his mount and he and his escort clopped off. I watched until the last glimmerings of torchlight disappeared into the surrounding gloom.

"Caesar's wife must be above suspicion," I yelled after them. In spite of everything, I couldn't help laughing.

These were the events of eleven days in the year 693 of the City of Rome, the Consulship of Calpurnianus and Messala Niger.

GLOSSARY

(Definitions apply to the last century of the Republic.)

Acta: Streets wide enough for one-way wheeled traffic.

Aedile: Elected officials in charge of upkeep of the city and the grain dole, regulaton of public morals, management of the markets and the public Games. There were two types: the plebeian aediles, who had no insignia of office, and the curule aediles, who wore the toga praetexta and sat in the sella curulis. The curule aediles could sit in judgment on civil cases involving markets and currency, while the plebeian aediles could only levy fines. Otherwise, their duties were the same. Since the magnificence of the Games one exhibited as aedile often determined election to higher office, it was an important stepping-stone in a political career. The office of aedile did not carry the imperium.

Ancile: (pl. ancilia) A small, oval sacred shield which fell from heaven in the reign of King Numa. Since there was a prophecy that it was tied to the stability of Rome, Numa had eleven exact copies made so nobody would know which one to steal. Their care was entrusted to a college of priests, the *Salii* (q.v.) and figured in a number of ceremonies each year.

Atrium: Once a word for house, in Republican times it was the entry hall of a house, opening off the street and used as a general reception area.

Atrium Vestae: The Palace of the Vestal and one of the most splendid buildings in Rome.

Augur: An official who observed omens for state purposes. He could forbid business and assemblies if he saw unfavorable omens.

Basilica: A building where courts met in inclement weather.

Caestus: The Classical boxing glove, made of leather straps and reinforced by bands, plates or spikes of bronze.

Caliga: The Roman military boot. Actually a heavy sandal with hobnailed sole.

Campus Martius: A field outside the old city wall, formerly the assembly area and drill field for the army. It was where the popular assemblies met. By late Republican times, buildings were encroaching on the field.

Censor: Magistrates elected usually every fifth year to oversee the census of the citizens and purge the roll of Senators of unworthy members. They could forbid certain religious practices or luxuries deemed bad for public morals or generally "un-Roman." There were two Censors, and each could overrule the other. They wore the toga praetexta and sat in the sella curulis, but since they had no executive powers they were not accompanied by lictors. The office did not carry the imperium. Censors were usually elected from among the ex-Consuls, and the censorship was regarded as the capstone of a political career.

Centuriate Assembly: (comitia centuriata) Originally, the annual military assembly of the citizens where they joined their army units ("centuries"). There were one hundred ninety-three centuries divided into five classes by property qualification. They elected the highest magistrates: Censors, Consuls and Praetors. By the middle Republic, the centuriate assembly was strictly a voting body, having lost all military character.

Centurion: "Commander of 100", i.e., a century, which, in practice, numbered around sixty men. Centurions were promoted from the ranks and were the backbone of the professional army.

Circus: The Roman racehorse and the stadium which enclosed it. The original, and always the largest, was the Circus Maximus, which lay between the Palatine and Aventine hills. A later, smaller circus, the Circus Flaminius, lay outside the walls on the Campus Martius.

Client: One attached in a subordinate relationship to a patron, whom he was bound to support in war and in the courts. Freedman became clients of their former masters. The relationship was hereditary.

Coemptio: Marriage by symbolic sale. Before five witnesses and a *libripens* who held a balance, the bridegroom struck the balance with a bronze coin and handed it to the father or guardian of the bride. Unlike conferreatio, coemptio was easily dissolved by divorce.

Cognomen: The family name, denoting any of the stirpes of a gens; i.e., Caius Julius *Caesar:* Caius of the stirps Caesar of gens Julii. Some plebeian families never adopted a cognomen, notably Marii and the Antonii.

Coitio: A political alliance between two men, uniting their voting blocs. Usually it was an agreement between politicians who were otherwise antagonists, in order to edge out mutual rivals.

Colonia: Towns which had been conquered by Rome, where Roman citizens were settled. Later, settlements founded by discharged veterans of the legions. After 89 B.C. all Italian colonia had full rights of citizenship. Those in the provinces had limited citizenship.

Compluvium: An opening in a roof to admit light.

Conferreatio: The most sacred and binding of Roman forms of marriage. The bride and groom offered a cake of spelt to Jupiter in the presence of a pontifex and the flamen Dialis. It was the ancient patrician form of marriage. By the late Republic it was obsolete except for some priesthoods in which the priest was required to be married by a conferreatio.

Consul: Supreme magistrate of the Republic. Two were elected each year. Insignia were the toga praetexta and the sella curulis. Each Consul was attended by twelve lictors. The office carried a full imperium. On the expiration of his year in office, the ex-Consul was usually assigned a district outside Rome to rule as proconsul. As proconsul, he had the same insignia and the same number of lictors. His power was absolute within his province.

Curia: The meetinghouse of the Senate, located in the Forum.

Dictator: An absolute ruler chosen by the Senate and the Consuls to deal with a specific emergency. For a limited period, never more than six months, he was given unlimited imperium, which he was to lay down upon resolution of the emergency. Unlike the Consuls, he had no colleague to overrule him and he was not accountable for his actions performed during office when he stepped down. His insignia were the toga praetexta and the sella curulis and he was accompanied by twenty-four lictors, the number of both Consuls. Dictatorships were extremely rare and the last was held in 202 B.C. The dictatorships of Sulla and Caesar were unconstitutional.

Dioscuri: Castor and Pollux, the twin sons of Zeus and Leda. The Romans revered them as protectors of the city.

Eques: (pl. equites) Formerly, citizens wealthy enough to supply their own horses and fight in the cavalry, they came to hold their status by meeting a property qualification. They formed the moneyed upper-middle class. In the centuriate assembly they formed eighteen centuries and once had the right of voting first, but they lost this as their military function disappeared. The publicans, financiers, bankers, moneylenders and tax-farmers came from the equestrian class.

Faction: In the Circus, the supporters of the four racing companies: Red, White, Blue and Green. Most Romans were fanatically loyal to one of these.

Fasces: A bundle of rods bound around an ax with a red strap, symbolizing a Roman magistrate's power of corporal and capital punishment. They were carried by the lictors who accompanied the curule magistrates, the Flamen Dialis, and the proconsuls and propraetors who governed provinces. When a lower magistrate met a higher, his lictors lowered their fasces in salute.

Flamen: A high priest of a specific god of the state. The college of flamines had fifteen members: three patrician and twelve plebeian. The three highest were the Flamen Dialis, the Flamen Martialis and the Flamen Quirinalis. They had charge of the daily sacrifices and wore distinctive headgear and were surrounded by many ritual taboos. The Flamen Dialis, high priest of Jupiter, was entitled to the toga praetexta, which had to be woven by his wife, the sella curulis and a single lictor, and he could sit in the Senate. It became difficult to fill the college of flamines because they had to be prominent men, the appointment was for life and they could take no part in politics.

Forum: An open meeting and market area. The premier forum was the Forum Romanum, located on the low ground surrounded by the Capitoline, Palatine and Caelian hills. It was surrounded by the most important temples and public buildings. Roman citizens spent much of their day there. The courts met outdoors in the Forum when the weather was good. When it was paved and devoted solely to public business, the Forum Romanum's market functions were transferred to the Forum Boarium, the cattle market, near the Circus Maximus. Small shops and stalls remained along the northern and southern peripheries, however.

Freedman: A manumitted slave. Formal emancipation conferred full rights of citizenship except for the right to hold office. Informal emancipation conferred freedom without voting rights. In the second or at latest third generaton, a freedman's descendants became full citizens.

Genius: The guiding and guardian spirit of a person or place. The genius of a place was called genius loci.

Gens: A clan, all of whose members were descended from a single ancestor. The nomen of a patrician gens always ended with -ius. Thus, Caius *Julius* Caesar was Caius, of the Caesarian stirps of gens Julii.

Gladiator: Literally, "swordsmen." A slave, prisoner of war, condemned criminal or free volunteer who fought, often to the death, in the munera. All were called swordsmen, even if they fought with other weapons.

Gladius: The short, broad, double-edged sword borne by Roman soldiers. It was designed primarily for stabbing. A smaller, more antiquated design of gladius was used by gladiators.

Gravitas: The quality of seriousness.

Haruspex: A member of a college of Etruscan professionals who examined the entrails of sacrificial animals for omens.

Hospitium: An arrangment of reciprocal hospitality. When visiting the other's city, ech hospes (pl. hospites) was entitled to food and shelter, protection in court, care when ill or injured and honorable burial, should he die during the visit. The obligation was binding on both families and was passed on to descendants.

Ides: The 15th of March, May, July and October. The 13th of other months.

Imperium: The ancient power of kings to summon and lead armies, to order and forbid and to inflict corporal and capital punishment. Under the Republic, the imperium was divided among the Consuls and Praetors, but they were subject to appeal and intervention by the tribunes in their civil decisions and were answerable for their acts after leaving office. Only a dictator had unlimited imperium.

Insula: Literally, "island." A large, multistory tenement block.

Itinera: Streets wide enough for only foot traffic. The majority of Roman streets were itinera.

Janitor: A slave-doorkeeper, so called for Janus, god of gateways.

Kalends: The first of any month.

Latifundium: A large landed estate or plantation worked by slaves. During the late Republic these expanded tremendously, all but destroying the Italian peasant class.

Legates: Subordinate commanders chosen by the Senate to accompany generals and governors. Also, ambassadors appointed by the Senate.

Legion: Basic unit of the Roman army. Paper strength was six thousand, but usually closer to four thousand. All were armed as heavy infantry with a large shield, cuirass, helmet, gladius and light and heavy javelins. Each legion had attached to it an equal number of non-citizen auxiliaries consisting of light and heavy infantry, cavalry, archers, slingers, etc. Auxilia were never organized as legions, only as cohorts.

Lictors: Attendants, usually freedman, who accompanied magistrates and the Flamen Dialis, bearing fasces. They summoned assemblies, attended public sacrifices and carried out sentences of punishment. Twenty-four lictors accompanied a dictator, twelve for a Consul, six for a propraetor, two for a Praetor and one for the Flamen Dialis.

Liquamen: Also called garum, it was the ubiquitous fermented fish sauce used in Roman cooking.

Ludus: (pl. ludi) The official public Games, races, theatricals, etc. Also, a training school for gladiators, although the gladiatorial exhibitions were not ludi.

Munera: Special Games, not part of the official calendar, at which gladiators were exhibited. They were originally funeral Games and were always dedicated to the dead. In munera sine missione, all the defeated were killed and sometimes were made to fight sequentially or all at once until only one was left standing. Munera sine mis-sione were periodically forbidden by law.

Municipia: Towns originally with varying degrees of Roman citizenship, but by the late Republic with full cit-izenship. A citizen from a municipium was qualified to hold any public office. An example is Cicero, who was not from Rome but from the municipium of Arpinum.

Nobiles: Those families, both patrician and plebeian, in which members had held the Consulate.

Nomen: The name of the clan or gens; i.e., Caius *Julius* Caesar.

Nones: The 7th of March, May, July and October. The 5th of other months.

Novus Homo: Literally, "new man." A man who is the first of his family to hold the Consulate, giving his family the status of nobiles.

Optimates: The party of the "best men"; i.e., aristocrats and their supporters.

Patria Potestas: The absolute authority of the pater fam-ilias over the children of his household, who could nei-ther legally own property while their father was alive nor marry without his permission. Technically, he had the right to sell or put to death any of his children, but by Republican times this was a legal fiction.

Patrician: A descendant of one of the founding others of Rome. Once, only patricians could hold offices and priesthoods and sit in the Senate, but these privileges were gradually eroded until only certain priesthoods were strictly patrician. By the late Republic, only about fourteen gens remained.

Patron: A man with one or more clients whom he was bound to protect, advise and otherwise aid. The rela-tionship was hereditary.

Peculium: Roman slaves could not own property, but they could earn money outside the household, which was held for them by their masters. This fund was called a peculium, and could be used, eventually, to purchase the slave's freedom.

Peristylium: An open courtyard surrounded by a collon-ade.

Pietas: The quality of dutifulness towards the gods and, especially, toward one's parents.

Plebeian: All citizens not of patrician status.

Pomerium: The line of the ancient city wall, attributed to Romulus. Actually, the space of vacant ground just within and without the wall, regarded as holy. Within the pomerium it was forbidden to bear arms or bury the dead.

Pontifex: A member of the highest priestly college of Rome. They had superintendence over all sacred observances, state and private, and over the calendar. There were fifteen in the late Republic: seven patrician and eight plebeian. Their chief was the pontifex maximus, a title now held by the Pope.

Popular Assemblies: There were three: the centuriate assembly (comitia centuriata) and the two tribal assemblies: comitia tributa and consilium plebis, q.v.

Populares: The party of the common people.

Praenomen: The given name of a freedman, as Marcus, Sextus, Caius, etc. i.e., *Caius* Julius Caesar: Caius of the stirps Caesar of gens Julii. Women used a feminine form of their father's nomen, i.e., the daughter of Caius Julius Caesar would be named Julia.

Praetor: Judge and magistrate elected yearly along with the Consuls. In the late Republic there were eight Praetors. Senior was the Praetor Urbanus, who heard civil cases between citizens. The Praetor Peregrinus head cases involving foreigners. The others presided over criminal courts. Insignia were the toga praetexta and the sella curulis, and Praetors were accompanied by two lictors. The office carried the imperium. After leaving office, the ex-Praetors became propraetors and went to govern propraetorian provinces with full imperium.

Praetorium: A general's headquarters, usually a tent in camp. In the provinces, the official residence of the governor.

Princeps: "First Citizen." An especially distinguished Senator chosen by the Censors. His name was the first called on the roll of the Senate and he was first to speak on any issue. Later the title was usurped by Augustus and is the origin of the word "prince."

Proscription: List of names of public enemies published by Sulla. Anyone could kill a proscribed person and claim a reward, usually a part of the dead man's estate.

Publicans: Those who bid on public contracts, most notable builders and tax farmers. The contracts were usually let by the Censors and therefore had a period of five years.

Pugio: The straight, double-edged dagger of the Roman soldiers.

Quaestor: Lowest of the elected officials, they had charge of the treasury and financial matters such as payments for public works. They also acted as assistants and paymasters to higher magistrates, generals and provincial governors. They were elected yearly by the comitia tributa.

Quirinus: The deified Romulus, patron deity of the city.

Rostra: A monument in the Forum commemorating the sea battle of Antium in 338 B.C., decorated with the rams, "rostra" of enemy ships (sing. rostrum). Its base was used as an orator's platform.

Sagum: The Roman military cloak, made of wool and always dyed red. To put on the sagum signified the changeover to wartime status, as the toga was the garment of peace. When the citizens met in the *comitia centuriata* they wore the sagum in token of its ancient function as the military muster.

Salii: "Dancers." Two colleges of priests dedicated to Mars and Quirinus who held their rites in March and October, respectively. Each college consisted of twelve young patricians whose parents were still living. On their festivals, they dressed in embroidered tunics, a crested bronze helmet and breastplate and each bore one of the twelve sacred shields ("ancilia") and a staff. They processed to the most important altars of Rome and before each performed a war dance. The ritual was so ancient that, by the first century B.C., their songs and prayers were unintelligible.

Saturnalia: Feast of Saturn, December 17–23, a raucous and jubilant occasion when gifts where exchanged, debts were settled, and masters waited on their slaves.

Sella Curulis: A folding camp-chair. It was part of the insignia of the curule magistrates and the Flamen Dialis.

Senate: Rome's chief deliberative body. It consisted of three hundred to six hundred men, all of whom had won elective office at least once. Once the supreme ruling body, by the late Republic the Senate's former legislative and judicial functions had devolved upon the courts and the popular assemblies and its chief authority lay in foreign policy and the nomination of generals. Senators were privileged to wear the tunica laticlava.

Servile War: The slave rebellion led by the Thracian gladiator Spartacus in 73–71 B.C. The rebellion was crushed by Crassus and Pompey.

Sica: A single-edged dagger or short sword of varying size. It was favored by thugs and used by the Thracian gladiators in the arena. It was classified as an infamous rather than an honorable weapon.

Solarium: A rooftop garden and patio.

Spatha: The Roman cavalry sword, longer and narrower than the gladius.

SPQR: "Senatus populusque Romanus." The Senate and People of Rome. The formula embodying the sovereignty of Rome. It was used on official correspondence, documents and public works.

Stirps: A sub-family of a gens. The cognomen gave the name of the stirps, i.e., Caius Julius *Caesar:* Caius of the stirps Caesar of gens Julii.

Strigil: A bronze implement, roughly s-curved, used to scrape sand and oil from the body after bathing. Soap was unknown to the Roman Republic.

Strophium: A cloth band worn by women beneath or over the clothing to support the breasts.

Subligaculum: A loincloth, worn by men and women.

Subura: A neighborhood on the lower slopes of the Viminal and Esquiline, famed for its slums, noisy shops and raucous inhabitants.

Tarpeian Rock: A cliff beneath the Capitol from which traitors were hurled. It was named for the Roman maiden Tarpeia who, according to legend, betrayed the Capitol to the Sabines.

Temple of Jupiter Capitolinus: The most important temple of the state religion. Triumphal processions ended with a sacrifice at this temple.

Temple of Saturn: The state treasury was located in a crypt beneath this temple. It was also the repository for military standards.

Temple of Vesta: Site of the sacred fire tended by the vestal virgins and dedicated to the goddess of the hearth. Documents, especially wills, were deposited there for safekeeping.

Toga: The outer robe of the Roman citizen. It was white

for the upper classes, darker for the poor and for people in mourning. The toga praetexta, bordered with a purple stripe, was worn by curule magistrates, by state priests when performing their functions and by boys prior to manhood. The toga picta, purple and embroidered with golden stars, was worn by a general when celebrating a triumph, also by a magistrate when giving public Games.

Tonsores: A slave trained as a barber and hairdresser.

Trans-Tiber: A newer district on the right or western bank of the Tiber. It lay beyond the old city walls.

Tribal Assemblies: There were two: the comitia tributa, an assembly of all citizens by tribes, which elected the lower magistrates—curule aediles, and quaestors, also the military tribunes—and the concilium plebis, consisting only of plebeians, elected the tribunes of the plebs and the plebeian aediles.

Tribe: Originally, the three classes of patricians. Under the Republic, all citizens belonged to tribes of which there were four city tribes and thirty-one country tribes. New citizens were enrolled in an existing tribe.

Tribune: Representative of the plebeians with power to introduce laws and to veto actions of the Senate. Only plebeians could hold the office, which carried no imperium. Military tribunes were elected from among the young men of senatorial or equestrian rank to be assistants to generals. Usually it was the first step of a man's political career.

Triumph: A magnificent ceremony celebrating military victory. The honor could be granted only by the Senate, and until he received permission, the victorious general had to remain outside the city walls, as his command ceased the instant he crossed the pomerium. The general, called the triumphator, received royal, near-divine honors and became a virtual god for a day. A slave was appointed to stand behind him and remind him periodically of his mortality lest the gods become jealous.

Triumvir: A member of a triumvirate—a board or college of three men. Most famously, the three-man rule of Caesar, Pompey and Crassus. Later, the triumvirate of Antonius, Octavian and Lepidus.

Tunica: A long, loose shirt, sleeveless or short-sleeved, worn by citizens beneath the toga when outdoors and by itself indoors. The tunica laticlava had a broad purple stripe from neck to hem and was worn by Senators and patricians. The tunica angusticlava had a narrow stripe and was worn by the equites. The tunica picta, purple and embroidered with golden palm branches, was worn by a general when he celebrated a triumph.

Usus: The most common form of marriage, in which a man and woman lived together for a year without being separated for three consecutive nights.

Via: A highway. Within the city, viae were streets wide enough for two wagons to pass one another. There were only two viae during the Republic: the Via Sacra, which ran through the Forum and was used for religious processions and triumphs, and the Via Nova, which ran along one side of the Forum.

Vigile: A night watchman. The vigiles had the duty of apprehending felons caught committing crimes, but their main duty was a fire watch. They were unarmed except for staves and carried fire-buckets.